Foundation for Love by Gail Sattler
After a heart-wrenching breakup with her fiancé, Carla Wainwright is not looking for romance. . .just help building her dream house. Contractor Jack Dugan isn't looking for romance, either, especially with Carla. He knows there are two sides to every story, and he has only heard one. Can Carla and Jack trust in God to settle their mutual distrust and make the place they met, the location for the future foundation of her house, the firm foundation for their love?

Love's Open Door by Susan May Warren
Paul Stoneman fears he will never be able to find a wife whom he can bring home to the harsh Siberian village where he works as a missionary. Ellen White is afraid to surrender to God's call to missions, preferring the safety of her career in interior decorating. But when Ellen offers to help Paul decorate his rented home, love comes knocking. Paul and Ellen are about to learn that only love, and faith in God, will give them the courage to walk through Love's Open Door.

Once Upon an Attic by Tracey Victoria Bateman
Professor Angela Cooper has given up on ever finding Prince Charming and decided to get on with her life. She leases a cozy little home, but her tranquility is shattered when a family of squirrels moves into her attic. Kendall Tyler's repeated attempts to remove the squirrels and his bumbling attempts to repair the damages he caused keep him coming back to her house—and to Angela. In the same way the squirrels have filled her attic with nuts, can God fill her heart with love?

Mending Fences by Susan Downs
When a storm wreaks havoc on widow Winnie Wainwright's new home and yard, she hires retired carpenter and widower, Handy Dan Parker, to repair the damage. Can he fix the hole in Winnie's grieving heart as well? Is Winnie the one God intends to use to fill the void in Dan's life? Or does a single misheard word create a rift in their relationship too deep to mend?

The House Love Built

FOUR ROMANCES ARE BUILT ON THE FOUNDATION OF FAITH

Tracey Victoria Bateman
Susan Downs
Gail Sattler
Susan May Warren

BARBOUR
PUBLISHING

Foundation of Love ©2003 by Gail Sattler
Love's Open Door ©2003 by Susan May Warren
Once Upon an Attic ©2003 by Tracey Victoria Bateman
Mending Fences ©2003 by Susan Downs

Illustrations: Mari Goering

ISBN 1-58660-799-5

Published by Barbour Publishing, Inc., P.O. Box 719, Uhrichsville, Ohio 44683,
www.barbourbooks.com

 Member of the
Evangelical Christian
Publishers Association

Printed in the United States of America.
5 4 3 2

The House Love Built

Foundation of Love

by Gail Sattler

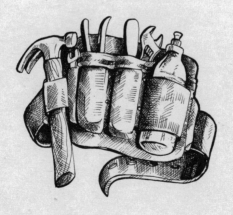

Dedication

Dedicated to Sandie. Again.

Chapter 1

C arla Wainwright stood in the middle of the empty lot, not far from the grand old pecan tree. Closing her eyes, she inhaled deeply while the wind tousled her hair.

If her calculations were correct, very soon this would be her living room. Here, she would be stretched out on the couch, enjoying a cup of warm herbal tea, and reading a good book.

But first, she had to build the house.

She opened her eyes and pressed her finger onto the blueprints for the cute little two-bedroom home she had selected. The house wasn't big or fancy, and it only had one story, but it would be hers, and hers alone—her refuge and her fortress— and no one could ever take this victory from her.

At the sound of a vehicle approaching, Carla stopped dreaming and turned her head.

A rusty, red pickup truck that had seen better days pulled up to the curb and stopped. A man wearing well-worn jeans and a light jacket slid out and began walking toward her. His slightly uneven gait told her he was the man she had been expecting.

While he walked, Carla studied him. He looked to be about thirty years old. His dark brown hair appeared neat, although a bit too long.

As he approached, Carla's breath caught. Ellen hadn't warned her about his height. At five feet four inches, Carla considered herself average, yet he towered above her by a foot. The girth of his shoulders and the muscles in his arms made her think of Paul Bunyan. She'd never met anyone so large in her life.

"You must be Carla Wainwright." He extended one hand and waited.

Carla gathered her nerve and returned his handshake. His large hand completely swallowed hers. "You must be Jack Dugan."

He nodded. "I understand you want to build a house."

Carla nodded. "Yes. Ellen recommended you highly. But if you don't mind, I have a few questions."

"Of course. Ask away."

Carla's carefully rehearsed speech deserted her when she looked up into his eyes. She'd never seen eyes so green or so beautiful. Even more striking than the deep sea color, his eyes seemed to bore into her, stalling her thought processes.

Carla sucked in a deep breath and stiffened her back to make herself as tall as possible. She couldn't let him make her nervous. She was here only to interview him for a job she needed done.

"Ellen said you were just getting back to work after an

accident and might be available to start right away. I'm going to be blunt. This may not be a big, executive home, but I need a commitment that you won't divide your time with other projects and that you'll do my house as quickly as possible."

His face tightened and he cleared his throat. "I don't know what Ellen told you, but the reason I'm not working now is because I'm caught in the middle of a gray zone technicality. Worker's Compensation says my claim is up and I should be back to work; but Rick, the main guy I work for, doesn't think I'm ready. Basically, we parted with a 'don't call me, I'll call you.' Therefore, my schedule is open."

Carla gasped. "I thought by law an employer was obligated to take someone back after an accident."

Jack shoved his hands in his pockets and shrugged his shoulders. "I'm different because I'm considered self-employed. Technically, Rick subcontracts me separately for each job. Sometimes it's for just one portion of a single home, sometimes it's overseeing a whole subdivision, or anything in between. Legally, he doesn't offer any guarantees because I'm a subcontractor, not an employee. In this business, word travels. No one else is hiring me while Rick considers me a liability. Being self-employed, I don't qualify for unemployment insurance, so I'm actively looking for something to start on right away, or I don't eat. That may sound harsh, but that's the reality of it. So, if you have a house to build, I'm available."

Carla clenched her jaw and swallowed hard. She didn't want Jack to do her house as a last resort because he was desperate, but his current situation suited her needs.

Jack came highly recommended. He'd done an excellent job renovating Ellen's basement. Likewise, Ellen promised that Jack would give her an honest quote and build her house at the best value for her money without compromising quality or taking shortcuts. She also said Jack was a good and honorable Christian man. Not that Carla would trust him because of his claim to faith. She only trusted him because Ellen did.

Carla stiffened her back and cleared her throat. "Are you sure you're ready to take on a whole house? I don't want you to discover halfway through it was too much for you and then have to find someone else."

He shook his head. "I assure you that even though I'm not going to be dancing on the rooftops for awhile, I'm more than ready and capable to get back to work. Building houses is what I do."

Ellen's assurances echoed through her head. If Ellen said Jack was the best, she would take Ellen's word for it and ignore the fact that no one else would hire him.

"Okay. I guess you're hired. The first thing we should agree on is the cost for labor and materials and exactly what it is you'll do."

He let out his breath in a deep whoosh of air. "Ellen told me a bit about your house. How about if we go sit down somewhere and we'll talk. My truck isn't exactly an office, but I've got a calculator, my laptop, and a thermos of good, strong coffee, if you're interested."

Carla sucked in a deep breath, repositioned her purse strap on her shoulder, and rolled the blueprints into a tube.

This was it. There was no turning back. Through diligence and hard work and a lot of help from God, she had overcome what for so long had held her down. She could move forward with confidence and determination and not look back. Building her house was the start of her new beginning.

"I'm interested. Let's go."

Jack Dugan hoisted himself up into the cab of his truck and watched as his newest, and currently his only, customer jogged to her car to retrieve her file folder. She looked to be about a year or two younger than he, in her mid to late twenties. Overall, the woman appeared more average than average could be. Average height, average brown hair, average build. She even wore average, sensible shoes.

When he'd told Ellen that he was interested in bidding on Carla's house project, instead of learning more about the house, he found himself learning about Carla. Ellen told him that Carla had been struggling for the last few years to pay for the lot, and likewise, she had to make every penny count in building the house too. Ellen then proceeded to tell him all Carla's hobbies and interests, her favorite colors, where she grew up, what she did for a living, and that she was handy and resourceful, just like him. He now also knew Carla's birthday, which he hadn't needed to know to build a house for her.

He didn't usually mix business with pleasure, but Ellen had presented Carla as a very likable Christian woman. As a single Christian man, if he felt God's leading with Carla Wainwright, Jack wasn't closed to pursuing the idea.

Carla hopped into the truck and slid the folder across the seat. "Here's all the stuff I've been accumulating."

He began to pick through the mass of papers. She had everything from handwritten notes to newspaper articles to paint chips to brochures for cabinets and appliances, and quotes from subcontractors, all neatly in alphabetical order. "Some of these quotes are two years old and no longer valid." He continued to flip through the pile. "This guy's even gone out of business." He laid the folder down beside him. "It looks like you've been collecting all this for a long time. Why are you suddenly in such a big rush?"

"I have to coordinate this with my holidays. I'm an administrator at the college, and I only get July and the usual school seasonal holidays off. Since we're already into June, if I don't do this now, I'll have to wait a full year for next summer's vacation."

Jack had a feeling she was leaving something out, since she would have known as much in advance about this year's vacation as next year's. Since he needed the job, he said nothing.

"Do you have a contract for us both to sign?"

He thought it interesting that she'd already said he was hired before she knew his price. Word of mouth from a satisfied customer was indeed the most powerful form of advertising. "I'll give you a written quote on the whole job, my labor as well as materials." Jack unrolled the blueprints and studied them. "This looks pretty basic. A 1,013-square-foot, two-bedroom ranch-style house, slab foundation, truss roof, double-hung windows, one bathroom, standard utility room, and single-car garage. Nice touch with the vaulted ceiling in the living room, especially in this size house. You'll probably want vinyl siding exterior and a shingled roof since you're watching your budget." He waited for her nod, then flipped to the next page. "This is good. There's a list of materials here too."

She nodded again, this time so fast her bangs bounced on her forehead. "I bought the plans and blueprints off a place on the Internet."

He rolled up the blueprints. "This is everything I need. Let me take this home tonight, along with that folder of yours, and I should be able to get you a fairly accurate estimate within a couple of days. If everything meets your approval, I can start Monday."

She smiled from ear to ear and clapped her hands in front of her. "That's great! I'm so excited! I know you'll be able to keep costs within my budget. What do we do first?"

"First, I'll rent a small tractor and clear the land."

"Clear the land?"

Jack swept his hand to the side to encompass the small lot, the last left in the subdivision of Brook's Country without a dwelling. He estimated the rest of the neighborhood had been completed two or three years earlier. "Since this lot appears to have been vacant for a long time, there's a lot of growth on it. Unfortunately, people also tend to use vacant lots as a free garbage dump. Plus, you'll have to get rid of those trees."

Her smile disappeared, and her eyebrows knotted. "I wanted to keep the trees. They're pecan trees, the last ones left in the neighborhood. I did some research on them. They were planted by the settlers before the land was divided up in the early 1900s. They have great pecans. I've picked them myself for the last three years. You can't cut them down. They're two stories high, and they'll look great beside the house. Just look at the picture."

Once more, Jack unrolled the blueprints and flipped to the exterior elevation page. He had been looking at more important things than the landscaping. Now that she mentioned it, he saw that she had hand drawn three large trees, two in the backyard and one at the side of the house. "Everyone else in the neighborhood has cultivated trees, planted after the houses were finished."

"I don't care. I want these pecan trees. They're one of the main reasons we, er, I bought this lot in the first place."

Jack had been in the process of flipping back to the page for the foundation plan when his hand froze. All indications from Carla so far also led him to believe that this house was to be hers and hers alone. She had previously given no mention of a second party's involvement. Unless she wasn't as single as he'd been led to believe, although he couldn't fathom why Ellen would lie to him. He stopped looking at the blueprints, waiting for Carla to elaborate on the "we."

"That's also one of the reasons I picked these plans. I want to look out my bedroom window and see the trees and hear the leaves rustling in the wind." She reached over and pointed to the sketch for the master bedroom window at the side of the house, right beside the tree she'd drawn in.

Jack nodded. The second party involved was obviously Ellen, giving advice. "These trees are taller than the rest of the ones in the neighborhood due to their age. Don't you think

16

they will look strange? Yours will be the smallest house in the neighborhood, but you'd have the tallest trees."

"But I just love the trees. It would be like living in a campground, don't you think? I've even seen squirrels running up the trunks. I can't destroy their home."

Jack rolled his eyes. "Squirrels are pests."

"The trees stay. I've already had everything surveyed, and that one is going to be right outside my bedroom window."

"That will make it more difficult to do the excavating."

"I don't care. I really want that tree."

"You're the boss," he mumbled, trying to think of how much longer it would take to work around the tree and how much extra the time would cost. "Is there anything else I should know about? Any modifications to the plans?"

"No, no changes. I have to do this as cheaply as possible, and that means sticking to the plans."

"Sticking to the plans, except for the trees."

"The trees are there. I drew them in. See?"

Jack made a mental note to study every detail and pencil mark more closely.

"It should only take me a day to clear the lot. I have a friend who's an excavator. He does good work, and he'll bend his schedule for me. He can have a site for a slab foundation excavated in one day, but he won't be happy about having to work around the trees. You never know how the root systems go, and they can make the excavation difficult."

"Thanks. I appreciate it. Will you still be ready to start Monday?"

He rolled up the blueprints. "Yes. But before we start, I'd

like to do one more thing. Ellen said we all go to the same church, but I don't remember seeing you there before. I always go to the early service. I'm used to getting up with the birds."

"I always go to the late service. I'm not a morning person."

"I'm going to do my best to do this for you as cheaply as possible without compromising quality in the time frame you need, but a little divine intervention wouldn't hurt. Before we go our separate ways, I'd like to pray about this with you." Jack smiled and reached toward her, encouraging her to hold hands as they prayed together.

Her eyes widened for a brief second before she squeezed them tightly shut. She quickly clasped her hands together in her lap, hunched her shoulders, and bowed her head, almost curling herself into a ball as she sat. "Okay," she mumbled, not opening her eyes. "You can start."

Jack momentarily let his hands hover in the air, then he, too, clasped his hands in his lap. The tightness of her expression and the awkwardness of her posture made him want to apologize, even though he didn't know why. It was normal for him to hold hands when praying with someone, especially since they had the bond of attending the same church, regardless if they'd met before or not. Unless she wasn't comfortable praying. If so, then they needed to pray more than ever.

Jack closed his eyes, cleared his throat, and centered his thoughts on asking for God's guidance and wisdom in both the construction and the purchasing of materials. He especially prayed concerning the short time frame Carla wanted to build a house from bare ground. Carla echoed his thoughts in prayer very fluently and comfortably, which told him that it wasn't praying in general that bothered her. Therefore, it had to be him, although he had no idea what he did wrong. He tried to be personable and agreeable, but sometimes everyone struck out. The thought bothered him, although he already knew it was a bad idea to mix business with pleasure.

At their closing "amen," he tried to ignore his hurt feelings and smiled politely.

She didn't even look at him. Carla scooped up her purse, slid to the door, and spoke as she pulled up the door handle. "My phone number and E-mail address are inside the folder if you have any questions."

The door closed, and she was gone before he had a chance to reply.

Chapter 2

Carla stood at the curb as the smallest tractor she'd ever seen pushed dirt, rocks, and plants into a mound at the front of her lot.

She knew she would be excited when the process began; but seeing the ground being cleared and hearing the roar of the little tractor working, it was all she could do to keep from dancing on the spot.

It was really happening. Her house was being built.

When Jack saw her, he waved, finished moving a large boulder to the rest of the pile, cut the engine, and emerged from the small cab.

Knowing what to expect, she was ready to face him.

"Hi," he said, smiling brightly as he walked toward her. "What are you doing here?"

"I was on my way home from work and wanted to see how things were coming."

"I'm nearly done. Tomorrow morning at sunrise, the excavation will begin."

She turned her head to look at the big pecan tree to her

left. She opened her mouth to speak, but Jack cut her off before a word came out.

"Don't worry," he said, raising one dirty palm in the air. "No one will hurt your trees. See the red tape? That's our signal that the trees aren't to be removed. I also saw your other pencil marks. I'll be putting in a sliding glass door instead of a window at the back of the house from the second bedroom, which I saw you relabeled as a den. That's to give access to your 'future deck' notation. And speaking of your den, I assume your note for a 'retractable stair thingamajig' meant you wanted a pull-down ladder access to the attic there?"

Carla smiled openly. So far, Ellen had been right. Jack really was diligent with customer requests. "Yes, that's exactly what I meant. Thank you. I brought a copy of the signed contract for you. I didn't know what you called your company until I saw your letterhead on the quote. Jack of All Trades?"

Jack grinned from ear to ear. Carla's breath caught.

Yesterday, she had been too caught up in the shock of Jack's physical presence to have a really good look at him. Overall, he was quite handsome, and his warm smile made him even more so. She didn't know if he hadn't shaved in the morning or if his beard simply grew quickly. Either way, between his stubbly chin, the messy hair, his vivid green eyes, and his well-worn workingman's attire, added to the sheer size of him, he exuded a bad-boy appeal that approached dangerous. As a Christian man, he wasn't supposed to look that way, although to put him in a respectable suit and tie doing the job he did was beyond ridiculous.

21

The allure of his smile magnified tenfold as he winked playfully at her and splayed one hand in the center of his muscular chest. "Yeah. Jack Dugan, Jack of All Trades, Incorporated. That's me."

Carla lowered her head, refusing to look at him. She'd been taken in by a trustworthy face before and vowed it would never happen again. She trusted him only as far as the distinct lines of their contract, which they now both had signed.

She quickly mumbled a good-bye, ran to his truck, left the contract upside down on the dash, then hurried home.

Despite Mr. Jack of All Trades, at sunrise, she knew where she was going to be.

"Good morning, Carla. What are you doing here?"

Carla dug into her purse, pulled out her camera, and held it up. "This is why I'm here. Since you're not actually doing the digging, what are you doing here?"

Jack crossed his arms over his chest. "I'm supervising and making sure the job is done right. Isn't that what you're paying me to do?"

"Of course," she mumbled.

He looked up at the sunrise, which was by no means spectacular and pretty much over. "What's with the camera?"

"I'm going to make an album of the construction of my house from the ground up. I'm making a before and after collection. Like when you go on a diet."

"I wouldn't know." He lowered his hands to rest on his stomach. "Although I have put on a bit of weight since my accident."

Carla couldn't help but follow his hands with her eyes. In general, she could see nothing wrong with his waistline or any other part of him. His jeans fit him well, not too tight and not too loose. This morning he wore a jacket; but when she'd seen him yesterday, he was wearing a well-worn T-shirt, which fit him just as well as the snug jeans. From a distance, as a woman she could appreciate his fine physique and his good looks. From close up, he outright frightened her.

She couldn't let him bother her. The important thing was her house, which she was paying him to build.

She quickly took a picture of the man doing the excavation. "Done. I'll be back tonight. Tomorrow you start the foundation, right?"

"Maybe. It depends what time the inspector gets here. Once he finishes and gives us the okay on the excavation, then we build the frame for the foundation and call the inspector back. After the second inspection, then we pour."

"And then you can start building?"

Jack shook his head. "No. Then we have to seal it, put in the drainpipe and the rest of the services. We'll also pour in the sand to four inches from the primal floor level. After that, we pour the floor. Then we backfill. Doing it that way takes an extra day before we start framing the actual house, but it saves the cost of bringing in the heavy equipment a third time. This is also when we'll do the final grading. Then, when the floor is perfectly set, we start framing the actual house."

Carla muttered her approval, pretending to understand the steps. "This all seems so complicated."

"Not really, but this is the most important stage in the

construction. Like anything else in life, a firm foundation is the most important part. I make sure I'm always on the site to supervise a foundation for a house I'm building."

Carla nodded, happy to hear that he had high standards, from the ground up.

"Just like the foundation of our faith is knowing that Jesus Christ is the Son of God, that whoever believes in Him shall have eternal life. I build all my houses on solid rock." He grinned. "Or solid cement."

She didn't know how their conversation shifted from house construction to doctrine, but she obviously agreed with his statement.

"Excuse me. One of the guys needs me for something."

"Yes, and I should get going before I'm late for work."

Once at her desk, Carla buried herself in her job, which was considerable since the college faculty was in the throes of marking final exams. Carla's main function for now was to assist students who hadn't passed connect with remedial help and set up summer school courses as required.

Throughout the week she stopped by the site both before and after work to watch the foundation going in. The process was exciting to watch.

During the actual excavation, when Jack wasn't working, he spent his time talking to her. Carla didn't mind, because it gave her time to get used to Jack and get to know him a little. She wanted to be prepared for when her vacation came and she would be spending more time with him.

By the weekend, everything for the foundation was complete. She spent Saturday morning standing on the curb watching the crew pour the concrete for the floor, then smooth it out.

According to Jack, Sunday was not only the Lord's day of rest, it was also his crew's day of rest. Sunday they would leave the floor to set, and work would begin again on Monday.

Carla arrived for church earlier than usual on Sunday morning. Since no one she knew had yet arrived, she walked into the sanctuary alone and sat in her usual seat to wait for Ellen. She read the bulletin quietly until someone called her name. However, instead of Ellen's soft, high-pitched voice, this voice was low and definitely male.

She crunched the bulletin in her hand as she turned toward the aisle. A man who could have been Jack's twin brother stood beside the pew with a Bible tucked under one arm. Except Ellen had told her that Jack was an only child, as was she.

Jack grinned. "Hi."

Carla opened her mouth to speak, but no words came out. If it wasn't for the same vivid green eyes and the perfect, mesmerizing smile, she would have had doubts this was the same man she'd seen twice every day for the past week.

Today, not only was Jack perfectly clean, he was clean-shaven. Instead of snug jeans so worn they were nearly white, he wore loose-fitting black slacks. Matching black leather shoes replaced the brown, beat-up safety work boots. The typical snug T-shirt had been exchanged with a neatly pressed, blue cotton shirt, which was covered by a black sport coat and accompanied by a black tie. His hair wasn't any shorter, but it was neatly gelled into place. The transformation made him into everything she had imagined earlier, and more. And it made him more dangerous.

"I decided to take in the late service this week. Mind if I join you?"

Whether she wanted to sit with him or not, she couldn't be rude. Carla shuffled to the side and checked her watch. "Ellen should be here soon too."

"That's great," he said as he slid into the pew beside her. "I haven't seen Ellen for a couple of weeks." He turned to her and smiled again, the same smile she'd seen many times all week, but yet different with the new packaging. "Before Ellen gets here, can I ask if you would like to join me for lunch after the service?"

Carla's stomach did a flip-flop. Jack seemed to be a nice man, at least while they were in public for anyone else to see. Her heart sank at the thought that he wanted to speak to her. That could only mean he had something important to discuss with her about the house.

She steeled her nerve, but she couldn't manufacture a smile. "I guess so. What's wrong?"

"Don't worry. Nothing's wrong. I thought we could just sit and talk."

If they weren't going to talk about the house, she didn't want to go; but now that she'd agreed, she had to.

"Talk?"

Before he could respond, Ellen joined them. Since the lights had begun to dim, Jack shuffled down the pew, making Carla also shuffle in, positioning them so that Jack sat between herself and Ellen.

The service was over before Carla was ready. She tried to delay the inevitable by asking Ellen if she was interested in joining them, but Ellen already had other plans.

And that meant she would have to face Jack alone.

Chapter 3

Jack smiled brightly as Carla approached him. Ellen had been right. He did like Carla. She had an easy smile, a kind and gentle spirit, and a genuine love for people. He knew she was some kind of administrator high up in the ranks at the local college. Yet, despite the uneducated status of the men on the various construction crews, she treated them all as equals, unlike how many other people who paid for custom-built homes treated the manual laborers, including himself, even though he'd been to business college. He liked that.

He'd learned that she had fully intended to subcontract all the work to build the house herself, but discovered the hard way that she was in way over her head. Still, he admired her spunk, as well as everything else he'd seen so far. He wanted to get to know her better. Yet, every time he tried to steer their conversations away from the house and onto more personal matters, she changed the subject back to the business of her house.

Today, away from work, he had the opportunity to talk

to her about other things.

After a very short wait, they were seated at a nice, cozy table for two. A server quickly took their orders and left them alone with a carafe of coffee.

Jack slowly sipped his coffee, trying to think of a way to start the conversation.

Carla leaned back in her chair and cradled her cup in her hands. Instead of looking at him, she stared intently into the cup. "What did you want to talk about?"

You. Me. The possibilities of us.

At his own thoughts, Jack struggled not to sputter into the cup. Slowly, he set it down on the saucer, barely managing not to spill any. "Nothing in particular. I just thought this would be a good time to talk without something distracting us."

"Oh."

A silence that threatened to hang forever hovered between them.

Jack cleared his throat. He didn't want to, but it appeared the best subject to start a conversation would be what got them together in the first place. "I didn't mean to pry, but Ellen said you're on a tight budget. Buying land is always a good investment, but why did you pick the Brook's Country subdivision? You could have bought something in the suburbs, where the land is cheaper, and spent more of your budget on the dwelling versus the land. Your house isn't going to be as big as the others in the neighborhood or as fancy. I know you wanted to start right away, but if you waited until next year, you could save more money."

Carla set her cup down, but kept both hands firmly wrapped around it. "I have my reasons."

Jack frowned. "I hope there aren't going to be any unpleasant surprises, and I'll have to shut everything down."

She shook her head. "No. The exact opposite. Once the house is finished, all my problems will be over."

"I don't understand."

Carla lowered her head and stared down at her cup, not making eye contact with him as she spoke. "I was engaged once. We had bought this piece of land to build a house on, but things didn't work out and the wedding was called off."

Jack's throat tightened, and his stomach started to churn. Now he understood the "we" reference that had puzzled him earlier. But just as it explained things, it didn't make him feel any better. It didn't sound like there was any chance of reconciliation, but now he also wondered if she'd been too burned by a love gone bad and wasn't open to try again. "Then why the rush? Ellen said you've had the land for a few years."

"My fiancé wasn't working at the time, so I paid the whole down payment. He said it would be best if his name wasn't on the loan, which I later figured out was because he didn't want to be obligated to help with the payments. But then, after we broke up, he said because it was a joint decision, I owed him half of any profit when the land was sold, less the down payment, which was mine. He doesn't have a case legally, since I've made all the payments myself, but I know he'll come after me on his own for what he thinks is his portion if I sell it. So I struggled to pay it off, telling myself that if nothing else, it was a good investment."

"Why does that make it different if there's going to be a house on it?"

She raised her head and finally looked at him. She smiled, but her smile didn't reach her eyes.

"Building the house on the land proves I'm not going to sell it, and then he doesn't have a chance of collecting a dime. I told him what I was going to do, but he didn't believe me. He's always asking me when I'm going to put the lot up for sale, and he won't take no for an answer. Now he'll see that I meant what I said. It's mine, I paid for it, and I'm keeping it. Once the house is built, I'm going to live in it forever. I'll never sell it. It's my trophy of how I've over-come my hurdles."

Jack had never been engaged before and could only imagine the anguish of breaking up after a relationship had progressed that far. Still, he would have considered such an occasion more a heartache than a hurdle.

"You said he keeps asking you about the lot. Does that mean you still see him? If he's bothering you, is there any-thing I can do?"

Carla shook her head. "No. You're doing the best thing by helping me build the house at a price I can afford, as quickly as it can be built. I didn't think I would be done until next spring, but something unexpected came up and I managed to pay it off early. Because I'm living on a single income, I didn't qualify for a mortgage the size I need. But the manager at the bank told me I could get a mortgage on the house once I paid the land off. Owning the land also gives me some equity." All the sadness left her face, and her previously sad eyes now absolutely sparkled. "So now I'm the proud owner of my very own twenty-year mortgage."

Jack had never seen anyone so happy to be in debt, although admittedly most people didn't consider the mortgage for their house a debt, but a normal cost of living.

"Is that why you chose those plans and wanted to do it yourself? Because that's all you could get for your allowable mortgage?"

She shook her head. "No. A single person doesn't need a big house. As far as I'm concerned, a bigger house would just mean more for me to clean."

"Not many people think of it that way."

"Housecleaning isn't my favorite leisure activity." Her eyes became unfocused as she stared at some undefined spot on the wall behind him. "I'd much rather come home from a hard day and lay back on the couch with a good book than wash floors."

Jack thought of his own house. Being in the construction industry, he'd built his house himself. With visions of middle-class grandeur and wide-open spaces, he'd constructed a large home fit for a family with two or three kids and a big dog. For now, though, also being single, he lived alone in his big empty house. Many days, he did think of the big house as a curse. As a subcontractor, he needed to keep it clean and available as a showpiece for potential clients to view on short notice. He'd even had to furnish all the rooms, even though he didn't use them, which meant even more cleaning.

He gave a humorless laugh. "I know what you mean.

When I built my house, I didn't think of what it took to keep it clean."

Carla grinned again. It was a beautiful sight. "See?"

He leaned forward over the table and dropped his voice to a whisper, compelling Carla to meet him halfway. "Let me tell you a secret. When the youth group has their annual fund-raiser and they hire themselves out for odd jobs, I always hire a bunch of them to give my house a good cleaning. I guess I'm just a typical man."

Suddenly, Carla's beautiful smile disappeared. Her face paled, her whole body stiffened, and she sat back in her chair, taking the coffee cup with her. "Well, that's why I picked a small house, and that's why I wanted to build it now. I have the whole month of July off, and I intend to use every day of it to build my house."

At the sudden change, Jack blinked and also sat back in his chair. He didn't know why the mention of the youth group caused her to withdraw. Ellen was very active with the church's youth group. Even if Carla didn't participate, she should have at least been supportive. If anyone wouldn't trust teens, it should have been himself, after his accident.

He wanted to defend the youth group, but after accidentally getting her to tell him her troubles, he didn't want to make their first time together away from the house a complete disaster.

Their dinners arrived, sparing the need to say any more. He led in a short prayer over their meal, including a request that their time together would be productive as he worked on her house. Carla's enthusiastic "amen" made his heart pound.

First, he was happy beyond words that she didn't feel awkward praying in the public setting of a restaurant. That said a lot about her faith and commitment to Jesus as her Lord and Savior. It made him like her even more, and now, in light of what he knew, he wanted to help her as much as he could.

"Tomorrow we'll start with the framing. The foundation will be set, so we can start with the house itself."

"Is there anything I can do to help at this point? I want to do as much as possible to keep costs down."

"There's always plenty to do. I usually hire kids to do cleanup, sweeping, gathering cut pieces, stuff like that. I was going to do it myself to save you some money. But if you want to do the grunt work, then I can move on to the next step, and the process can be somewhat sped up."

"That's great. I can be at the house right after work and help until sunset. I guess there isn't going to be any lighting, is there?"

"Lighting needs electricity. That won't happen until later. For now, we only work during daylight."

He kept the conversation light and cheery, and the rest of their meal together progressed well. They parted on good terms, making reference to seeing each other at the house in the morning.

Jack stopped hammering and watched Carla exit her car. She jogged over the dirt toward the house, hopping over a few stray two-by-four pieces as she ran. Instead of the nice clothes she wore to work, today she wore jeans with a hole in one knee and a T-shirt proclaiming the concert tour of a popular Christian musician from about three years previous. He kind of liked the casual side of her.

"Hi, Jack. What can I do?"

He pointed to the broom lying on the ground nearby. "You can sweep up and throw away anything that's on the concrete floor." He paused. "I missed you this morning."

She picked up the broom, but instead of sweeping, she looked at all the sections of partially assembled walls lying on the ground. "I had to give someone a ride, and I couldn't make it. I can't believe how much you've done in one day."

Jack and Frank, the framer he'd hired, had managed to nearly finish the sections for three of the four exterior walls. Frank had left after eight hours, leaving Jack to do anything else he wanted alone. Of course, he'd known Carla was coming.

Jack lifted his baseball cap off his head, ran his fingers through his hair, and replaced the cap. "It's going well. We should be able to lift everything up tomorrow and start the interior walls by Wednesday. The framing and the roof could be done in a week and a half, and then we'll start the interior."

Her eyes widened. "Wow. That's so fast."

"I suppose. But this is the fastest part of building a house." Jack checked his watch. "I've only got another couple of hours before the sun goes down, so I have to get back to work. When you're cleaning up, make sure you don't sweep off the chalk lines."

At his words, Carla dropped the broom and ran into the center of the foundation to stare with undisguised awe at the blue lines that were to be the interior walls of her house.

"This is going to be the door to the utility room. And this is my living room." She ran a few steps away, grinning from ear to ear. "This is where the couch is going to be! This is it! My house!"

Jack watched as Carla walked across the concrete, from "room to room," taking great care not to step on any of the blue lines, until she stood at the opening of what would eventually be the bedroom doorway.

In all his years building, Jack had never seen anyone so enamored with a foundation before. He couldn't help but be just as enamored with her honest enthusiasm. He found her simple joy in something he'd come to think of as trivial absolutely charming. He wondered if he might be starting to fall in love, right there on the foundation of her house.

"I know I've looked at the plans a million times, but it's so different, standing here, with it all marked out like this."

"I guess. Now would be a good time to sweep up your house for the first time. There's still plenty to do before you move in." He raised one eyebrow and looked pointedly at the broom on the ground.

Without another word exchanged, Carla began cleaning up. Being the first day, there wasn't a tremendous amount of litter, so Carla finished quickly. However, Jack had lots to do before the light dwindled to nothing.

Jack felt Carla behind him, watching, without having to turn around.

"Is there anything else I can do?"

"No, you can go home. I'll stay for about twenty minutes, and then I'll be back tomorrow just after sunrise."

"I don't know if I'll be back in the morning. Sal might need a ride to work again."

Jack tried not to care if Sal was a man or a woman. "If I don't see you in the morning, then have a nice day."

"I guess. Good night, Jack."

Chapter 4

"Hi, Jack!"

Jack steadied himself as he waved down to Carla from atop the roof.

In only a few days, the exterior walls were assembled and lifted into place, the interior walls were positioned and fastened. None of the doors or windows were in yet, but they'd put up some of the panels for the start of the exterior walls. Today, Friday, they'd finished the roof trusses and nailed down the plywood shell for the roof.

But now, Frank's five days of work were up. Saturday Jack would be alone to shingle the roof, a job that would take him until Tuesday because he refused to work Sundays. He planned to get the tar paper stapled into place before nightfall to be ready when the conveyor truck arrived Saturday morning. He'd finished one side, but now Carla had arrived with some food, so it was time for a break.

Very slowly, Jack crept downward, keeping his knees bent and one arm down to steady himself if he lost his balance or slipped. He hadn't anticipated how he would feel being back up on a roof again. He told himself, over and over, that getting back up was like falling off a horse. Once you fell off, you were supposed to get right back up again, and then everything would be fine, just as it was before. Except falling off a roof was a lot farther than falling off a horse. And potentially more fatal. God must have decided it was not his time to die that day, and therefore, here he was, back on another roof, once more able to earn a living.

Only, he didn't feel quite as confident as he did before. He muttered a prayer of thanks for his safety as his feet settled on the ladder. He said another prayer when Carla came running to steady the ladder before he began his descent. He needed the extra minute to stop his legs from shaking.

When both feet finally touched terra firma, it was all he could do not to bend down and kiss it.

"Jack? Are you okay? You look funny."

He lifted his cap and swiped his fingers through his hair. "I'm fine. A little shaky, but fine. This is the first time I've been back up since my accident. I found it a little unnerving."

Carla looked up to the edge of the roof, from whence he'd come. "I don't understand."

"I fell off a roof on my last job."

Carla pressed her palms to her cheeks. "I didn't know! I only knew you were hurt. What happened?"

"It's a long story. Can we eat those hamburgers before they get cold?"

"Oops. Of course."

As they did every day, they walked into Carla's future kitchen, where she laid an extra-thick blanket on the concrete floor where she said the table would be. Jack lowered himself slowly onto the blanket, wanting to tell her they would be much more comfortable sitting on the padded bench seat inside his truck. However, she wanted so much to eat in the "kitchen," he couldn't burst her bubble.

After they prayed over their meal, Carla distributed the hamburgers and fries.

He had barely taken his first bite when Carla spoke.

"What happened? Are you sure you're okay to be up there again? If you're not, you can hire someone else to do the shingles."

He shook his head while he chewed. "No way," he mumbled through his mouthful, then swallowed quickly. "Too expensive, especially with no notice on a rush job. I counted on doing it myself as part of the contract. Don't worry. Before long it'll be like it never happened."

"Didn't you have special boots so you don't slip?"

"I wasn't wearing my work boots at the time, actually. I was wearing my leather shoes because I was on the way to a Bible study."

"Then how did you end up on a roof?"

Jack sighed. He really didn't want to tell her, but if there was anything he'd learned about Carla Wainwright, it was that she was like a dog with an old bone when she wanted something.

"Remember that really bad storm we had at the end of February? The ice and wind were so bad it knocked out the power in a good portion of the city. Me and another guy were starting on a shake roof when the storm started. When the wind whipped up really strong, we decided to call it quits and go home. I had just changed and was on my way to the Bible study when I realized I left my tool belt on the site. Not wanting it to get stolen, I detoured back."

Carla nodded. "I remember that storm. I could feel the draft along the floor of my apartment, the wind was so strong. I'm on the third floor. I stood at the window for awhile, watching. I was so glad to be home."

"Well, I wasn't home. I had just picked up my tool belt when I heard someone calling from the roof. Some kid had climbed up on a dare and couldn't get down. His friends took off when they saw me drive up, and the poor kid was stuck up there all alone. The ladder had blown down, and the storm was in full force."

"Don't tell me you went up on the roof in that storm?"

Jack stared blankly at the hole that would soon be Carla's kitchen window. He would never forget that day. "I didn't have a choice. The kid was starting to panic. He looked like he was going to jump, so I went up and got him. To make a long story short, he was okay until we got to the eaves. I was lying on my stomach on the freezing, slick plywood, holding him with one hand and steadying the ladder with the other. Then he jumped too fast onto the ladder, and it started to go down with him on it. I slid forward and stopped the ladder from falling, but I couldn't grab anything to keep myself from falling. I slid right off the roof and landed on the ground. He scuttled down the ladder and ran away."

Memories of lying semiconscious on the frozen ground, unable to move and being pelted by the ice pellets hit Jack so vividly, it was like he'd stepped back in time. Half conscious, half frozen, and unable to move, he really thought he was going to die out there. As visions of death crossed his mind, he found he had no major regrets—he had no one to whom he owed compensation, he had no outstanding debts besides his house, for which he had life insurance. He'd led a good, clean, Christian life. His only regret was that if he didn't make it home, which he didn't think he was going to, no one would miss him or even realize he was gone.

The touch of Carla's warm hand on his arm brought Jack back to the present. "What happened?"

"Believe it or not, my cell phone rang. I don't know how it stayed on my belt or how it still worked. Even more of a miracle was how I answered it. It was Josh, wondering why I was late. I was so dazed, I don't remember telling him where I was. In fact, I passed out before we finished the conversation. But I remember waking up in the hospital. I had a major concussion, a couple of cracked ribs, a lot of bruising, and a broken leg."

"That's awful! But it could have been worse."

"Yes, it could have. I don't know why God spared me, but He did. I thank Him every day."

"I guess you never saw or heard from that kid?"

"Nope. Between the dark and the pelting rain and ice, I wouldn't recognize him if he sat next to me."

"Didn't you tell anyone? You're a hero!"

"No, I'm not. I'm an unemployed subcontractor who did something stupid. Under those conditions I should have moved slower and made sure I had something to keep myself steady instead of running in there without a plan. You're only a hero if you come out smelling like a rose or die trying, and I did neither. Let's just eat. I have to get back up there and finish stapling down the tar paper before it gets too dark to see what I'm doing."

They ate quickly, and Jack returned to the roof while Carla cleaned up below. As he expected, the second time up the ladder was easier than the first, and he expected the next time would be easier still.

Every once in awhile, he saw Carla come out from the house to dump more debris into the roll-away trash container.

He felt bad for being so abrupt with her, but he hadn't wanted to talk about what happened. While he was more than thankful his life had been spared, he still struggled with why he'd been hurt and subsequently lost his job when he was only trying to help someone. He kept telling himself that he would feel differently when he no longer felt the residual effects in his leg and was back to working steadily.

When he finished stapling down the last of the tar paper, he found Carla waiting for him at the bottom of the ladder.

He hadn't felt tired; but the moment his feet touched solid ground and he knew he wasn't going back up, a wave of exhaustion washed over him. He didn't mean to be rude, but he actually yawned.

Too late, he tried to cover his gaping mouth with his hand.

"Sorry. I guess I should go home and get to bed. Tomorrow's going to be a long day. The shingles will be delivered first thing in the morning."

Carla checked her wristwatch. "Okay. I'll see you then."

Carla watched Jack scale the ladder and scramble up onto the roof as a flatbed truck loaded with shingles backed up toward the house.

She didn't know Jack well enough to know if he was trying to look brave in front of her or if he really wasn't that affected by facing what surely must have been his greatest fear—falling off the roof again. She could only imagine what it must have been like. The sheer solid weight of him, being the size he was, surely had made the landing so much worse.

She pushed Jack's fears from her mind and tried to deal with her own.

Over the last couple of weeks she'd managed to get used to him. In some ways, she even liked him. From Jack's words and actions, she knew his faith was solid and good. But then again, so was Lyle's, and that had been the biggest disaster of her life. She would never again allow the same thing to happen. Soon her house would be built and she could close the door to her past and start anew.

Once the flatbed truck was in position, the driver maneuvered a large conveyor to the roof. Jack and the driver slowly sent all the bundles of shingles onto the roof and distributed them in numerous piles. As soon as the truck left, Jack ripped apart a bundle and started laying shingles in a row across the peak.

Instead of returning to the inside, where she really didn't have anything worthwhile to do, Carla stood and watched.

Jack pulled his hammer and some nails from his tool belt

and methodically fastened down the row he'd just laid. He then shuffled to the edge of the roof, laid a row of shingles down, and began hammering.

The whole process didn't look too hard.

Carla sucked in a deep breath, scaled the ladder, and scrambled onto the roof. She was glad to discover that while she was experiencing somewhat of an adrenaline rush, she wasn't afraid of heights.

"Can I help?" she asked when she thought she was close enough for Jack to hear over his hammering.

He fumbled with the hammer, coming just short of dropping it. "Carla! You startled me. What are you doing up here?"

"That looks like something I can do. If I can pitch in, it could be done faster."

He stood, lifted his cap, ran his fingers through his hair, then replaced the cap. "I don't know. Have you ever done this kind of thing before?"

"No, but I know how to work a hammer. If you give me something easy, I know I'll be a little slow, but I'm better than nothing."

He grinned. "You're much better than nothing. Here. I'll show you what to do. I only brought one hammer; you can lay the shingles down, and I'll nail them into place."

Very patiently, Jack showed her how to line them up and how much overlap to allow, and Carla began her task. While she worked, she smiled. Her help would not only save money, but also speed up the project.

Spreading the shingles went much faster than the actual nailing. After she had a row laid out, instead of sitting and

The House Love Built

waiting for him to nail it down, she descended the ladder and went home for her own set of tools.

She wasn't gone long; but even in the short time, she noticed how much Jack had done. She also noticed it was much hotter on the roof than it was on the ground, even at the early hour.

Jack waved to her from atop the roof as she walked toward the house, then rescaled the ladder.

"Welcome back. You didn't by any chance bring something to drink, did you?"

Carla said nothing as she produced a water bottle from a pocket on her tool belt, pulled up the nozzle, and handed it to him. Jack immediately raised the bottle to his mouth, mumbling a quick thanks as his lips covered the nozzle.

She patted a now empty pouch as Jack guzzled the cool water. "This tool belt has all sorts of handy pockets and loops and secret compartments. I have to be careful not to put in too much stuff, or it gets really heavy."

He smiled and swiped his forearm over his mouth after drinking half the bottle in a single round. "That's a really nice belt. I'd like one like that."

Carla ran her hand over the soft leather. The tool belt had been her father's pride and joy, one any man would have envied, Jack included. Up until today, she hadn't had a chance to use it.

Memories of her dad nearly brought tears to her eyes. He was a kind and gentle man, and she'd never known anyone like him—before he died or after. Even after two years, she still missed him dearly.

46

"Yes. It's very special to me."

"Now that you have a hammer, you can start nailing at one end, and I'll start at the other."

A rush of uneasiness passed over Carla. Jack really was a typical man and all that went with it. She already knew he loved tools and loved to work with his hands. Now, as they started to work together instead of her just watching, he was starting to give her orders. The way he turned around and started walking back to where he was working showed that he expected his orders to be carried out without question.

She swallowed hard, telling herself that he was supposed to be giving orders. It wasn't personal. While they were working together, even though she was paying for his labor, she had put him in charge. That was why she'd hired him in the first place. He knew what he was doing. She didn't.

"Jack? I need you to show me where to nail."

He turned around and grinned. "Sorry. Do it this way."

Jack showed her how many nails to put on each shingle and where and went to work.

At first he hammered five nails to her one, but by the time they stopped for lunch, she was hammering in three nails to his five. They stopped only long enough to eat the picnic lunch she'd brought, then continued until suppertime. Because it was hard work, Jack insisted they quit for the day.

Carla couldn't remember any other time she'd been so tired. With the exhaustion came the feeling that tomorrow she would be stiff and sore, so Carla didn't argue. Tomorrow was Sunday, the Lord's day of rest.

She had a feeling she was going to need it.

Chapter 5

J ack? What are you doing here?"

He didn't give her a chance to protest as he slid into the pew beside her. Carla squirmed a foot down the polished surface to give him room, torn between wanting to move as far away as possible and not wanting to move more than she had to. Every muscle and tendon in her body hurt.

"I'm here because I go to church faithfully every Sunday."

"But this is the late service."

"I could say I slept in, but that would be lying. I just wanted to sit with you. Is that okay?"

Carla forced herself to breathe. "I guess," she muttered, not at all sure what she thought.

"Where's Ellen?"

"She's not coming. She's sick."

His smile widened. "Then it's a good thing I decided to come. You wouldn't want to sit alone, would you?"

Actually, she did want to sit alone. She needed the time to pray about what was happening with Jack. Without him sitting beside her.

She couldn't help it, she was starting to like the man. Today, his presence and his words confirmed her suspicions. He liked her too. And that was bad. She wanted to trust him, but she couldn't.

"What about lunch? Would you like to join me after the service?"

"I can't. I've already promised my mother I'd meet her halfway and we'd go out for dinner."

"Halfway?"

"My mom still lives on the farm, and it's a five-hour drive. I'm trying to convince her to move into the city. She says she needs good reason to sell the farm and move closer. Once a month, if I don't go visit, we meet halfway."

The lights dimmed to signify the start of the service, sparing her the need to keep talking.

After the close of the service, Jack walked to her car and stood beside it while she unlocked the door. "You'll be doing the roof all day, right? What's next?"

"It's a small house, so the roof will be done Monday. It will take a couple of days to do the back-framing, putting in the doors and windows, and the finishing. Then everything stops, and we wait for the framing inspection."

"Will that take long?"

"Not usually. But after that, it can get a little unpredictable for awhile. That's when I call in the trades to do the plumbing, electrical, telephone, and cable hookups. We'll hook up the furnace, maybe the hot water tank; and when the preliminary electrical and plumbing inspections are done, then we start the drywall."

Carla pictured the house in her mind. So far, it was a hollow shell. Some of the panels were on, but it was barely more than two-by-fours outlining the walls. It was still a far cry from the cute little picture she'd seen on the Internet when she chose the plans.

"Am I going to see you tomorrow? I hope so." He paused and grinned.

All Carla could do was stare up at him. The way she was hanging around the job site and being a pest to all the workers, his attitude should have been one of sarcasm. Something in his eyes told her that he was very serious, and she didn't know how to take it.

She didn't want him to want to see her.

For the first time since the project began, she didn't know if she was doing the right thing by hanging around to see the progression on her house. But she had to help as much as she could to save both time and money, so she didn't have a choice. For the next week, she would have the protection of other people always being around, working. After that. . .

"I'll see you Tuesday. Good-bye, Jack."

Carla hurried home to her apartment, then drove to the small town café where she always met her mother. She told her mother all about how the house was progressing and how good it looked.

She avoided telling her mother about Jack. She didn't know what to say.

She had a feeling the next couple of months were going to be the longest of her life. She'd never felt so unsettled, not even during her breakup with Lyle.

When she could finally move in, she could hide away in her little fortress, and all would be well.

Jack sucked in a deep breath, lifted his baseball cap, ran his fingers through his hair, and plunked the cap back on his head.

"What do you mean, you're leaving? You're only half done."

"I've got something else to do first. This is taking more time than I thought it would, and I have a better offer across town. I'll be back when I'm done there."

Jack gritted his teeth. He didn't often contract a house from start to finish, and this was one of the reasons why. He much preferred being a subcontractor rather than having to work with one. He did his best to ignore all the swearing and cursing when a work in progress didn't go as planned. What he couldn't handle was someone leaving him high and dry in the middle of a job. As it was, the gas fitter didn't show up when he was supposed to, coming on Wednesday, instead of Friday like he was scheduled.

He'd had no trouble with the phone company or the cable company. While they worked, he'd roughed in the piping for the built-in vacuum himself.

The electrician had shown up on time and done his job quickly, but he had done it too quickly. When Jack called for the electrical inspection, the inspector had insisted on a few changes, and it was hard to get the electrician back to make the corrections and complete his work. Of course, that meant calling the electrical inspector back a second time.

And now, to top everything off, the plumber was pulling the same stunt as the gas fitter.

"But you're the last one I need before I can start the drywall. You're putting my whole project behind."

"Look, Bud, the one I contracted across town pays double what this job pays, so I'm going to do it first."

Jack crossed his arms over his chest and stretched to his full height to accentuate his authority. "I don't care about your other jobs. You knew your deadlines and what this job paid when you signed the contract with me."

"The other job pays cash."

Jack squeezed his eyes shut and pressed his thumb into the knot between his eyebrows. In other words, the plumber was accepting money under the table to do a rush job, putting all else aside, in order to collect his "bonus."

While such deals were not uncommon, Jack refused to work that way. He paid by check, paid all his taxes and levies, and deducted everything he was supposed to when he paid a subcontractor.

"I'm not going to condone that. I'll let you go today, but I expect you back tomorrow. You can finish this job in one day, and then I don't care what you do. If you're not here tomorrow, know that I'll never use your services again; and if anyone asks, I'll be honest and say you left my job half done to do another."

The plumber checked his watch and glowered at Jack. "I don't know what this job is paying you. I hope it's worth it. I'll be back tomorrow."

Without giving Jack a chance to reply, the man stomped

away and roared off in his car, the squealing tires leaving a patch of rubber on the road.

Truthfully, Jack was doing Carla's house for less money than any job he'd taken since he first started out ten years ago. At first Ellen's begging had influenced him, but he found himself doing many extras for Carla that weren't in their contract.

Carla.

He didn't know what was bothering her, but behind her smile was something painful, something she didn't want to talk about. Up until now he hadn't pushed it, but he wanted to know, and he wanted to make it right and make her happy—really happy.

In a few days she started her vacation. He didn't know what she had planned, but he knew she intended to spend most of her time at the house, and he could hardly wait.

In order to save her more money, even though it would take a little longer, he hadn't subcontracted out anything else on the house except for the cabinets. The insulation and drywall were jobs he did often as a subcontractor. This time, he was doing it for his own job, just like he'd done the roofing and most of the framing. Between all the delays, he'd already managed to put up most of the vinyl siding, since none of what happened on the inside of the house affected what had to be done to the outside. By the time the plumber finished and the last inspection was done, he would have most of the exterior work completed.

In a few days, he could move to the last step, which was finishing off the inside of the house.

If only he could get the plumber straightened out.

Jack couldn't hold back his smile. "Hi, Carla. I've been expecting you."

"You were?"

He smiled even wider. He should have seen it coming. Carla was dressed to work, wearing a T-shirt and jeans, and her tool belt complete with her hammer and water bottle.

"Your vacation started today, didn't it?"

"Yes. I'm off for a whole month, so I plan to help as much as I can. I want to be able to move in by the time I have to go back to work."

The smile left Jack's face. "I can't finish this in a month. I know the house looks nice from the outside, but the inside is hollow."

"I know. So let's get busy. I plan to do more than sweep. I plan to work. I've got my hammer, and I know how to use it. I'm pretty good with a paintbrush too."

"You're kidding, right?"

She crossed her arms. That bulldog expression he was getting so used to was in her eyes. "Do I look like I'm kidding? For your information, I have a stool in my car so I won't have to bother you for the places I can't reach. I believe today we put in the insulation?"

He didn't dare to question the *we*. "I guess the insulation isn't a difficult job. Come on, everything is stacked inside. We might as well get to it."

When he grabbed a bale of insulation, she did the same and followed him into the den. Before they started, he pulled two dust masks out of his tool belt and handed her one.

"What's this?"

"It's a dust mask. You don't want to breathe in the fibers. I also wear gloves, because handling the insulation can make you itchy."

Gloves on and dust mask in place, Jack showed her how to place the batting properly, then staple the plastic sheeting over top.

He turned around, stepped back, and pulled the mask down, letting it dangle beneath his chin. "You do the next section, and I'll watch."

Jack tried not to shake his head, watching her. She had to use the stool so she could get high enough to place the insulation properly at the top. He only had one pair of gloves, so he'd given them to her. They were ridiculously large on her, making her movements so awkward she could barely hold on to the fiberglass pieces as she pressed them into place.

Worse, she had to take the gloves off and use both hands to squeeze the trigger of the staple gun. Then she couldn't handle the kick of the unit. The force of impact of each staple into the two-by-fours caused the gun to bounce so much that the staples weren't all the way into the wood. She ended up having to finish sinking them with her hammer. Then she missed half the time.

"I have an idea. I've only got one pair of gloves and one staple gun because I wasn't expecting help," he said, being very careful to choose his wording. "I do this faster than you. How about if I put the insulation in, and you can be the gofer and run and get the bales for me? We can speed up the process if I don't have to run back and forth."

She sighed, handed him the staple gun, and shook her hands at her sides. "This is much harder than I thought it would be. Maybe that's not such a bad idea."

Ever since they had parted on Sunday, Jack found he had been looking forward to talking to Carla as he worked. Instead, with Carla running away to bring more insulation and rolls of plastic as he needed them, they couldn't do more than make polite chitchat. He wanted more, and he found himself getting frustrated when every time he turned around to say something, all he saw was her back.

On the bright side, he finished the job of applying all the insulation much faster than usual because every other time he'd done it, he'd done the job alone.

When the last section of plastic was in place, Jack left a message on the insulation inspector's voice mail asking if he could come early.

As Jack tucked the phone back onto his belt, Carla glanced around them, appraising their work. "Now what?"

"We can go outside and do some finishing work until the inspector gets here, but that's all we can do for today. I counted on a whole day for the insulation and inspection, but thanks to your help, I'm done hours early. Tomorrow I have a guy coming to put up the drywall with me. Two people can get it all up in one day, and then it'll take a couple of weeks for me to do the seams and sanding."

"There sure are a lot of inspections."

He nodded. "The next ones will be after the lighting and

plumbing fixtures are in. Then the last one will be the occupancy permit. But until then, there's a lot of work to do."

As Jack gathered up his tool belt and hammer, he tried not to smile as Carla did the same.

"Okay. Let's go outside."

Chapter 6

With the wooden platform and step that would make the small porch already set in place, all Jack had left to do was to hammer the wood spindles to the top railing bars and hammer them into place beside the posts by the door. Then the front entrance area would be complete. It was a treat to have Carla steady the wood as he hammered the pieces together.

They had just lifted one of the assembled units to slot it into place when Carla gasped, stiffened, and fumbled with her side of the railing, causing Jack to scramble to keep it from falling.

When he was sure he had the section supported, Jack looked up to see what had startled her.

A car he knew he'd seen before but couldn't quite place turned the corner at the end of the block.

"Carla? What's wrong?"

She steadied her grip on her side of the wood piece. Her voice came out in a tight squeak. "That was Lyle. I knew he would have to see the house going up with his own eyes once he heard I was actually building. I just didn't expect him to drive by when I was here. He was going to stop, but when he saw I wasn't alone, he took off." She looked down at the section of the railing. "I'm so sorry. I hope I didn't break anything."

Gears started turning inside Jack's head. He'd thought the car looked familiar, but now that the name had been said and the connection made, he started to feel ill.

"Lyle McLaughlan is your ex-fiancé?"

Carla's face turned ashen. Fortunately he already had the base of the railing on the ground and he was supporting the weight himself, because this time she outright dropped it. "You know Lyle?"

"No, not really. I play football with him a few times a year through the interchurch league. The guys go out for coffee and donuts after the games." He didn't know Lyle all that well, but Jack remembered about three years ago, Lyle had gone through a rough breakup with his fiancée. Without naming names, Lyle had said some very unkind words—that the woman was a flake and a loser. He said she'd overreacted to something to the point of mental instability. Lyle said he would have forgiven her, but she refused to work it out, and they split up.

He didn't think Carla was any of the things Lyle had said, but then again, he also knew there were two sides to every story.

Carla backed up a step. Her voice came out in a strained squeak. "Please don't tell him any of the stuff I told you about him and the lot."

Jack shook his head. "Don't worry. Anything you've told me stays between us. Besides, I never see him except for football games since he doesn't go to our church." Not moving, Jack stared at Carla. It really wasn't any of his business, but some sick little part of him had to know. "Lyle seems like an okay guy. Do you mind me asking why you split up?"

She backed up another step from him and crossed her arms over her chest. "I didn't like it when we had a fight."

"No one likes to fight, but every couple does."

"I've been told that, but my parents never fought. My father was kind and gentle and never raised even his voice to my mother. I learned my lesson the hard way with Lyle. If that's the way it is when you're tied down with someone, then I'm never getting married. That's why I'm building this little house just for myself."

A sinking feeling washed through Jack. He knew she'd been burned by a past relationship, but knowing the other party changed everything. Lyle was a Christian, with good morals and high standards, just like himself. He didn't want to be cynical, but it was human nature to only remember the best of a loved one after they died, instead of their faults, especially as time went on.

If the only man good enough for her was someone as perfect as the best memories of her dead father, he knew he never stood a chance. He couldn't compete with a memory. Obviously Lyle couldn't either.

"The Bible tells us how to have good arguments. I know they cover that kind of thing in premarital counseling."

"You don't understand. Sometimes he really hurt me."

Jack hadn't talked much to Lyle, so he didn't have any experience to know if Lyle had a sharp tongue. For that, he would have to take Carla's word at it.

"But I know Lyle. That doesn't make sense."

"I'm not expecting you to believe me. No one believed me. No one except Ellen. I think your inspector is here."

Jack had been so lost in thought that he hadn't noticed the inspector's car pull up. "I have an idea. While I'm showing the inspector around, you think about what you want to do with your fireplace. Next week we'll have to place the order, so you should decide exactly what kind of facing you want."

They walked into the house together. Carla stopped at the black fireplace insert, while Jack walked from room to room with the inspector.

While the inspector checked the attic, Jack leaned against the two-by-four that was the start of the door frame to the room and waited. Instead of thinking about the house, Jack thought about Carla.

In the short amount of time since they'd met, he'd really begun to care for her.

He sighed and watched her as she stood, lost in thought, staring at the fireplace.

He'd prayed for God's will to be done. The thought that the answer might be *no* never crossed his mind. He'd never considered that Carla would be carrying too much emotional baggage to at least give a relationship with him a chance.

Once he had the form in his hand certifying that the house passed the inspection, Jack saw the inspector to the door.

Carla appeared behind him. "What now?"

"All we can do is finish putting up the railing, and that's the last of the exterior work except for the painting." He tucked the inspection paper into his pocket. "It will only take one day for me and Rob to put up the drywall. After that, I think we can count on a week and a half to two weeks to do the mudding and sanding."

"Let's get to it, then. I can hardly wait."

Carla thought she would beat Jack; but when she arrived, hammering was already in progress. She walked inside to see that Jack had already installed the vaulted ceiling in the living room with fake wood paneling, just like he'd said. He warned her that it wouldn't look great at first, but when he touched it up with some stain and applied a few coats of varathane, being so high, no one would notice that it wasn't real. So far he was right.

The ceiling was up in the kitchen, too, as well as the short hallway. She walked a few more steps and stood in the bedroom doorway and watched Jack and another man hard at work.

Both men stood on some kind of stilts in the middle of the room. The man she didn't know was steadying one end of a large sheet of plasterboard with both hands above his head. On the other end, Jack was so tall that from atop the stilts, he pressed the plasterboard to the ceiling stringers with his head while he used both hands to nail the section in place.

Already both men were damp from hard work, and she could see why. Carla couldn't imagine hammering upward, to head height or higher for a prolonged length of time. Yet except for the dampness on Jack's brow and the obvious wet stains on his T-shirt, he didn't appear to be struggling or tired. Watching him work in the awkward position, it was no wonder he had the biceps of a pro wrestler. His obvious strength and stamina were both to be admired and feared.

"Hi, Carla. I didn't see you come in. Carla, this is Rob. Rob, Carla."

They nodded polite greetings, and Carla turned back to Jack. "You guys look like you're hard at work. Is there anything I can do to help?"

"I've seen you at work with a hammer. I matched that chip from your folder and bought some nice green paint and a couple of brushes. How about if you go outside and paint the wood spindles and trim around the windows?"

"That's a gentle hint if I've ever heard one."

He grinned. "I can be subtle when I need to be."

Carla didn't dignify his comment with a response.

Today she didn't mind not being included in doing any real work. Going outside to paint gave her time to think.

Part of her wanted to explain to Jack what had happened with Lyle, to defend herself and clear her name, as she could well imagine what Lyle had said about her. She could see in Jack's face that he thought it was her fault, and perhaps it was, even though her counselor told her it wasn't. When it came down to actually talking about what had happened between herself and Lyle, the only person Carla had been able to talk to who wasn't a professional was Ellen. First she'd been too embarrassed, and then she'd been too ashamed. Of course,

Lyle's threats that if she ever said anything to anyone about his actions always hung over her head.

She had worked for years not to be afraid of him, but at times, she still was. She knew what he was like, and the good sense the Lord had given her told her she was right to be afraid.

But now, just as her counselor warned her, she was carrying over her fear of Lyle to other men. Jack was an ordinary man, in many ways not too different than Lyle, but in many ways, completely different. She wanted to trust Jack. But she had trusted Lyle, which proved what she couldn't trust was her own judgment.

When lunchtime came, the three of them stopped working. With all the dust and materials strewn everywhere inside the house and only mud to sit on outside, they all climbed into the back of Jack's pickup for an impromptu picnic. Rob complimented them on how well the house was coming, and Carla had to agree. Jack had every right to be proud of the job he was doing.

It gave her goose bumps inside to think that maybe, just maybe, when Jack prayed the first day they met, that God really was listening. In addition to Jack's hard work, God really was providing a little divine intervention for the smooth progress of her little house.

Carla poured a cup of iced tea for each of them. "I only have one piece left to paint. Do you have something else I can do?"

Jack looked down to the white plastic pails they were sitting on. "You can probably start doing the seams and filling in the nail holes in the rooms we've already done. I know you can't reach the ceiling, but you can certainly start the walls."

After lunch Jack carried a pail of filler into the house. Carla followed him with a large roll of white mesh tape.

"Here's what you do. Watch me."

In only a few minutes, Jack filled in a seam, applied the tape, topped it with filler, filled in the nail holes, then smoothed everything with the trowel.

"Now you do it. Don't worry about it being rough. When it dries, we sand it smooth, then put on another coat."

Carla ended up putting on too much filler, then spread it too far in her attempts to smooth it.

"No, like this," he mumbled. Instead of taking the trowel from her, he gently covered her hand with his and guided her movements as she made a second attempt at spreading. "Don't press so hard. Follow my movements. Relax."

The second the word came out of his mouth, he shuffled in closer. He rested his free hand on her left shoulder while his right hand guided hers to do a better job. As they leaned forward together and he hunched down to her level, she could feel the heat of his chest and the movement of his breathing against her back.

Relaxation was the farthest thing from her mind. She felt like a child pressed up against a big bear—a bear who could crush her at will. She had no escape. Jack completely surrounded her from the back. To her front, she was only inches from a solid wall. The panic she hadn't felt for so long threatened to overtake her.

"See? You're doing a good job."

As quickly as he'd come up behind her, he released her and was gone. All that was left was the residual warmth where their bodies had pressed together, and it was fading fast.

Carla forced herself to breathe.

He hadn't called her stupid. He hadn't criticized her inexperience. He hadn't pointed out every mistake.

He hadn't hit her for being inept, then told her she deserved it.

He had very gently showed her what to do and left, trusting that she would do it right.

Carla squeezed her eyes shut, but she couldn't stop the silent tears from flowing. She'd been so frightened. . .cornered. . .trapped. Yet she hadn't been. She repeated over and over in her head that just because Jack thought Lyle was a nice guy, it didn't mean Jack was like Lyle or would justify Lyle's actions.

Suddenly, Jack appeared beside her. "I forgot something. It might help if you. . ." His voice trailed off when he saw her face. "What happened? Are you hurt?"

Without waiting for a reply, he picked up her hand and started examining her fingers.

Carla couldn't stop her lower lip from quivering as she brushed away her tears with her free hand. "I'm okay. It's nothing. What did you want to show me?"

He continued to hold her hand. With his other one, he reached up and gently brushed a new tear from her cheek. The concern in his beautiful green eyes touched her soul, which only made her feel worse. "This doesn't look like nothing. What's wrong?"

"It's nothing. Really. What did you want?"

His brows knotted, and one eye narrowed. He remained silent for a few seconds, then shook his head. "I can't remember."

"You should get back to work. I'm sure Rob is waiting for you."

As Jack left the room, he paused and glanced over his shoulder just before he disappeared down the hallway.

Carla meant to concentrate on filling the holes. Instead, she thought of Jack's kindness, his gentleness, and his concern. While Lyle was nice at first, he'd never treated her the way Jack did.

Jack really was a nice, decent man. She knew it in her head. Now, if only she could believe it in her heart.

She had almost finished the wall when Rob and Jack appeared.

"We're done putting up all the plasterboard. Rob's got another job after this, so it's up to us to do the rest. You said you wanted to work, so from now on, it's just you and me."

Carla's heart stopped, then started up in double-time.

She didn't know if that was good or bad. Words failed her, so she nodded instead.

"I'll see you tomorrow morning, say, seven o'clock?"

Chapter 7

When Jack arrived at the house promptly at seven o'clock, Carla was already there. He inhaled deeply and walked inside.

For the next few weeks, except for when the plumber and electrician came back, it would just be the two of them, working side by side, all day long.

He knew she didn't know what she was doing, but she was eager to learn. He could give her the simple jobs; and for the times she couldn't help, her being there with him was enough.

He found her already hard at work, finishing her work from the previous day.

"Good morning."

As Carla looked back at him over her shoulder, a smudge of white marred her cheek. "Good morning to you too."

Jack's breath caught. He wanted to wipe the offending blob away.

And he wanted to kiss her while he did it. And that was wrong.

He still didn't know what the problem had been between Carla and Lyle. If the things Lyle said were true, he was taking his chances that history might repeat itself. As it was, yesterday he'd found her crying for no reason.

Even if he did find out that Carla was the wronged party and Lyle had made the whole thing up to salvage his pride, Carla had still seemed to have an unrealistic view of marriage. Every couple argued now and then. He was sure her parents had too, only she hadn't seen it.

He'd never felt so torn in his life. Even though he knew he was setting himself up for heartbreak, he couldn't stop himself from wanting to be with her.

Jack cleared his throat. "Looks like you're making progress. I'll go into the kitchen and start the ceiling. By the way, I brought coffee."

"That's great."

Working with Carla was different than working with anyone else. More words passed between them in one day than a whole week of working with a man, even his best friend. He couldn't believe how quickly the days disappeared as they continued with their task.

On the downside, she worked much more slowly than he was used to. By the time they'd finished texturing the ceiling and filling the last nail hole in the wall, four days had passed, an unheard-of amount of time for two people working on such a small house.

At first he'd found her attention to detail admirable; but as time wore on and the project extended into a longer and longer time frame, he caught himself becoming irritated.

Carla wanted the job done quickly, yet she was the one slowing it down.

It was a relief to load up all the supplies in his truck when they were done.

While he opened all the windows a crack, Carla looked around at their work.

"What now?"

"Now it sits for a few days to dry. Then we sand it and do the whole thing all over again."

"Why?" Her eyes widened, and she hunched her shoulders. "Did I do a bad job? I'm sorry. I tried to be so careful."

He reminded himself that she was doing her best.

Jack sighed. "You did a great job. This is just the way it's done. For the next few days we'll be outside. First we'll frame the driveway and walkway, and then I'll call in the cement truck to fill it. While that's setting, we'll do the second application."

The following morning they arrived back at the same time.

They stood side by side as Jack inserted the key into the lock. "I know we're going to be working outside today, but I want to see how everything is progressing in—" His voice trailed off as he opened the door. "It's cool in here."

Carla nodded. "You won't believe what happened. I forgot my lunch pail, so I had to come back last night. When I walked in it was so hot. I found the furnace on full blast. So I turned it off."

Jack bowed his head, squeezed his eyes shut, and pinched the bridge of his nose. "I turned the furnace on."

"Why? It's the middle of summer."

Over and over, he told himself that she didn't know any better. "To dry out the house. Otherwise it takes forever for the filler to be ready to sand. It's going to take three days at best."

"I'm sorry. I didn't know."

Jack raised his head and forced himself to smile. "It's okay. It was warm yesterday, so hopefully it won't delay things too much."

Jack walked to the wall and ran his finger down the center of the seam, confirming that it was far from dry. "I'll turn the furnace back up. Please. Don't touch it again."

With the furnace reset, he unloaded the wood for the driveway forms and a couple of shovels from his truck.

She turned and looked into the yard. "Don't you think it's a little too soon to be planting flowers? I don't even have any grass yet."

"You might notice you don't have a sidewalk or a driveway either. The excavator took a layer off where they go, but there's been a lot of movement in the yard, and the rain makes it settle too. Today we dig where the driveway goes, measure it, and frame it. When that's done, I'll call the cement truck, and they'll pour it."

"Why don't you rent one of those cute little tractors again?"

"Cute little tractors?"

"Like that one you used to clear the land before the excavator came the first time."

Jack grinned. "Those are expensive, and they have to be

booked in advance. Besides, we've got nothing else to do, so we have the time to dig this by hand. We're only going down a couple of inches."

"Oh."

At first Jack thought Carla's efforts to help dig and level out the bed for the driveway were cute. After the third time she accidentally nailed him with a wad of dirt, he began to change his mind.

He bent at the waist and shook the mud out of his hair. "I forgot my cap today, so I think I'll work over there, where it's safer. Okay?"

"I'm so sorry, Jack. I'll be more careful."

"It's okay. I know you have an office job and you're not used to this. Maybe you should call it a day and come back tomorrow when they pour the cement. You might want to write your initials in the corner."

Her eyes lit up, and she smiled from ear to ear. "Really? I can do that?"

"It's your house. See you tomorrow. If not, the day after we should be able to start sanding and do the second application of filler the next day."

Jack squeezed his eyes shut and pinched the bridge of his nose. "You're kidding, right?"

"Why would I kid? I hate that awful off-white base color you guys use for new homes. I'll paint the rooms different colors later, when I have more money to decorate properly. But until then, I want the whole house painted a real color."

"Yes. But pink?"

"I like pink."

Jack refused to comment.

He waited while the clerk mixed the required quantity of paint, all pink, and they returned to the house.

Fortunately Carla was better at painting than she was at filling and sanding or anything else she'd helped with. They'd had a few tense moments when she oversanded a whole wall, forcing yet another delay while they did a third application of filler. All Jack could think of was that he was glad he wasn't paying her. If he was, he would have fired her ten times over. Still, he admired her tenacity, although he had to admit that at times her lack of ability and her many blunders got on his nerves.

Mistakes aside, finally, they were hard at work, painting. With any luck, they could be finished in a couple of days and get back on schedule.

"Jack? This is the wrong color."

He stepped off the raised plank and turned around to see Carla studying the wall. "I know. It should be a neutral beige."

"That's not funny. This isn't the pink I picked. We have to go back."

Still holding the paintbrush, he swept his arm through the air to encompass all they'd done. "What are you talking about? We've nearly finished two rooms."

"That doesn't matter. This is the wrong color."

Jack gritted his teeth rather than say what was on his mind. Because of the difficulty in not slopping paint on the textured ceiling, painting was his least favorite job of the entire procedure of building a house. "Paint always dries lighter than it goes on."

"How much lighter?"

"I can't give you a percentage. It just dries lighter."

"I don't think it will be light enough. I think we should go back and get this paint lightened."

He lifted his baseball cap, ran his fingers through his hair, then rammed it back on his head. "They can't lighten paint. It's not like just mixing in more white. Even if it was, these are full tubs, there's no room to add anything significant. With one half used, they'd never get all three the same. We'd have to buy all new paint." Besides the expense, Jack thought of the hassle of taking the three tubs back to the store and the time they would waste.

She turned her back to him and again held the paint chip to wall. "But it doesn't match the chip. Don't they have a guarantee?"

"Maybe if we'd only opened it, but we've used half a tub. Besides, I already told you, it will be lighter when it's dry."

She turned around and glared at him. "And if you're wrong? Will you come back and repaint the whole house?"

Jack held his breath. He'd worked harder on Carla's house than anything he'd ever built. Her little house had become a trophy for him as much as her. He'd put all his best efforts into it. He'd put extra care into the unique way he finished the vaulted ceiling. He'd done endless bickering and bartering with all the suppliers. He'd called in personal favors from subcontractors he knew.

He'd been so proud of the house. Until she decided to paint it pink.

As hard as he tried, he couldn't keep the tight edge out of his voice. "I'd repaint the whole house myself just to get it a neutral beige."

She frowned and rested her fists on her hips. "I don't want beige. I want pink. The right pink."

"I'll pay for new paint out of my own pocket if you pick a beige tone," he grumbled between his teeth.

Once again, she stepped up to the wall and held up the paint chip. "I know it was hard to paint up to the vaulted ceiling, but this really isn't the right color. They know you at the store. Surely they can do something."

Jack stomped across the room, stopping inches from her back. "You don't understand." He raised one hand to encompass his hard work up at the join of the vaulted ceiling, at the peak of the ceiling, which matched the peak of the house. Except that level was infinitely more difficult to work at from inside the house. "Think of what you're asking me to do."

At the sound of his voice suddenly behind her, Carla turned quickly and stared at his hand in the air above her head. Her eyes widened, and she inhaled sharply.

In a split second, she covered her head with her arms and hunched down. "I'm sorry," she whimpered. "You're right. I'll keep what I've got."

Jack opened his mouth, but no words came out.

She acted like he was going to hit her.

He would never hit her. He'd never even think of hitting her, for any reason, no matter how angry he was and no matter what she'd done.

Brief snippets of different times they'd been together fell into place like dominoes. Not wanting to hold his hand when they prayed together. Her tears the day he'd first shown her how to do the seams. How she was always so quick to apologize when she'd done nothing wrong.

He didn't think he'd acted aggressively, but her response had been too automatic.

She was afraid of him.

But he'd done nothing. Which meant something like this had happened before.

Jack lowered his arm and backed up.

Lyle. That was why she left him. That was why Lyle was so quick to discredit anything she said by talking ill of her. She'd said that Lyle had really hurt her. Now he understood. It was more than cruel words. Lyle had hit her and apparently more than once.

"Carla. . .I won't hurt you. I would never hurt you."

Very slowly, she lowered her arms. Her eyes were too bright and welled up with unshed tears. "I didn't mean to make you angry."

He wanted to step closer—to touch her, to hold her in his arms, and to tell her everything was okay. That she had nothing to fear. He would rather die than cause her pain.

At that exact moment, he realized he loved her.

But he didn't dare touch her. He didn't know what to do.

Jack shook his head. "I'm not angry. I'm just frustrated. If you want to change the paint, that's fine with me."

She looked up at him, swiped her arm over her nose, and

sniffled. "No, you're right. I have to trust this will be the same as the chip. We really don't have time to buy new paint and start again. I've already delayed this so much. I have to go back to work on Monday, and the cabinets and floors aren't even in."

"I didn't mean to scare you. If you want you can go home. I'll understand. I can finish the painting."

"Please don't feel sorry for me. I'm okay. Let's get back to work."

Jack's feet wouldn't move. "Do you want to talk about it?"

"No."

To prove her point, she turned around, picked up her brush, and resumed painting. Jack could see her hand shaking as the brush moved up and down, but she didn't say a word.

They painted for the rest of the day. Jack tried as much as possible to be in the same room as Carla, even though he didn't know what to say. Not that he wanted to hear anything about Lyle. He thought that if he saw Lyle now, he didn't know if he could be held accountable for his actions.

He wanted to just talk, to hear Carla say she trusted him, that she knew he was nothing like Lyle.

Instead, they chatted about nothing of consequence while they worked diligently all day. They called out for pizza for supper. They were both starting to yawn by the time they were done.

Tomorrow they would do it all again with the second coat. As well, the electrician would put in proper light fixtures to replace the bare light bulbs he currently had hanging in the center of each room. Then came the flooring, cabinets, the final inspections, and occupancy permit, at which point Carla could move in.

Jack looked around him. He saw the potential, but he didn't want the project to end. He wanted her to stay with him forever.

He pressed the lids back onto the pails. "Want to make it earlier tomorrow, and we can have breakfast together?"

"I don't think so. I'm not very fit to look at before my morning coffee."

He doubted that. He wanted to be able to look at her twenty-four hours a day. He wanted to protect her and shelter her, especially from people like Lyle.

"How about if we come just a little early, and I'll bring breakfast here?"

Her eyebrows knotted. "I guess. If that's what you want."

Jack couldn't stop himself. He crossed the room to where she was wiping some spilled paint. "That's not what I want. I want you to trust me. I want you to know how very much I, uh, like you and that I'd never hurt you."

Very slowly, he reached toward her. Carla lowered her head and watched as he gently touched her arm with only his fingertips, then slowly trailed his touch up to her chin. She tilted her head up and looked at him with those big, sad, puppy dog eyes. Jack's heart pounded so hard he could feel it.

He felt a slight stiffening of the muscles in her neck. Immediately, he lowered his hand, even though it almost hurt to give her the space he thought she needed. "Tell me what to do," he ground out.

"Don't move," she whispered.

She shuffled closer to him and rested her hands on his chest. His heart pounded more than ever as she leaned into him, not moving her hands. He forced himself to breathe as she nestled her cheek to his heart, then slipped her arms around his back.

He wanted to hold her so badly he hurt, but she had told him not to move. Jack remained as he was, with his hands at his sides.

She spoke so softly he could barely hear her. "Hold me, Jack."

So as not to overwhelm her, Jack very slowly moved his hands around her back. He struggled to increase the pressure of his embrace gradually, even though he wanted to squeeze her tight and kiss her until they melted.

He nestled his face into the hair on the crown of her head, not caring when his nose touched a gooey blob of wet paint. He couldn't help himself. He kissed the top of her head. "I think I'm falling in love with you," he murmured into her hair.

For a second she stiffened, then snuggled in closer. "I'm not sure how I feel, but I think I'm falling in love with you too. It terrifies me."

He could only guess at what she was going through. He hadn't been afraid of a person since he was ten years old and the neighborhood bully had given him a bloody nose. Since he turned thirteen, no one had been a physical threat to him. Now, as an adult, he was well aware that when he entered a room, he was bigger than most people by a head and outweighed the average man by at least thirty pounds. He didn't want to intimidate people, but he knew his size did.

He didn't want Carla to feel threatened by him. He wanted her to feel safe and secure in his presence. He wanted to grow old with her.

"This might be a little fast, but how do you feel about marriage? In general."

She backed up so fast he felt a rush of cool air between them. "I'm never getting married. I won't allow anyone to ever have control over me or have the right to order me around ever again."

All Jack could do was blink. "But marriage is a partnership. It's not about control or giving or following orders. It's about being in love and sharing everything. Love is patient. Love is kind. And all that stuff God says."

She backed up a few steps. "I'm really tired. I should get to bed. Good night, Jack. I'll see you tomorrow."

Before he could respond, she was gone. He took one step, intending to follow her, but suddenly, he froze. His heart sank as he suspected she was running from him. He couldn't take the chance that she might think he was chasing her and make everything worse.

Jack stood still, watching her through the window as she drove away.

He knew he wouldn't get much sleep tonight, but for tomorrow, he already had plans.

Chapter 8

When Carla pulled up to the house, Jack's truck was already there.

She tried to be bold as she pushed the door open and walked inside the house. She'd been such a ninny yesterday, and she wanted to make it right. When she got home, she had phoned her counselor for the first time in over a year and poured out her heart. All the woman would say was that Carla had to decide for herself if she could trust Jack or if she couldn't. No amount of talking or reasoning would make a difference. It was something Carla had to do alone.

She followed the music of the local Christian radio station to find Jack in the kitchen, painting.

In the center of the room, he'd laid out a blanket. Beside a bag from the local fast-food restaurant was some kind of plant with pink flowers.

Jack saw her when he turned sideways to dip the paintbrush in the pail. "Hi. I didn't hear you come in. Breakfast is ready. I do a great drive-thru."

"What is that?"

His green eyes sparkled as he grinned. "It's the first plant for your flower bed."

She stared at the bright flowers. "I thought you didn't like pink."

"It doesn't matter what I like. It's your house, and you do. Enjoy it."

"Thank you," she mumbled, too stunned by his actions to say more.

Except for the engagement ring, the only time Lyle gave her a gift was after the first time he hit her. As time went on, he was filled with less and less remorse as he got rougher and rougher, until finally he told her she deserved it in the first place. By then, she'd come to believe him. Still, even the first time, when he really appeared to be very sorry, the gift he'd bought was something he liked more than she did.

The memories caused her to lose her appetite, but she ate the breakfast Jack had worked so hard to buy and quickly resumed her painting.

She wanted to be alone, not only because she needed to concentrate on doing a good job, but also because she needed time to think. However, every time she turned around, Jack appeared, offering to help or simply checking on her to make sure she was okay. Before she knew it, he'd moved his painting gear into the same room where she was, following behind her to do everything she couldn't reach instead of working a room ahead.

The entire time they painted, he teased her about being so short and not being able to reach the high spots. Carla therefore told him he was no better, because he was too tall to reach the low spots.

As the days progressed, Jack never once criticized her. She found she could relax, although feeling relaxed while working hard at doing the finishing and painting was a foreign combination for her.

Once the painting was done, people started coming and going in a whirlwind of activity. The floors were laid, then the kitchen and bathroom cabinets went in. Next, the plumber installed the sinks, toilet, and the dishwasher. The electrical inspection had been done, and Jack was currently with the plumbing inspector, who was nice enough to come on Saturday as a favor to Jack.

She stood to the side and watched as Jack saw the plumbing inspector out.

"I can't believe it's almost done," he said as he closed the door. "All that's left is the carpeting next week, then the occupancy permit, and then you can move in."

"I can't believe how fast it went, either. Monday I have to be back at work. It's hard to believe I've been off a month. I don't feel very rested."

"I know what you mean. I've got a couple of new jobs lined up, so I'm not going to get much of a rest other than just Sunday. But it's good to be back on the job again."

Carla scanned the living room. Her living room. Except for the carpet, the house was done. For the first time, she could really envision her furniture here. She was currently standing where her new couch would go, the same spot she was standing, minus the house, when she first met Jack. Only now, she would be saying good-bye.

Jack left his spot at the door and joined her where she stood. "So what now?"

"I guess I'll notify the bank to submit the final payment to you."

He stepped closer. Very gently, he picked up her hands, then closed his fingers around them. His large hands swallowed hers up completely. "I meant what about us?"

His gentle touch set her insides quivering, but not from fear. She felt shaky and couldn't define why. "I don't think there is an us."

He shuffled closer. "I'd like us to start seeing each other. How about after church tomorrow?"

"I'm going to my mother's tonight, so I won't be here tomorrow. After that, I don't know. I like to think I would be okay, but the thought of putting myself in the same vulnerable position scares me to death."

"Then could we work on being friends first?"

She looked up at him. The man was six feet four inches tall and towered over her by a foot. His shoulders were so broad he had difficulty buying nice clothes. She didn't want to think of his shoe size. Since he did manual labor for a living, he was strong and fit and well toned all over. If he wanted to, he could squash her like a fly. At the same time, his sincere smile and his dazzling sea green eyes took her breath away. He had a simple, honest charm that drew people to him. He hadn't seemed to notice, but she'd seen women at church almost swooning over him. From a safe distance, he made her swoon at times too.

Yet, close up and personal, Carla wanted to run for the hills.

"I don't know if I'm capable of being friends."

He gave her hands a gentle squeeze. "I don't know what Lyle did to you, but I can promise I would never hurt you. If you want, I can give you references." He gave her a weak smile.

"I'm sorry, Jack. It's not you. It's me. This is something I have to work out myself."

He released her hands, and immediately Carla felt the coldness of the loss. She was almost ready to ask him to touch her again when his large palms cupped her cheeks. All she could do was look into his soulful eyes.

"I love you, Carla, but I'm not going to pressure you to go beyond what you can handle. Above all else, I want you to be happy. When you're ready, you've got my number. Until then, may I kiss you good-bye?"

Carla's heart pounded, and she broke into a cold sweat. That he was saying good-bye made her want to tell him not to go, but she had to be fair and honest. When this moment was over, would she be able to feel safe? For now he was being gentle and tender. But what about when he was angry with her? Or what about when he was angry about something else and she was the nearest scapegoat?

Her eyes fluttered shut. "Good-bye, Jack."

She truly had expected him to brush a quick kiss on her cheek and back up, but he didn't. He settled his warm, moist lips on hers and took his time, touching her heart and soul with the most mind-blowing kiss of her life.

"You know where to find me if you want me," he murmured in a low, shaky tone, and then he turned and walked out the door.

She ran to the window and watched Jack's big red truck disappear from sight.

Numbly, Carla walked around her home, truly alone in it for the very first time in its nearly completed state. She tried to picture her furniture in every room. She could, except at the same time she also saw Jack, working at something there.

She squeezed her eyes tightly shut, but that didn't stop the images of Jack from appearing or the tears from pushing their way out. She had never been so mixed up, not even when she couldn't understand why Lyle would hit her when he professed to love her so much. At the time she knew it was very wrong. When Ellen figured out what was happening and dragged her to the counselor, it was a relief both to end the relationship and not to be told that she was crazy and stupid for allowing it to happen.

But knowing that she'd made such poor judgments before, she didn't trust herself to make the right one now.

Carla checked all the windows, locked up the house, and went to her car, where she already had her suitcase for the night in preparation for the long drive home. She didn't know if she would talk about Jack with her mother; but the time away would give her time to truly be alone, give her a unique opportunity to detach herself from everything, and pray properly.

God had helped her before, when she poured out her heart and problems about Lyle. She knew He would help her now with Jack.

Chapter 9

T hanks for calling, and I'll see you in September."

Carla hung up the phone, made the appropriate notes on the calendar on her desk, and looked up at the clock.

She stood. "It's my lunch break. I'm leaving the building. Page me if you need me."

Sal folded her hands on her desktop and grinned up at Carla. "Let me guess. Going after something for the house?"

Carla nodded as she grabbed her purse. "Yes. I got the occupancy permit yesterday. Believe it or not, the inspector pointed out that Jack and I both forgot to get the numbers for the front of the house."

"When are you actually moving?"

"I don't know. I can move in any time; but because I missed the end of the month for giving notice, I have the apartment almost two months. I could move everything in my car, one box at a time, and save on a moving truck with that kind of time frame."

Sal laughed. "Have fun shopping."

Fortunately Carla caught every light green and arrived at the store in record time. As she walked through the parking lot, she nearly tripped over her own feet when she saw a very familiar huge red pickup.

Jack.

It had been over a week since she'd seen him, and she missed him more than words could say. After they parted, she spent most of the next day talking to her mother about him. Her mother hadn't given her any advice either way on what to do. All her mother had said was to pray diligently and an answer would come.

Carla had prayed diligently, night and day. When she wasn't praying about him, she was thinking about him.

The only decision she'd come to was that she loved him deeply. She knew in her head that he would never hurt her. She'd seen him angry many times in the time it took to build her house. She'd been too afraid to let him see her, so she'd hidden. He didn't swear or throw things or hit things. He stood in one spot, breathing deeply, almost like he was counting to ten. When he calmed down, he rectified whatever the problem had been and carried on.

Yet, even though she knew he wouldn't hurt her, she was still afraid. Therefore, coward that she was, she'd done nothing.

She quickly selected some brass numbers for the front of the house, then glanced at her watch. If she hurried, she would have time to buy some wood pieces to make a plant shelf in the utility room.

Carla ran outside to the lumber section. At the sound of

a familiar, deep voice, she skidded to a halt and ducked behind the rack of mesh wiring.

Automatically she looked up, but she couldn't see Jack, which was odd. When she heard his voice again, she lowered her sights to see him hunkered down so low he was nearly sitting on the ground, talking to a little girl.

"You shouldn't touch a baby bird. I know it's on the ground, but it's probably not hurt. See up there?" He pointed to the overhanging roof, where a nest was tucked under the eaves. "It's fallen out, and the mother will be back soon. If we can put it back without touching it, she will probably take care of it. But if a human touches it, she'll push it out of the nest and it will die."

The mother, who was standing nearby, looked up at the nest. "They're just starlings."

Jack shrugged his shoulders as he reached for a broken piece of plastic sheeting lying on the ground. "It's still one of God's creatures. If the mother pushes it out, so be it. But until that happens, we should do what we can to help."

Very gently, Jack nudged the baby bird onto the plastic with a stick. He hoisted himself onto one of the shelves, balancing on his toes, and carefully deposited the bird back into the nest.

Without a word spoken, the three of them stood to the side while other customers, oblivious to what had just happened, continued to walk by. Finally, the mother bird returned. Immediately she shoved some food into all three babies' beaks as if nothing had happened.

"Look, Mommy! The baby bird is okay!"

"Yes. Let's thank the nice man and get going. We have to pick up your sister."

The little girl said the quickest thank-you Carla had ever seen and dashed off with her mother. Jack turned and started walking to the cash register.

Carla's heart pounded as she recalled Jesus' words from Luke 12.

Are not five sparrows sold for two pennies? Yet not one of them is forgotten by God. Indeed, the very hairs of your head are all numbered. Don't be afraid; you are worth more than many sparrows.

It wasn't a sparrow, but it was close enough.

"Jack! Wait!"

His feet skidded to a halt. "Carla? What are you doing here?"

"I changed my mind."

He blinked and his eyebrows rose. "You'll let me repaint with a neutral off-white?"

"No. Not in a million years." She cleared her throat. "Tell me. How do you feel about marriage? And not in general."

"Marriage? I. . ." His voice trailed off, and his eyebrows knotted. "Is this a real question?"

Ignoring the handful of brass letters in her hand and the spool of wire Jack had, Carla did her best to wrap her fingers around Jack's hands. "It's more than a real question. It's the question."

He stiffened from head to toe. "I hope you know what you're asking me, because my answer is yes. Are you sure?"

"Yes, I'm sure."

She looked down as he plucked the numbers from her numb fingers and laid them and the spool of wire on the ground beside them. "I've never been proposed to before, so I hope I'm doing this right."

Ignoring everything around them, Jack wrapped his arms around her and kissed her well and good—in the middle of the lumber section. Carla also ignored the whispering of people as they walked past—and kissed him right back.

When they finally separated, Carla ran her fingers through her hair and gasped. "Oh, no! I have to get back to work! I'm late!"

Jack grinned. "I'll pay for those. Meet you at the house after you get off?"

"Yes! Thanks!" she called out as she ran for the parking lot.

The whole way back to the college, Carla couldn't wipe the grin from her face.

She was getting married, but this time, she could hardly wait. She had only one problem, and that was her house.

The house they had just worked so hard to build.

Carla hurried as fast as she could, but Jack still arrived at the house before she did.

The first thing she noticed were the bright brass numbers, proudly displayed beside the front door.

"Very nice," she said. "But what are we going to do? We both have our own houses."

He picked up one hand and slowly intertwined his fingers in hers. They remained standing in the center of the sidewalk, looking at the front of the house. "It would make more sense to live in my house. It's bigger and more suited for a family." He turned and grinned at her. "And dogs. I've always wanted a dog. How about you?"

"I'd love a dog." She turned back to face the house and sighed. "I don't want to move in for a couple of months and then move again. I gave notice at my apartment already, and I have to be out in seven weeks. I don't know what to do."

"We could get married in seven weeks and move you right into my house. And that will make it our house."

She sighed again. Her house was small, but it was cute and built by the best contractor in the business, at least in her opinion. "I guess I'll sell it, then."

"I've been thinking about that. It's special to you for your own personal reasons, and I think you should keep it. Why don't you rent it out?" He stepped in front of her, and without letting go of her hand, he gently ran the fingers of his free hand on her cheek. "If you decide to stay home for awhile when we start our family, that would give you your own income, independent of me. You've more than earned the equity in it."

"That's a great idea!"

She smiled as Jack bent over and gave her a gentle peck on the cheek. He really was a kind and wonderful man, and she knew she would thank God every day of the rest of her life for him.

At the same time as Jack opened his mouth to speak, his stomach gurgled. His cheeks and his ears turned a charming shade of red. "How about if we go grab some supper. I'm not exactly dressed for it, but I want to take you out for dinner to celebrate our engagement."

"Just a minute."

Carla left Jack standing on the sidewalk while she walked to the doorway. She ran her fingers over the smooth numbers and then the pristine freshly painted wood trim. She'd fallen in love in that house, but she had no regrets about someone else living in it. She doubted a family would rent such a small house, making her wish that if a single person moved in, they would receive the same blessings of love that God had given her.

Jack appeared beside her, and she turned to face him. "You probably hear this a lot, but this is the house that Jack built."

He picked up one hand and once again twined his fingers with hers. "No, it's not. We built it together. This is the house that love built."

Carla smiled. This was where God had helped her get over her fears and where God had connected her with Jack.

"Yes," she said. "It certainly is."

GAIL SATTLER

Despite the overabundance of rain, Gail Sattler enjoys living on the West Coast with her husband, three sons, two dogs, five lizards, and countless fish, many of which have names. Gail Sattler loves to write tales of romance that can be complete only with God in their center. She's had many books out with Heartsong Presents and Barbour Publishing. In 2002, 2001, and 2000, Gail was voted as the Favorite Heartsong Author. Visit Gail's Web page at http://www.gailsattler.com.

Love's Open Door

by Susan May Warren

Dedication

Being a missionary is, in my mind, one of the hardest jobs in the world. The personal sacrifices are high, and the rewards. . . sometimes delayed. However, every year thousands of missionaries raise their own support, sell everything they own, and trek across the world to learn another language and culture so they can share the good news of salvation. I admire them more than I can express.

This book is dedicated to a few missionaries who have blessed my life with their commitment and sacrifice:
Randy & Robin Covington, Kamchatka Peninsula, Russia
Dwayne & Carolyn King, Russia
Mark & Julie Morgenstern, Ukraine
Dale & Emily Vajko, France
The SEND Team, Far East Russia and especially,
Andrew Warren, my dear husband and, by far,
my favorite missionary.
Thank you for letting me join you in the backwoods of Siberia.

"I said, 'You are my servant'; I have chosen you and have not rejected you. So do not fear, for I am with you; do not be dismayed, for I am your God. I will strengthen you and help you; I will uphold you with my righteous right hand."
ISAIAH 41:9–10

Chapter 1

Ellen White leaned forward in her seat, her hymnal clutched to her chest. She clung to every word that rolled from Paul Stoneman's lips. Bold words. Words that stirred a longing in her heart.

"God loves the Chukchi people." Mr. Stoneman's right hand gripped the pulpit. His tanned skin seemed to blend with his corduroy jacket. "He wants to see His word in their language." His piercing green eyes scanned the audience, intense in their scrutiny, as if searching for someone in particular. When his gaze paused on Ellen, she shivered.

"God is calling you to love the Chukchi people. To get involved. To walk through the door of missions. You never know what will happen when God gets ahold of your heart." He opened his leather Bible. "In Isaiah 41:9 and 10, God says, 'I took you from the ends of the earth, from its farthest corners I called you. I said, "You are my servant"; I have chosen you and have not rejected you. So do not fear, for I am with you; do not be dismayed, for I am your God. I will strengthen you and help you; I will uphold you with my righteous right hand.'" He closed the Bible, and again those depth-charged eyes grazed the audience. "Don't be afraid to follow His call. Now, please pray with me that the Lord of the harvest would send out workers. For the fields are white unto harvest."

Ellen nearly forgot to bow her head. Her entire body tingled as his fervent prayer sizzled inside her. Tears edged her eyes. The missions committee had really done their homework this year. Someone would surely respond to the call to full-time missions after Paul Stoneman's emotional plea.

She watched the missionary take his seat on the platform, noticing how even his hair had been affected by his heart-wrenching description of his ministry as a Bible translator among the Chukchi people of Siberia. Unruly and the color of a rich mahogany, his hair scraped his shoulders like some sort of Native American warrior. He tucked his hands in his lap, and she frowned at a stark white bandage around his left hand. He stared out into the audience, unsmiling, his jaw tense, as if evaluating each one of the members of his supporting church for their commitment to Jesus Christ.

There was a time, perhaps not so long ago, when such a plea would have made her reevaluate her commitment to Christ and His calling. But that day had come and gone, and she was safely on her career path. She leaned back in her seat and paged to the right hymn. Next to her, Mitchell Frank, her business partner, gripped his half of the songbook. Ellen sang the words, "So send I you to labor unrewarded, to serve unpaid, unloved, unsought, unknown. To bear rebuke, to suffer scorn and scoffing. So send I you to toil for me alone."

"If they are trying to inspire new missionaries, they ought to pick a different song." Mitchell's nasal voice hissed in her ear. She gave him a scowl.

"So send I you to loneliness and longing, with heart a hung'ring for the loved and known, forsaking home and kindred, friend and dear one—so send I you to know my love alone."

Ellen glanced up at Paul Stoneman. He'd stood with the rest of the congregation, and she was surprised to see he wasn't holding a hymnal as he sang. His eyes were closed and something written on his face made her hurt. She looked down and finished the song, her eyes burning. There was something about this missionary that tugged at her heart. She'd have to avoid his Sunday evening presentation if she wanted to escape the feeling she wasn't doing her part in the scope of missions. She suspected that significant time spent with Missionary Paul Stoneman could alter a person's life forever.

Ellen had never seen the sanctuary so decked out for a mission's conference. Red and gold banners with portions of the Matthew Twenty-eight Great Commission hung along both walls between the stained glass windows. In the back, above the pulpit, hung a black-and-white poster of a scraggly Chukchi child holding a Bible. Stoneman was obviously their featured speaker this week. His pictures of a remote village somewhere in a frozen place were plastered in the foyer, on the bulletin board, and in her bulletin. She opened it and found his name. Paul Stoneman, serving with Bible for All Nations Translators in Chukchotka. Where did he say that was—Russia?

As the organ began to play, Ellen watched Mr. Stoneman walk up the aisle with the pastor to the back of the sanctuary. She sighed deeply and her chest loosened as if she'd been holding her breath the entire service.

"Would you like to get a bite to eat?" Mitchell picked up her purse and handed it to her. "They have a lunch special at the diner on Oak Street. All you can eat for—"

She screwed up her face. "I don't do 'all you can eat.'"

"I know, but I hear they're looking to remodel. I thought we'd do some research." He smiled, and she couldn't help notice how pale his skin was in comparison to Paul Stoneman's. His gray eyes seemed dull, his hands small. Mitchell spent most of his days bent over wallpaper books or matching swatches of fabric. Paul Stoneman looked like he could wrestle a grizzly or a polar bear or whatever wildlife they had in Chukchotka. Mitchell spent his time wrestling down the estimates their interior contractor gave them.

She pushed Mitchell gently out of the aisle. "I also don't do diner decorating."

"You might, if we don't get the First Citizen's Bank contract." Mitchell placed his hand on the small of her back, leading her up the aisle. "How are the drawings coming?"

She stepped up her pace and drew away from his touch. How many times had she told him—

"Ellen!"

She turned and spied Duncan Parks threading his way up the aisle. "Ellen, wait!"

She stopped and braced herself. The new youth pastor had been dogging her for weeks to join the youth staff.

"Are you busy tomorrow?" he asked, looking like a man with an agenda.

She took a deep breath, scrambling for an excuse. It was hard to turn down a pastor who looked like a chipmunk— short brown hair puffed up behind his ears, round cheeks, soft shoulders, and a belly to match. She heard he got on well with the kids, however. His gentle brown eyes spoke trust.

"I'm not sure," she replied, wondering if getting a manicure and brushing her cat counted as a busy Labor Day.

"Great! You can help me." Duncan rubbed his pudgy hands together and his eyes gleamed. "The kids and I are going to spend the day painting a fence, and we need your help."

"Why?" She shot a "help me" glance at Mitchell, but he was absorbed in conversation with Mrs. Guinn, obviously giving out advice, the way his hands were working the air.

"You are the local decorating expert, Ellen. What with your company and all—"

"That's interior decorating." Why did everyone think she spent her time building decks or selling lawn art? Ellen's Elegant Interior Design didn't stock porcelain deer, plastic mallards, or even an occasional birdbath. Design. Elegant. Inside.

She saw Duncan grimace and guilt stabbed at her. "But of course I'd be glad to help." Maybe she couldn't be a missionary, but certainly she could reach out to her fellow man. "Whose house are we painting?" Probably Mrs. Gilstrap's. Ellen noticed the paint peeling off in sheets last time she'd whizzed by the widow's house.

"Paul Stoneman's."

101

Duncan left her speechless as he dashed to his next victim.

Paul Stoneman dropped his army duffel bag with a thump in the tiny living room. Home sweet home. He unlaced his hiking boots and toed them off, leaving them in the middle of the floor. He didn't even bother to drag the duffel into the bedroom. . .just made straight for the long couch. He eased himself onto it, stretched out, then propped his right arm over his eyes to shield them from the streetlights that poured artificial brightness into the room. His left hand throbbed. He rested it on his stomach, winced, and slowed his breathing, hoping pain relief would follow.

He was exhausted to the bone. His stomach churned, a reaction to the lasagna he'd eaten at Pastor Evans's house this evening. A diet rich in spices and anything other than potatoes and venison would take some acclimation. He'd have to work up to the buffalo wings he'd longed for many a Siberian night if he wanted his stomach to cooperate.

His mind scanned over the marathon day. First Sunday school and the morning service, then a potluck lunch with the missions committee, then the evening service, and finally a luscious dinner that he was too tired to eat that stretched out into a goals and strategy session for the next term. Still, twelve hours after the morning service, his spirit remained on full charge. Something desperate had taken hold of him this morning staring at a healthy, groomed audience freely worshiping God. It probably had something to do with the lingering image of Milla, her frail two-year-old body wasted away by famine, or with Yuri and the memory of his fingers, frostbitten blue-white after traveling ten miles by dogsled for church. Suddenly he'd wanted to point an accusing finger at the congregation and challenge, no, *dare* them to follow God's call into missions.

He sat up to shake himself free of the feeling and found he was sweating. The pain, obviously. Or the mild September climate of Oklahoma. Anything was warmer than the tip of Siberia, the Chukchotka Peninsula, just south of the Arctic Circle. He suddenly longed for his furry reindeer skin bed, the smell of campfire smoke seeping into his thick reindeer skin *Khonba* jacket.

Home.

He gave a wry chuckle. The only real home he'd known he'd left sixteen years ago when he'd packed his bags and headed north as a career missionary.

No, make that he'd found his only home sixteen years ago. His family was Yuri and Valya and their children, Milla and Sasha. The memory of their leathery faces framing gap-toothed smiles warmed him from the inside out. He could nearly hear their voices, "Pasha, return soon." He put a hand to his chest, feeling his heart begin to ache. Oh, how he hoped Travis and MaryJo found the same peace among the people he'd long ago adopted as his own. The Chukchi. The native people of the north, with chocolate eyes, wide faces, and ebony hair the color of a Siberian night.

Paul hadn't seen blond hair for four years. Perhaps that's why the lady in the congregation had caught his eye this morning. Her hair gleamed like spun gold, with snow-white highlights. It draped down to her shoulders and framed a flawless heart-shaped face.

Then he'd caught her expression and just about stuttered. Enraptured. She hung on his words like they were sustenance, her face full of urgency. He half expected her to rise from her pew and run forward.

He'd been oddly disappointed when she didn't.

He pushed himself off the sofa with a groan, grabbed his duffel, and turned it upside down. Out tumbled a sleeping bag, ratty jeans, long underwear, wool socks, a number of worn turtlenecks, two fraying sweaters, his reindeer jacket, and finally, a plastic bag that held his shaving kit and a prescription bottle of pain reliever with codeine. He wrestled with the lid and, too tired to search for a glass in his new digs, gulped two tablets down—dry.

This furlough house was certainly a blessing. He'd have to get used to things like running water, a flushing toilet, and neighbors who didn't walk in uninvited. He vaguely remembered an agreement to do some decorating in exchange for low rent. Cupping his good hand around his neck, he kneaded a stiff muscle. The place looked comfortable enough. No pictures, but he could fix that. Maybe he could build a deck. He had a fairly decent hammer swing.

Grabbing his sleeping bag, he dragged it to one of the tiny bedrooms. Moonlight streamed through the wide windows onto the pale walls. They shone like a new snowfall under a glorious aurora borealis. He'd definitely have to buy a shade for this room. He noticed a tall privacy fence out back, but the neighbor's second story loomed above it like a watchtower.

Some kind soul had made the single bed, adding a homemade quilt with a floral pattern. He smiled, touched that he'd been thought of, the bachelor missionary.

He shrugged out of his jacket and draped it over the straight-back chair, wishing for the thousandth time that he might find someone with whom to share such a quaint house. Someone who responded like the blond in the audience. . .and then carried it through to commitment. It was a pretty tall order, even for God. Such a woman would not only have to be willing to fly to the end of the earth, cook over a fire, learn to skin a fresh salmon, and speak Chukchi, she'd have to love Paul Stoneman too.

He winced. Without God's intervention, his continuing existence as a bachelor was in no significant danger. He knelt beside his bed and lifted a quick prayer, ending with, "and Lord, she has to be called to missions separately, not because of me." The last thing he wanted was to drag a lady into a remote Siberian village, knowing she did it only because of him. He couldn't live with that kind of guilt. Or responsibility. He knew firsthand the sacrifices a missionary woman made, and she couldn't do it without her own personal "burning bush" experience to sustain her.

A wife for Paul Stoneman would have to be someone extraordinary.

Not only that, but once he found this extraordinary human being, he had his own personal nightmares to overcome before he'd drag anyone he loved to the backwoods of Siberia.

He sighed as hope died a quiet death in the recesses of

his mind. Perhaps singleness did have its perks. Like now, for instance, when he was allowed to flop onto the bed, wrap himself up in his smoky sleeping bag, and fall asleep in his church clothes.

Chapter 2

Orange, hot waves seeped under Paul's eyelids. He blinked them open and winced. Sunshine trumpeted into his room, and was that a mangy golden retriever licking his window? He rolled over, and his hand thumped against the bedside table. Pain shot up his arm. Where was the cover of darkness when he needed it? He'd just been reeling in a whopper salmon from the Kolyma River, dreaming of fresh roe and salmon steaks.

That definitely was a dog slobbering his window, and the mutt was barking like he'd seen a squirrel instead of the local new neighbor/missionary trying to get some shut-eye. . .in his dress pants and oxford shirt. Paul grimaced. No wonder he'd had a nightmare about drowning. He was still wearing his tie. Paul sat up and worked the noose from his neck and tossed it into the closet. His hand burned. He raised his hand to eye level and peeked beneath the bandage. The stitches were still there, mocking him for his recklessness.

He checked his watch and his pulse rocketed. He bolted to his feet, his head spinning, and staggered toward the bathroom. It wouldn't do to have the local youth group seeing the sainted missionary looking like he'd spent the night under a dumpster.

He was splashing water on his face and glaring at his reflection when the doorbell rang.

Grabbing a towel, he wiped his dripping face on the way to the door. Duncan someone smiled through the glass, his image distorting at odd angles like a Picasso painting. Paul jerked the door open and draped the towel over his shoulder. "Good morning." He tried to ignore the fact he sounded like he'd just gargled in motor oil.

Duncan held out his hand, a wide smile pushing back bunched cheeks. "Good morning, Paul. I wanted to tell you that the gang is already hard at work." He gestured to the fence, a simple picket affair running around the small property. Ten Tom Sawyers were painting themselves and a bit of the fence a yellowish brown. Paul grinned at the smeared face of a ten year old. At this rate, painting the fence would take his entire furlough.

"I'll be out in a minute to help." He closed the door and leaned against it. In the daylight, he had to admit the house needed some amenities. The pink base paint definitely had to go. Something, anything, to make him feel like he wasn't living in cotton candy.

He searched for a room in which to change and finally picked the bathroom, hoping the dog, which he confirmed was a golden retriever, couldn't find him through the frosted glass window. Paul shucked the suit pants and climbed into a baggy pair of jeans. Now this was more like home. Emerging from the bathroom, he unbuttoned the oxford and stripped it off, hoping he'd remembered to pack his favorite college sweatshirt.

"Excuse me, where can I find a step stool?"

He froze. The voice, sweet and feminine, with a Southern twang and a slight gasp at the end reminded him he wasn't wearing a shirt.

He turned and cringed at the startled, reddened expression of a petite blond.

"Sorry," she squeaked.

Of course, it had to be her, the blond from yesterday. He wanted to crawl under the orange sofa. He kicked up the first article of clothing he could find, his reindeer jacket, and shoved it on. "Howdy."

"I. . ." She looked away, her face wry. "I wanted to start on the storage shed in back, but it's too tall."

"Right. Well, I've lived here about eight hours so far. How about a kitchen chair?"

She made a quick exit, but left in her wake a fragrance that filled the room with fresh roses. His feet shuffled after her but stopped when his toe stubbed on the doorjamb. He blinked, registering her blue-green eyes in his memory, the way they'd blinked in surprise, the blue in them as deep as the Arctic Ocean. He rubbed his chest. So she'd made an impact yesterday. So she appeared in his kitchen today and was right now painting his back shed. It didn't mean he had to stumble outside after her—in his socks—like a puppy.

He picked up a chair and carried it outside. The Oklahoma wind stirred the leaves of the pecan tree in the front yard, and the sun winking in the cloudless sky made him glad he'd agreed to spend his furlough at his parents' home church. He wished his folks' furlough from their ministry in Papua New Guinea had coincided with his. He hadn't seen them in six years and the space of time made him ache. Perhaps life in this small town, among a caring body of believers, would heal his tired body and lonely spirit.

"Excuse me, did you need this?" he asked as he approached her.

She turned, and he was swept away by the surprise on her heart-shaped face. She looked so clean in her pink sweatshirt and blue jeans, he wanted to run back inside and throw on the monkey suit.

"Oh, yes, thank you." She looked away, obviously as flustered as he.

"Where do you want it?" He plopped it next to the corner, where he noticed someone had painted a small brown square.

"That's perfect, thank you." She came up to stand beside him, and he marveled that a woman so petite could make a grown man's knees turn to jelly. She hopped up on the chair with the agility of a dancer. "Could you hand me that paint can?" She pointed and he couldn't help notice her fingers, long, slender, and manicured, with pristine white tips. He reached for the paint can, feeling a bit guilty that she was about to get dirty on his behalf.

"I can hold it for you."

He was rewarded with a smile so warm it burrowed right into his heart. "Thank you, Mr. Stoneman." She dipped the brush in. "I appreciate your help."

"Paul." He forced his gaze away, to the golden retriever that continued to bark into his window as if seeing his lingering shadow, to the kids painting the fence and themselves, to Duncan the youth pastor talking on his cell phone and gesturing like a mime. Anywhere but the gentle slope of her jaw and the way she bit her lower lip.

He winced in self-disgust. Four years in the backwoods and he turned to mush at the first blond he met? And normally he'd dated brunettes. He amended that thought. He'd only dated *one* woman, years ago, who'd dumped him faster than a hot poker when he'd revealed his call to missions. But *she* had been a brunette.

"Glad to meet you, Paul." The blond dipped her brush in again. His arm muscles were starting to burn. "I'm Ellen White."

Ellen. "I appreciate your coming out here to help me today." He took a deep breath, wondering if there might be a step stool in the tool shed. "I guess I'm supposed to put some decorative touches to this place, but well. . ." He made a face.

"It's such a pretty house. I know Carla invested everything she had into it." She giggled. "I'll bet she's not too sad she can't live in it."

"Why not?" He liked the way her eyes lit up like jewels in the sun when she laughed.

"Because she married her contractor!" She laughed, and then her eyes widened as the chair tottered. She clamped a hand on his shoulder to right herself. "Uh, sorry."

She quickly gathered her balance. "What kind of decorative touches are you going to add?"

His shoulder tingled where she'd touched it. "I think I might build a deck."

He saw her raised eyebrows. "Or maybe paint," he added. "Painting's not hard."

He watched her even strokes, the way the paint seemed to go on like butter on bread. "You do that well."

She arched a brow. "Anyone can paint a wall. It's wallpaper that takes real talent."

He grimaced. "I think I'll stay clear of wallpaper." What had his pastor gotten him into? When Pastor Evans mentioned low rent in exchange for household decorations. . . well, Paul hoped a bird feeder and a deck qualified. But wallpaper? He felt the muscles in his neck start to scream.

"By the way, I like your jacket."

His eyes widened, suddenly aware he was wearing his furry jacket, made from the skin of caribou. He'd brought it home to show the kids when he made missions presentations. No wonder he had sweat running between his shoulder blades. "Thank you. It's called a Khonba. A friend of mine made it."

"In Siberia?"

He was pleasantly surprised she knew where he worked. "Yep. Even fifty below, this thing will keep you toasty warm."

"It gets that cold where you're from?"

"Colder. Breathtakingly cold." He thought of the wind that lifted the snow in a solid sheet and carried it across the frozen tundra. The biting chill that found a man's bones and turned them brittle. The rich smell of caribou stew filling every crack in a log house. The sun at dawn, turning the ice plain into a field of tiny gemstones—amber, ruby, amethyst, and turquoise. Chukchotka was breathtaking in so many ways.

She shivered, a playful response to his words, and he regretted she couldn't see what he could.

"Can I ask what happened to your hand?"

He'd nearly forgotten the dull throb. "I cut it." He didn't add that it had happened trying to save a starving child from an even hungrier dog. Some things were better not to remember.

"Hey!"

Paul frowned at the high-pitched shout behind him. Craning his neck, he saw the neighbor's mutt running along the fence, darting in and out of the legs of the painters.

"Hey, Pooch!" Paul yelled, wondering where the dog's master was. The retriever bounded over, knocked him against the knees, then jumped up and thumped two bushy paws on his stomach. Paul stumbled back, aiming for escape, and tagged the edge of the kitchen chair with his heel. The chair wobbled, and he looked up just in time to see Ellen's face go white.

The next second, she was crashing down on him, hands aiming for his shoulders. She missed and hit the paint can. Paul watched in slow motion as she fell, followed by a wave of paint. She landed with a thud, drenched in "terra sienna," a color that would have made a nice tan, under different circumstances.

"Oops." Paul winced. He knelt beside her. "I'm so sorry. Are you okay?"

"Ouch." She rolled over onto her back and flicked her hair

back with a saturated finger, painting a line across her cheek. He resisted the urge to wipe it off and instead reached out and fingered a strand of dripping hair.

"Whoa. Does this stuff come off?"

She flicked her eyebrows, and his chagrin was immediately balmed by the humor in her eyes. "You know, I've always wanted to be a brunette."

She lay there in the grass, hair dripping brown paint, eyes shining, grinning at him through a wash of sticky paint, and something went weak inside him. Swallowing hard, he held out his hand and pulled her to her feet. "Let me see if I have anything to clean you up."

He ran into the house, more terrified than when he'd been chased across the frozen tundra by a pair of mangy dogs. He leaned against his doorway, chest heaving. *Lord, this is crazy! A kind look from a pretty lady and my heart leaps through my chest! If this is what is going to happen every time I'm on furlough, please, just send me back. . .and soon.*

The last thing he should do was unlatch his heart for a woman who had no place in his life. And Miss Ellen White, with her long manicured nails, highlighted hairdo, and was that her bright red Mercedes parked in his driveway? Well, she was just about the worst definition of a frontier missionary he could conjure up.

Except for that yearning look on her face yesterday in church that fairly screamed *Here I am, Lord, send me!*

Paul looked heavenward. "Lord, help me keep my focus. Help me not to get sidetracked by a cute blond with beautiful eyes."

He nearly jumped out of his skin when the door squealed open. Miss Ellen, the half brunette, stuck her head in. "Can I wash my hands in here?"

She'd piled her hair up in his bath towel, which he'd abandoned on the lawn, to wipe her neck. Still, her face was streaked brown, like war paint, and her sweatshirt was surely ruined. She ran her hands under the water. "I'll get you a new towel. Do you have any soap?"

"I don't think that's coming off with soap." He turned toward the living room and was aghast to find his toiletries scattered about the floor. He kicked his clothes into a pile, scooped them up, and ran to his bedroom, where he threw them into the closet.

"Just a second, I'm still looking for it!" He closed the closet door, noticed a gray tube sock straggler, scooped it up, and threw it in with the other renegades. Then he returned to the living room, found his soap, and sauntered back to the kitchen area.

She lathered up to her elbows with the deformed soap chip he gave her. He averted his eyes, cringing.

"I just need to get the first layer off," she said as brown paint swirled in a tempest in the sink. "I'll get back to work in a minute."

"Back to work?" He cupped a hand behind his neck. "Uh, I think you've done your time."

"No." She turned, wiping her arms. "I'm here to help. In fact," she let her gaze wander around the room. "I'd say you need a woman's touch here."

He followed her gaze and saw nothing but pink base

paint on every wall. "It looks pretty feminine to me."

The sound of her laughter was sweet music to his ears. "I'm not talking about the paint." She rearranged the towel into a secure turban. "You need curtains and wallpaper and maybe even some stenciling." She peeked into the family room. "And I'd strongly suggest a slipcover for that sofa."

"I was thinking I might build a deck." He smiled and raised his eyebrows. Certainly she wasn't serious. "Miss White—"

"It's Ellen. Listen, Carla Dugan is a woman of taste. A deck is a nice idea, but I think she might want you to pay attention to the inside of this cute house."

Paul swallowed hard. He could almost see gears working in her head as she bit her lip and turned in a circle, surveying the house again.

"You're in luck, however." She turned those jeweled eyes on him, and he knew she was telling the truth. Luck was one word. Blessed, perhaps, might be a better vocabulary choice.

"I'm an interior designer."

"An interior what? Like someone who arranges furniture?" His mind went blank, and he forced himself to smile.

She smirked. "I can help you decorate the house? Pick out wallpaper that matches? Paint and stencil the kitchen?"

"Ah, I see." He nodded, but something inside him began to tighten. Would that entail her working alongside him? Together? Alone? He continued to nod, hoping his face didn't betray terror.

She walked into the living area, and in that moment he was profoundly thankful his clothing was safely piled in his closet. "This room has wonderful light. It just needs a valance and perhaps some sheers for nighttime."

He shuffled behind her. "I was going to build a deck?"

"A palomino beige would make a lovely base color for the room. We'd start with a border and perhaps run wallpaper up to a chair rail and paint above."

She began wandering toward the bedroom. He suddenly thought of his filthy sleeping bag.

"Ellen! Great, that sounds just great." He strode after her and nearly ran her over as she stopped and whirled. "Your help would be appreciated." He gently tugged at her elbow. "When can we start?" He kept backing up, toward the door, hoping she would follow and they'd both be able to get outside. . .to fresh air, sanity, perhaps a mangy dog that would convince her that bachelors were trouble. She had only to look in the mirror, at her once blond hair, to prove it.

"How about next Saturday?"

The soft breeze picked up her paint-splattered fragrance and did nothing to clear his mind. He tucked his hands in his jeans and tried a different tactic. "What is this all going to cost me? I'm a poor missionary, you know."

She smiled, and he noticed the slightest smattering of freckles dotting her nose. . .or was that paint? No matter, it looked delightful. He took a deep breath.

"Nothing. It's my contribution to missions. It's the least I can do for our visiting missionary. Everyone has to do their part." She smiled, and then, for the briefest moment, he thought he saw that look, that yearning he'd seen yesterday in church, flicker across her face. His mouth went dry, and his heart banged hard in his chest.

Then it was gone, and her face shone clear. "I guess I'd better get home and get cleaned up." She touched her turbaned head. "Sorry I made such a mess of the place."

He had no words to that but nodded stupidly as she walked away to her cherry red convertible. He waved as she drove away, feeling his heart fall somewhere in the vicinity of his shoes. Ellen White was definitely a dangerous woman to hang out with if he wanted to keep his mind on returning to the mission field in a year.

He cradled his head in his hand. "I was going to build a deck."

🏠

Ellen kept both eyes glued to the road, determined not to check the rearview mirror in hopes Paul Stoneman was watching her drive away. Her telltale heart would probably leap out of her chest and run back down the road. The last thing she needed was to fall for heartbreaker Stoneman. Even if he did have jade green eyes that made her pulse skip and begging-to-be-mussed mahogany hair with red highlights that turned to fire in the sun. Standing there dressed only in a pair of well-loved jeans and some sort of animal skin, with a slightly dazed "What am I doing here?" expression on his whiskered face, he looked every inch the backwoods renegade. Missionary indeed. He ought to produce pinup calendars—he'd certainly put a jump-start into his fund-raising.

And she'd just offered to help him decorate his house. Ellen cringed, realizing her idiotic, disloyal mouth had done it again. Run out before her to commit her to folly. "I was going to build a deck." His words rang in her memory, and suddenly she had the urge to hide under her floor mats. What had she been thinking? Not only wasn't a man like Paul Stoneman interested in frills and wallpaper, but she'd just flung herself into spending time with the magnetic Paul Stoneman—alone.

Ellen nearly ran the red light and slammed her brakes just in time to screech inches away from the car in front of her. She smiled sheepishly in response to the driver's rearview mirror scowl. Already Stoneman was fraying her concentration.

She didn't have time to dive into romance. . .she rolled her eyes as her thoughts spiraled out ahead of her. Romance? Paul Stoneman was the last man she should be dreaming about. Weren't missionaries married to God or something? The man had "bachelor to the rapture" written across him like a plaque. And he certainly hadn't done anything to encourage her babbling.

Besides, she wasn't looking for love. Hadn't she been pushing Mitchell away for the last year or more? Her career needed all her concentration if she hoped to establish Ellen's Elegant Design as the premier decorating firm for Milltown and beyond. No, she didn't have time to dally around with fancies of the heart. And she certainly wouldn't look for love with a man who was destined for the wilds of Siberia in a year's time.

She gunned it at the light and took the left turn with a screech. Maybe the paint can had jarred loose a few brain cells. The first thing she should do after diving in the shower and hopefully washing terra sienna brown out of her hair would be call the guy and apologize for running over him like a herd of buffalo. Had he even asked for her help? She puffed out a disgusted sigh. Exuberant Ellen strikes again.

Then again, the house needed some frills. . .at least window treatments. And didn't the pastor say the missionary needed to fix it up. . .something about rent exchange?

Ellen careened into her complex and hit the button for the automatic garage door. She cruised into her space in the underground lot, climbed out of the car, and slammed the door. The sound of the automatic lock echoed against the low-hanging cement beams. She'd been lucky to land a condo in the High Oaks complex. Her two-bedroom view overlooked Lake Mills and the sweep of jeweled oak and maple that hugged the sparkling lake. Just yesterday she'd awakened to her first gaggle of Canadian geese, flying in to holiday for the winter. The glorious view, especially with the dawn running like rose syrup over the landscaped lawns, reminded her each morning that life was indeed good. Full. Rich. She couldn't help but thank the Lord for giving her this little peek into His splendor.

But just think what beauty Paul Stoneman woke up to each morning.

Ellen pushed him out of her mind as she took the stairs two at a time to her second-floor unit. It wouldn't do her reputation any good to be seen drenched in paint—just what she needed to inspire confidence in her decorating abilities.

She had just turned the key in her door when she heard the step behind her and the tiny accompanying gasp. She turned, armed with a grimace.

Yep. Mitchell looked aghast. White hued his already thin face. "What happened to you?"

"I, uh. . .had an accident."

"I'd say." He put his hands on his hips. He was dressed for exercise—a pair of track pants, designer tennis shoes, and a navy sweatshirt. "I was just coming over to see if you wanted to play a round of tennis? But I'm thinking you need a bubble bath and a good Bogart movie to ease your pain." He smiled, and the friendship in it made her return the grin.

"At least a bath, yes. But I'm not up to tennis today, I'm sorry." She put a hand to her head and wrinkled her nose. "Besides I need to work on the bank drawings." A month stood between her and the deadline for her proposal to decorate the interior of the new First Citizen's Bank of Oklahoma City, as well as their chains, and she still couldn't nail down the color scheme. Rose was so passé, but she needed something that soothed, relaxed. . .especially in an institution that managed people's money. Her career, dreams, and hopes rode on her presentation. This one account could vault Ellen's business into the top decorating annals. Seven city branches, including the three-story headquarters. The thought made her dizzy. "Thank you for your offer, though. I'll play next Saturday, maybe."

Mitchell shrugged, but she saw disappointment line his gray eyes. "What if I come in and help you?" His smile quivered.

Now why couldn't she love a man like Mitchell? Decent, hardworking, and so obviously smitten with her? Wasn't he every woman's dream?

"Not today. But thank you. I'll call you if I need help." She gave him her warmest smile, wishing he didn't wear his heart on his sleeve. "See you in the office tomorrow."

She opened her door and heard him jog down the stairs, guilt piercing her heart with each step. Yes, Mitchell was the local catch of the year, with his rising talent in the decorating industry, his upscale condo, and his sporty silver BMW. And, the man loved God, or at least had the morals of a man who loved God. Didn't smoke, drink, or run with those who did.

But somewhere, deep in the recesses of her heart, she knew she wanted more. Just what, she wasn't sure. But she did know that the thought of a man sold out to God, surrendered, humbled, and passionate about serving his Savior, turned her weak. Unfortunately, her world seemed in short supply of God's kind of heroes.

Ellen locked the door behind her, kicked off her shoes, and made for the bathroom. She let the shower warm up while she peeled off her paint-soaked sweatshirt and jeans. Catching her reflection in the mirror, she scowled. Her blond hair, now effectively brown, hung in chunks over her face, also smeared in terra sienna brown. She looked like a drowned mouse.

No wonder Paul Stoneman had looked at her with horror in his eyes when she suggested she help him. It probably had nothing to do with the fact that she'd offered to invade his life with wallpaper samples and fabric swatches.

After this morning's escapade, he probably feared the havoc she'd wreak to the interior of his home.

She smiled grimly. Well, what Paul Stoneman didn't know was that she was not only a whiz with design, but she could slap up wallpaper faster than Martha Stewart. She wasn't a contractor's daughter for nothing. Ten-plus years working for her father had taught her not only how to paint a wall but also how to snap a plumb line and build a deck that would rival Bob Villa.

She couldn't let Stoneman's last impression of her be that of a soggy rodent. Ellen stepped into the shower and lifted her face to the spray. Paint dripped down her back, pooled at her feet. Besides, weren't they all challenged this week to do something for missions? Paul Stoneman wasn't the only one who wanted to be a part of God's work. It wasn't so many years ago that God's call to missions had pulsed in her heart. She swallowed back the memory of herself, young and naïve, on her knees, pledging her life to God, her vocation to His direction.

Thankfully, the Almighty hadn't taken her seriously. He must have known she wasn't the type to comb her hair with a whale bone. She'd last all of two hours in the wilderness Paul Stoneman had described. Yeah, she could see herself trying to skin a salmon. The very thought made her laugh aloud.

But she should do her part. And if that meant helping a missionary decorate his house, well, it was a small sacrifice. It wasn't like she was upending her life, was it? A few nights after work, a surrendered weekend or two. And when he headed back to the wilderness, she'd know she'd contributed to the great commission.

And honestly, it wasn't like it would be sheer torture to spend a little time with Mr. Paul Stoneman. Maybe she'd even enjoy it.

For the good of missions.

Chapter 3

Ellen cruised past the fast-food drive-in and turned onto Mistletoe Lane. She'd cranked the top down, and the wind in her hair, the kiss of the late afternoon sun, and the smell of freshly fallen leaves made her want to sing along with the Shania Twain hit blasting from her radio. Fridays were meant for celebrating, and this one had been particularly spectacular. Landing the Whitney account meant Ellen's Elegant Design had nearly arrived. Not only would decorating the century-old mansion notch up her status and add gold etching to her resume, but she and Mitchell would have a year of delight turning the sprawling mansion into an eighteenth-century French castle. Mitchell excelled in period decorating; and the new owners, some blue bloods out of the East, had given him carte blanche to turn the ivied thirty-room estate into a getaway into history.

She could almost see the spread on *Designer Today* magazine. And in three weeks, after her proposal to First Citizen's Bank, they'd have enough work to keep Ellen's Elegant

Design in significant cash flow for a year or more. The only glitch was Mitchell's sudden hint at partnership. Ellen slowed as she turned onto Pecan Crossing. She'd started the company with only a few fabric swatches and the sweat of her brow. Mitchell had been an asset, yes. But she just didn't see the sign saying, Ellen and Mitchell's Elegant Design. It sounded choppy, not a hint of singsong ring to it.

And if he became her partner, she had no doubt he'd curtail her little extracurricular activity. . .the one that had her emptying their remnant shelves into her backseat and donating her weekend to help a backwoods missionary tame his house. If she didn't know better, she thought Mitchell had actually taken on a lime glow when she'd mentioned it at lunch.

Good thing her mouth was too full of microwave popcorn to respond to his "What would a man like him want with matching curtains?" comment. So Paul might be heavily on the rustic side. Wouldn't any self-respecting male want to live in a house that didn't remind him of bubble gum?

And she'd even picked up some fried chicken on the way over. The last thing she wanted was for Paul to think he needed to cater to her. She was here to serve *him*.

She parked on the street, clicked off the radio, and instantly heard the swell of music, a tenor of some sort, filling the air. She pulled out the bag of chicken, her stomach lurching at the smell, and trotted up to the door.

She could barely hear the doorbell over the music; and when the buzz of a power tool added to the cacophony, she hiked around the house to the backyard.

Her heart nearly skipped a beat. Paul Stoneman, missionary to the north, was building a deck, looking every inch the rustic carpenter in a sweaty sleeveless T-shirt, thick arms working a circular saw, hair tousled by the wind, and singing at the top of his lungs to an operatic tenor blasting Italian from a boom box. He worked oblivious to her, cutting his board, then laying it over the studs of a very sturdy, very uniform deck outline. Sawdust and wood chips layered his jeans and, as if to add to his lumberjack appeal, the wind reaped his masculine scent—hard work and spicy soap—and sent it back to her like an incentive for her heart to roar to life in her chest.

Yes, Paul Stoneman was the poster boy for G.Q. missionary, and she suddenly wondered why he wasn't hitched to some hardy tomboy.

A smart woman would drop the extra crispy chicken she was holding and flee before he turned around and saw her wearing her heart on her face.

But Ellen stood there, listening to him sing in a glorious baritone, watching him hammer, his back muscles rippling, and wondered, insanely, what it would be like to work beside such a man in the outskirts of civilization.

Life certainly wouldn't be dull.

Then he turned, and those green eyes fixed on her, riveting through her; and her pulse confirmed, indeed, "dull" wasn't a word remotely in the same universe as Paul Stoneman.

"Hi," she said. *Oh, that was witty. Turn and run now, or regret it later.* She managed a shaky smile. He smiled back, and the warmth in his grin touched his eyes. Her knees nearly turned to rubber.

He sauntered over to the radio and flicked it off. The tenor died mid swell. "Hi. Ellen, right?"

Ellen White. Local designer. Age twenty-eight. Christian for twenty-plus years. And very, very single. "Yep."

With this clever repartee, she was bound to win his heart. Ellen sucked in a deep breath and scraped up her composure. She was here to help him pick out some wallpaper, not audition for a missions assignment. She nearly grimaced with the idiocy of her thought. Their future had zero-chance possibility. That thought slowed her heartbeat to quasi normalcy. So he had magical eyes. She'd simply avoid them.

"Are you hungry?" She held out the bag of chicken like a peace offering. "I tried to call, but there was no answer. But I thought you might be home and, well, I know I promised to help you, so I brought over some wallpaper samples and some fabric remnants, and. . .uh, I didn't know you were busy. I can come back, later. . .or never, or. . ." She gritted her teeth and dredged up a smile, hating the way her mouth had a mind of its own.

"I was building a deck." He looked at her, confused, like she'd just invited him to the prom.

"I see that." Certainly, if she left now, she could dodge him at church for the remaining eleven months. In a congregation of three thousand, how hard could that be?

"But I am starved." He smiled again, and it was so welcoming, she was having a hard time remembering what she'd just said. "I haven't eaten a thing all day."

Standing at least six foot two inches with muscles that filled out, and then some, his black sleeveless T-shirt, he didn't look underfed. But then again, maybe they ate reindeer three meals a day. Maybe the poor guy didn't know how to cook up macaroni and cheese. She heard that missionaries returning to the states often had reverse culture shock.

"How about a picnic? I even picked up some of that new Cherry Coke." Could she sound more desperate?

But Paul Stoneman was as gracious as he was beautiful. "Sounds like God sent you just in the nick of time." He grabbed a rag and wiped his hands. "I'm going to run in the house and wash up. Do you want to eat out here or inside?"

Outside sounded safer. "Let's eat here." She looked around, suddenly remembering their last adventure. "Is that dog still around? The hyperactive golden retriever?"

He laughed, and it loosened the knot in her chest. "I talked to the neighbor. I think Fido is safely under lock and key."

"That's a relief. I didn't bring enough for three. Do you have a blanket?"

"I'll see what I can dig up." He whirled and took the back entrance into the house, leaving Ellen to swat back recriminations. She was here to help. Do her part in missions.

And that did not include flirting with the local missionary. Her parents, God-fearing folks that they were, would be aghast.

She was inspecting his carpentry work when he returned, a green army duffel bag draped over his arm. "Will this do?"

"Sure." She spread it out on the lawn and opened the bag of food. "White meat or dark?"

He sat down next to her, legs drawn up, forearms resting on his knees. "Whatever you don't want. I haven't eaten chicken in four years."

She handed him the carton. "I like both. You choose. You're the one who's suffering for God." She meant it as a joke and chuckled.

He didn't.

"I don't suffer." His face turned solemn, his green eyes dark and piercing. "I love what I do; and if you could only see the joy that reading the Bible brings to the Chukchi, you'd know that it is the folks back home that are suffering. There is nothing more rewarding than seeing God change people's lives right before your eyes." His words tugged at her heart and, for a second, she felt an old pulse, as if something long dormant had budded to life.

"Wow." Her voice sounded odd, as if it had been roughened by surprise. "You make your work sound so—"

"Exciting? Rich? Rewarding?" His mouth tweaked in a slight smile.

"Bold. I can't even imagine what it must be like to live out on the edge of civilization, having to hunt for your meals or grow your own food."

He shrugged and took a drumstick. He had work-worn, tough hands. And his bandage, gray and torn around the edges, betrayed a hint of blood. "You get used to it. I lived with the Chukchi, and they taught me how to survive." He grabbed a napkin and held it under his chicken. "After awhile, just surviving becomes a triumph. There is nothing better than realizing that God has brought you through another winter, healthy and warm. It draws you closer to Him, knowing He's our provider."

She stared at him, this wilderness-honed man, the wind raking its fingers through his hair, and his simple faith kneaded a soft spot in her heart. It had been ages since she'd been on her knees, asking God to provide for her. The faith it took to do that on a daily basis made her tremble. And ache. She saw his faith in his eyes and for a moment jealousy flared in her heart. Hadn't she once longed to know God like that? Hungered to place her every moment in His hand and come out richer for it?

She bit back the yearning and reached for a piece of chicken. Even if God did seed in her a desire to be used by Him, certainly He wouldn't expect her, a woman who kept her weekly salon appointments, to fling her manicured life into the gutter and tromp up to the Arctic Circle with a way too handsome bohemian.

Even if the bohemian did have a smile that felt like pure sunshine.

"Shall we pray?" he asked.

She nodded and bowed her head. As Missionary Stone-man thanked the Lord for dinner, Ellen begged the Almighty to protect her rebellious, way too easily influenced heart.

She looked considerably better with the brown paint out of her hair. Considerably. That was an understatement. The twilight waxed her hair a deep gold and softened her smile until it was pure magic. She had incredible eyes—blue-green, the color of the Arctic Ocean in the morning, and just as deep, undulating with untold emotions. She smiled intermittently at him as she ate her chicken, and every time it felt like the sun had broken through the clouds.

"So, you grew up around here?"

She nodded and wiped her mouth with a napkin, then very carefully worked any grease off her incredibly groomed fingertips. He had never seen anyone with such long manicured nails, so perfectly white at the tips. "My dad is a contractor—he built most of the houses in this development, as a matter of fact. My mom helped him with the business, filing, billing, answering the telephone; and it seemed natural for me to help on the work site. More than once he had to finish the job on his own, for various reasons; and I've spackled, sanded, and painted more walls than I can count."

She had the most beautiful mouth and full lips and a smile that was pure radiance. And when the twilight breeze wafted her scent to him like a song, he could barely focus on her words.

"I guess it's natural that I went into the decorating business. I like to see something take shape, texture, and personality. I like to take four blank walls and make the room into a masterpiece of elegance and comfort." She sat cross-legged, at ease with herself in a pair of faded jeans and a crisp white sweatshirt. She wasn't gangly thin, but comfortably rounded, healthy. And so clean and bright, he felt like a mangy, unkempt wolf next to her.

"I finally started my own company. Ellen's Elegant Design. That's me."

She smiled again, and he suddenly had a hard time remembering his name let alone understanding why a lady like Ellen White was here, in his backyard, sitting on a grimy duffel bag, eating cold chicken with the likes of him. A missionary with four years' growth hanging down the back of his neck and sawdust flaking off him like fish scales. He tried to dredge up his voice and failed.

She gathered up the dinner trash. He knew he should say something.

"Um. . .thanks for dinner. It was delicious."

"Oh, I slaved all day." She wrinkled her nose at him.

He laughed, charmed. *Okay, Lord, if You want to send a gorgeous blond my direction, I won't turn around and run.* "Did you say you brought some wallpaper samples?"

He wanted to choke on his own words. Here he'd spent the entire week wondering if last Saturday, and her outlandish offer, had been a dream, convincing himself that no woman in her right mind wanted to hang out with a man who looked like he'd stepped out of a *National Geographic* magazine. She probably thought he ate polar bear or whale for supper.

But Ellen had returned, all five feet six inches of her, with supper and decorating samples. Maybe his parents had been right when they told him to furlough near their home church. They'd told him to expect warm fellowship from First Church. He hadn't expected this. Maybe God had found his extraordinary woman.

"I cleaned out our sample closet," Ellen said, "and found about thirteen rolls of a textured ivory that I think would be perfect as your base color. We can work around that."

He knew he was grinning like a goofball when she stopped and frowned. "Are you okay?"

He nodded. "I just. . .well, I just can't believe you're here and armed with wallpaper—"

"And fabric samples." She seemed to like his comment, for a blush pressed her cheeks. "Well, it's the least I can do to help our local missionary."

Ouch. He tried to keep the smile on his face, but his heart felt kicked. Why hadn't he parted the clouds of whimsy to see reality? The missions committee had probably sent her to make sure he could keep his end of the bargain. "Great. Yeah, thanks." He stood up, then reached out and helped her to her feet.

He tried not to notice the way her smile dimmed. "Lead on, oh, master decorator," he said, trying to keep things light. But as she jogged out to her car, her blond hair spilling out in the wind after her, he wondered just how he was going to keep from letting Ellen White and her sunshine smile into his heart.

Chapter 4

Ellen zipped into the church parking lot and parked next to a minivan. She waved to the Millers and waited for all six children to exit before she opened her door. Sandy Miller's brood always made her slightly wistful—they had been best friends in high school until life circumstances drove distance between them. Sandy had married Guy, her high school sweetheart, and ten years later had enough youngsters to form her own basketball team.

And Ellen had a luxury convertible and a condo with a view.

Ellen smoothed her brown gabardine pants, tucked her Bible under her arm, and marched into church. Someday, perhaps, children and accompanying husband were in her future. But today she had goals, dreams. . .

Who was she kidding? Hadn't she, only a year ago, been tempted to surrender to Mitchell's marriage proposal? Hadn't she paced a month away fighting the swell of despair in her heart? Good men were hard to find, even harder to catch. She should take Mitchell's offer and run with it, thankful she'd found a man who shared her dreams.

As if to add oomph to her thoughts, Mitchell pulled up and parked beside her car. "Ellen, wait!"

Ellen stopped and smiled at Mr. and Mrs. Anderson as she waited for Mitchell.

"Where were you yesterday? I called you all day—even your cell phone. Didn't you get my messages?" Mitchell looked sleek today in his black silk suit and teal tie, with just a hint of cologne to accent his suavity. He fairly glided into church, holding his leather gold leaf Bible in his soft manicured hands.

She couldn't help but blink back Paul's image, roughened hands folded in prayer, the wind toying with his unruly hair. "I'm sorry, Mitchell. I spent all day helping Paul Stoneman build a deck. And then we painted his bathroom."

"Paul Stoneman, the missionary?" Mitchell's gray eyes betrayed a swell of shock. "Why?"

She held her Bible against her chest as she walked, her spike boots clicking against the cement walk. "Evidently he made some agreement with the missions committee or maybe Carla Dugan, his landlord, that he'd do some enhancements to the house in exchange for low rent."

"And this means you have to surrender your Saturday to help him?"

Ellen shrugged, suddenly chagrined. "I was just trying to. . .to—"

"Is there something between you two?" He stopped, and his gaze held accusation.

"No. Of course not." Ellen's throat tightened. No, of

course not. So Paul laughed at her jokes and told her a few stories about life in the wilderness. They had a casual friendship. Nothing more. No. *Of course not.*

"Well, are you ready for our preliminary meeting with First Citizen's Bank tomorrow? Cynthia will be in at ten, and I don't want to disappoint her."

She gaped at him. Just who did he think was running this company? She'd had Cynthia Washburn's appointment on her calendar for the better part of three months and nothing short of a cyclone would keep her from being there, on time, dressed in her best designer clothes. "I'm not even going to justify that with a comment."

His eyes sparked. "Listen, Ellen. I just hope you know you can't run this firm without me. You need me." He leaned close. "And don't forget that."

She blinked at him, for once speechless.

"Ellen, are you okay?" Paul Stoneman's rich, strong voice felt like a balm on her hot skin. She turned and forced a smile.

"Yes, Paul. Thank you." She angled a look at Mitchell, who'd taken a step back. "Have you met my. . .associate, Mitchell Frank?"

"Nope, don't believe I have." Paul extended his hand, and even Ellen could see it dwarfed Mitchell's grip. Paul looked ruddy and only semi-tamed today, his long brown hair dragging on his white oxford collar, a hint of suspicion in his green eyes. She felt suddenly overdressed next to his black jeans and hiking boots. "Good to meet you, Mitchell," he said in his cheerful baritone. "You work with Ellen?"

Mitchell smirked at Ellen, and she saw something dangerous glint in his eyes. "I'm her partner."

If she weren't wearing her best pants, with a white silk top, and if she hadn't been balanced on a couple of three-inch spikes, she might have decked Mitchell right then and there.

Just let him try to steal her company from her.

Paul could tell by the flush on Ellen's face and the flashy smirk on Mr. Silk Suit that he'd stepped into something. He just hoped it wasn't some sort of couple's quarrel. The thought sent a flash of white pain into his chest, so sharp he had to stifle a wince. Of course. Mitchell was her partner. In a multidimensional definition. Paul would have to be deaf, blind, and dumb not to see how well they matched. Mitchell in his crisp three-piece and Ellen in her matching trendy boots, her hair gelled out in a floppy neo-seventies style. It hit Paul like a slap that Ellen White was so far out of his league he'd need oxygen just to exist in her atmosphere.

What had happened to the fresh scrubbed "I'm just here to serve" beauty with whom he'd spent all yesterday afternoon painting the bathroom?

Ellen turned to Paul, clearly ignoring Mitchell, and gave him a hundred-watt smile. "I'm glad to see you today. Are you speaking in church?"

He felt like something the dog had chewed. Scruffy hair—why hadn't he gotten it cut yet?—and wearing his father's coat, a treasure he'd unearthed in the box of goodies his mother had in storage, he had the sudden urge to run into church and hide under a pew. Or maybe just turn around, hop a plane, and jet back to the one place that seemed like home. "Nope. Off duty. Just here to worship."

Mitchell reached out and placed his hand possessively on Ellen's back. The gesture said *Hands off, Pal, she's mine.* "You did such an excellent job during missions week—really raised the awareness of missions." His straight teeth looked bleached. "If I didn't have a business to run, I might have signed up."

The thought of Mr. Suave field dressing a reindeer and making his own stew nearly made Paul laugh aloud. Not fair, he told himself. God could do anything, with anyone. A missionary didn't have to be made of chunky granola to be effective. Why, God could even take Elegant Ellen and turn her into a frontier woman if she let Him have control of the chisel.

Now that was an image worth smiling over. . .Ellen White baking bread and canning jam. Ellen White decorating his fur-lined teepee.

"What are you grinning about?" Ellen quirked a refined eyebrow, as if reading his thoughts.

Paul looked at the matched pair of dressed-to-impress decorators. "You never know where God may call you, if you let Him get ahold of your heart." He waggled his eyebrows and marched away, thinking how delicious it would be to see Miss Interior Decorator in the Siberian wilds and knowing those kind of whimsies could get him in big trouble.

"So, what happened to your hand?"

They sat on the deck, now completed, letting the late

afternoon sun bathe their shoes, enjoying the way the wind snatched jeweled leaves from the neighboring trees and tossed them hither. Still dressed in a black silk suit, she perfumed the night with the subtle fragrance of some sort of refined flower.

Ellen was here, again, and suddenly he knew why the sun had been hiding all day.

She was so beautiful it hurt.

What was she doing here with him? He tried not to feel like a hobo in his army fatigues and fraying gray sweatshirt, but he knew his hair needed a buzz and the work smell coming off of him would flatten a skunk. "I got into a land war with a wild dog."

"What?"

He liked her surprise. It lit up her face and peeled away the fashion model exterior. The girl behind it made his heart skip.

"The Chukchi people have a lot of wild dogs that run in packs through the village. We were having a cookout—the end of the summer celebration—and one of the toddlers wandered off with a piece of meat in his hand. It attracted the interest of the pack." He blinked away the sight of little Sasha, screaming, surrounded by bared fangs and enough wolf blood to make his own go cold. "I intervened, and well. . . ," he paused and lifted his hand, "souvenir."

He tried to scoot away from her, but Ellen grabbed his wrist, as if wanting to inspect his bandage. Her touch felt cool on his hot skin.

"It looks painful."

"It's getting better. Seventeen stitches."

She peeked under the bandage. "They look homemade."

"I thought Valya did a pretty good job, considering she only had fishing twine." He chuckled at the face Ellen made.

"Is this common? It sounds so dangerous."

He smiled, not wanting to tell her the truth, wishing suddenly that he could tell her that life in his village, in any remote missionary location, was just as safe as Milltown, Oklahoma. But missions' reality was that medical care was iffy at best, life was rife with peril, and sometimes people, especially children, died.

"It has its moments. I try to be careful. Most of all I remember that God is with me. When this happened, He provided the treatment I needed."

"Your faith amazes me." Her eyes were so wide, he wondered for a moment if they could swallow him whole. Not that he would mind. Since the moment she'd barreled into his life, he'd been fighting the fringe hope, and the voice of reason, that Ellen White would make room for him in her life.

"You have the same faith, Ellen. You just don't need to use it. If you were out in the bush, facing a pack of mangy dogs, you'd have no choice but to trust God. That's how it works. I'm thankful to be in a position to be forced to trust God on a daily, hourly basis."

He smiled, but he felt like a hypocrite. Yes, he trusted God, but even he, sainted missionary, had his threshold. He might be able to risk his life, but he couldn't imagine dragging a wife. . .or children. . .into the backwoods. He would never have the faith of Travis and MaryJo. . .trekking into the wilderness with her six months pregnant. Pure lunacy. He could never endure what his parents did. That kind of pain could cripple a marriage, shatter a faith.

"You're amazing, Paul." Ellen caught her lower lip in her teeth, staring at him like he was some sort of Hebrews eleven superhero. He wanted to shrink under the decking and hide. Thank the Lord she couldn't see into his heart with those captivating eyes.

He dredged up a smile and shrugged, calling himself a coward. He should tell her the truth, that even missionaries struggled with issues of faith. Instead he indicated her black portfolio. "Did you bring something?"

She blinked at him, as if traveling back from some distant planet. "Oh, yeah. Some fabric swatches and paint strips. I was thinking of sage for the bedrooms."

"Sage? As in green?"

She wrinkled her nose and nodded, again destroying her polished, out of his league, image. Unzipping the portfolio, she pulled out a board with fabric samples and paint strips attached. The portfolio fell open on the grass, and he couldn't help but notice the sketches on top. "Wow. Those are beautiful." He reached past her and picked them up. "Is it a bank?"

"It's a proposal to service First Citizen's Bank's main branch in Oklahoma City and all the regional branches."

"I like it. Very homey colors."

She giggled. "Oh, thanks. Actually, navy and brown are supposed to be calming colors. We're going to do the furniture in stressed leather, and the fireplace there is fake, but will add a sense of family and comfort to the lobby. People need to feel safe in a bank, and the aura of entering a family room type atmosphere, as if the man managing your money is your favorite uncle, will be an asset."

"I have to admit, I've never seen a bank lobby I wanted to stretch out and take a nap in."

"I'll take that as a compliment."

He whistled low. "You're very talented." Again, the question whizzed through his mind—what was a lady like Ellen White doing with him? Especially with the twilight painting them a perfect romantic backdrop? It was enough to make a lonely fella like himself conjure up faulty suppositions that might get them both in trouble.

"Thank you. If I land the account, it will really put Ellen's on the map."

She took the pictures and tucked them into her portfolio. "That is, if Mitchell doesn't try to steal the company from me." She muttered it, but he heard the hostility in it and jumped on the comment.

"Mitchell is trying to steal your company?" For a second, he couldn't bat away the urge to track down Slick and wrap him around his fancy car.

"Oh, I don't know. He's just been putting a lot of pressure on me lately. He wants to be my partner." She sighed and wove her hands through that silky blond hair.

Pressure? Partner? As in marriage? Another flash of pain speared his chest. No, he couldn't be jealous of Slick Mitchell, could he? Not when Paul didn't even have a prayer of a chance with Ellen White. "He seems nice." What could he say, that he wanted her to flee the one man that fit into her lifestyle, her image? She deserved a man who could build her a comfortable life.

"He is. Mitchell and I have been together for five years, nearly since I started the company. But now he wants more."

Paul tried not to let his face betray the way her words hurt. Stupid. She wasn't sitting here because she was interested in Paul Stoneman. The truth felt like a fist in his solar plexus. Ellen was on a goodwill mission. Pity, pure and untainted, sent her to his backyard with wallpaper samples and fabric and smelling like a dream come true. She was doing her bit for God to help the poor First Church missionary.

He wanted to groan. He should have guessed it. Still, the reality made his throat tighten. Why had he ever thought a lady like her would want a guy whose sum total of worldly goods consisted of a grimy sleeping bag and reindeer-skin jacket?

He was a real catch.

"When is your presentation?" His voice sounded like it had been through a meat grinder.

Thankfully she didn't notice. "In a couple weeks. I just have to decide on a few pieces of artwork and polish my pitch, and I'll be ready."

"I'll be praying for you."

The smile she gave him felt like an embrace around his heart. "Thank you, Paul. I've been praying about this too, and I just feel like God has something wonderful planned. I can't escape the feeling that He's planned something, just over the horizon—the culmination of my dreams and hopes.

I just know I'm going to land this." She shrugged, and the faith shining in her eyes made his heart skip.

Lord, this isn't fair. Here she is, a woman of faith, of purity, of purpose, right before my eyes. And so painfully opposite from me it hurts. Yet my heart is tumbling in my chest and right now all I can think about is getting on my knees and begging her to let me into her life. Have mercy!

"I guess you've always wanted to be a decorator, huh? It's a beautiful thing when dreams come true." He tried not to grimace at his words.

She gave a slight chuckle with just a hint of chagrin. "I suppose."

He frowned. "What do you mean? You sound like you've been dreaming this particular moment all your life."

She was biting her lip, obviously chewing over her next words. It was so cute, so totally unrefined. So completely winning. "Actually, I have a deep dark secret."

"Really?" He fought to keep a giddy grin off his face. If God wanted him to fall for Ellen White, the Almighty was doing a good job of setting the mood. The sun had dropped below the rooflines and dusky twilight hued the backyard in muted shades of lavender. The leaves had begun to rustle, caressed by a slight wind. He kept fighting the impulse to put his arm around her on pretense of warding off a chill. "I can keep a secret."

Was he flirting with her now? His heart expanded about thirty sizes when she smiled at him, a twinkle in her eyes.

"When I was a little girl. . ." Her voice lowered and she actually glanced around the backyard, as if someone besides the squirrels would hear her. He suppressed a grin. "I wanted to be a missionary."

Her confession had the impact of an Oklahoma tornado ripping right through his chest. He couldn't speak for the agonizing space of thirty seconds. He just stared at her, all his dreams whirling inside him. A missionary. Oh, yes!

And right then, hope took root.

"Really? How interesting." Was that really his calm, cool voice? Was that really him, sitting there, hands cupped over his knees, acting as if he didn't long to do a jig right in the middle of his new deck?

You never know what God can do when He gets ahold of your heart.

He always knew he wanted to be a recruiter.

Chapter 5

"Stop. Don't move."

Ellen's voice betrayed amusement, and Paul knew he'd done it again. Glued wallpaper to his arm or pants or maybe this time his hair. He stood on the stepladder, the wallpaper curling down over his head, wondering for the thirty-sixth time in the last hour just why he'd been finagled into this mess.

Then she laughed. . .and he knew.

Recruiting. Oh, how he liked that word.

He had to admit, Ellen had the patience of a saint. He had given her plenty of reasons to run for the hills over the past few weeks. Just three weeks ago he'd dumped paint into her golden hair. Then they'd spent last weekend painting the bedroom a death green that she'd called sage. Then, just yesterday, he'd had the brilliant idea to cook a chicken. . .oh yes, dazzle her with his culinary skills.

He was still trying to air the smoke fumes out of the house.

And this morning, he'd managed to work his tongue into

a knot, displaying his total ignorance. "A swag. . .as in. . . ?" Her sweet as candy laughter blamed his embarrassment. The closest thing he'd had to a swag window treatment in his entire life were the tea towels his mother had hung over their tiny windows in their hut in Papua New Guinea. And they hadn't done a thing to keep out the mosquitoes, the peering eyes, or the rats. "Why do I need a swag?"

Then again, if Elegant Ellen said he needed a swag or a swatch or a valance or—what did she say. . .café curtains?— then who was he to argue? He had about as much decorating savvy as a raccoon. Besides, it wasn't in the least painful to surrender to those blue-green eyes swallowing him like an arctic wave. In fact, he was starting to relish it.

The delight was something he was pretty sure God was okay with. Paul had spent plenty of off-decorating hours on his knees, trying not to asphyxiate from the paint fumes, begging God to spare his heart or deliver his dreams.

And here Ellen was, wallpapering his family room on a blue-skied Saturday. The wind sent leaves dancing in front of the window as if beckoning them to join in. For the first time in years, he felt like a red-blooded American male, enjoying the friendship of a blond with laughter that was honey to his soul. And the fact that he hadn't hidden his calling, but spun her stories she devoured with rapt attention, only made their friendship sweeter.

Recruiting, indeed.

"I thought you said this was a cinch." His triceps began to burn as he held the sticky wallpaper above his head.

She giggled. "It is. . .by myself. I have a system." She

peeled the wallpaper off his socks. His skin felt gummy through the cotton. "But you wanted to help, so. . ." She shrugged, but he saw mischief in her eyes.

He gave her a mock glare.

"Line the wallpaper along the ceiling, and we'll work from the top down." She smoothed the paper like a pro, her French manicured fingers delicate and smooth along the beige patterned paper. The color reminded him of the sand dollars he'd caught and dried while vacationing on the Sea of Japan. She'd called it a neutral palette, whatever that meant. It did look better than the cotton candy.

"So what kind of house do you live in. . .in. . .Cha. . . Cha—"

"Chukchotka." He stepped down from the stool and watched as she measured another strip of wallpaper. "The Chukchi people herd reindeer for the government for a living, or at least they used to. Many of them are beginning to run their own private herd. But they have to travel with the deer, so we have makeshift camps, somewhat like the Sioux tribes did."

"You mean you take your home with you? Like a teepee?" Her gape made him laugh. She had a way of turning his ordinary life into something of folklore.

"Yes. Well, many of the people do. Most of the Chukchi live in town in houses. They rotate out to tend the reindeer on dogsled or snow machines. But a select group are turning back to the old way, and yes, they travel with the herd, carrying their homes with them."

"You do that?" She folded the wallpaper strip like an

expert and climbed up the step stool. He stepped up behind her to spot for her, not minding a bit if she should happen to fall into his arms.

He tried to fight the image. After all, he was a missionary; and despite the fact that he hadn't kissed a woman since his senior year in college—and even then it had been with the promise of a future—he'd been spending way too much time wondering how it would feel to hold Ellen in his arms, run his fingers through her silky hair, and kiss those beautiful lips.

Oh, he'd really unleashed his heart this time. He hadn't come home looking for a wife, but God had dropped this very capable, very bubbly. . .yes, very cultured woman into his life—if her fingernails, her convertible, and her designer jeans were accurate indicators—but what was he supposed to do, slam the door in her face?

If he listened to the voice of reason screaming in the back of his head, he'd do just that. He'd wipe off her glue brush, pack up her rags and swatches and swags, and send her politely packing back to her safe, refined world. Far, far away from the stories of the Chukchi people, which were doing more to ignite his dreams than draw her into his world. Because anyone with all his brain cells firing would see that Miss Ellen White wouldn't last a day, no, an hour in a Chukchi village.

And he wasn't about to forsake his call to missions for anyone, even a lady who filled up all the lonely places in his life.

But "I wanted to be a missionary. . . ." Those quiet words drilled into his head in the quiet of the night and pumped a desperate, very tangible, hope into his veins.

"So, when you are overseas, what do you miss the most?" She smoothed the wallpaper down the wall.

That didn't look too hard. Why did his wallpaper strips look like he had covered over a spiny lizard? "Um. . .buffalo wings. And smooth roads."

She pushed her hair back with her wrists. "Smooth roads?"

"I love to ride my bike, but there are no paved roads in Chukchotka, and it's pretty painful. I left my bike behind last time."

"So what do you miss about Siberia?"

Now that was a question he liked. The fact that she assumed that he missed Siberia touched his heart. Yes, he missed the smell of waking up to a campfire, the sounds of children playing in the yard. The golden slide of the sun over ice-encrusted tundra. "I miss the sunrise."

She looked over her shoulder and gave him a strange smile. "Really? I have this great view from my apartment. I love to watch the sun rise over the lake. It's my favorite part of the day."

The way she said it, with that tiny golden smile, made him want to twirl her around the room. So she was a sunrise gal. Yes!

"Have you been a missionary all your life?" She stepped off the stool and finished smoothing the strip to the baseboard.

"Yes. I went to Moody Bible Institute, got a degree in missions, and headed out right after my senior year. God burned the desire into my heart to be a missionary since childhood, and I can't imagine doing anything different. Ever."

She turned and looked at him, her expression solemn. "Nor could I see you doing anything different. You amaze me. I realize now that I could never do what you do."

Then she smiled as if she hadn't just sent all his hopes scattering like wheat in the breeze. His heart took a wicked tumble to his knees.

He hadn't been imagining the way she gazed into his eyes with pure admiration, but it obviously wasn't the admiration he'd been hoping for. Ellen White saw him exactly the way every other layperson looked at a missionary. Untouchable. Righteous. Possessing some magical mustard seed of faith.

If only she knew how he wrestled with courage, with faith. If only she knew that he'd spent nearly a decade stalking the night, shaking his fist at God, tears streaming down his cheeks. If only she knew that deep inside his heart of faith lurked a fear so deep he was afraid to voice it. He swallowed hard and dredged up a smile.

"Hey, let's get out of here, huh? I think you've done enough work for one night."

She stood up and stretched her back. "Okay. Where to?"

He waggled his eyebrows, and wasn't it nice that she blushed slightly as she looked away? It felt like a dagger in his heart to think she wasn't the one God had picked out for him. Miss Ellen White was just a ray of sunshine in his lonely life, a friend who had laughter that made him want to dance. He should simply enjoy the gift and in a year walk away thankful.

Watching Ellen gather up her supplies, her golden hair falling like a waterfall over her beautiful face, a work of delight and beauty that *really* lit up his home, he knew he was destined to leave behind his heart, crushed and bleeding, on the Oklahoma prairie.

Ellen dug her fingers into the back of Paul's sweatshirt, sure she'd never had so much fun riding a bike. He'd rebuffed her suggestion to take her convertible, and the beat-up pickup in his driveway obviously didn't rate high enough because he went right for a much-used bike parked beside the garage.

"It only has one seat," Ellen commented.

He shrugged, but his smile seemed just a little too rapscallion. He'd changed into a pair of track pants and a green sweatshirt that matched his incredible eyes.

She felt like a vagabond in her faded work jeans and a flannel shirt. All she needed were a couple blackened teeth and she'd be the spitting image of a hillbilly. Fine for wallpapering, but suddenly he wanted to take her on a jaunt out in public? On the back of his bicycle?

He swung his leg over. "Hop on."

She'd clearly looked incredulous because he'd laughed, strong and deep and rich. It spiraled right to her heart and bolstered her courage. She stepped on the pedal, swung her leg over, and sat on the seat. She raised her hands. "And um. . . ?"

"Hold on to my waist."

Oh sure, she'd just wrap her arms around him and hang on like she hadn't been dreaming that particular fantasy for a week now. Paul Stoneman had invaded her thoughts with the force of an Oklahoma windstorm. All she had to do was merely let her brain relax, wander from her sketches, and suddenly there was Paul, complete with magical green eyes, tangled mahogany hair, singsong laughter, and stories so vibrant she felt like she was sitting near a Chukchi campfire. She felt guilty just for dreaming about the way he smiled and how it made her heart kick into overdrive. He was a missionary, after all! Still, although she couldn't deny he'd lit a fire in her heart—only half of it had to do with the fact that she went completely weak near the man. She couldn't pinpoint it, but she'd begun to feel like she had as a child, sitting on the edge of her seat, soaking in the reports of the missionaries.

Longing to be on the cutting edge of the gospel war. What it must be like to be a missionary and see people freed by the grace of God for the first time. The thought made her want to leap to her feet and shout, "Here am I, send me!"

And then, like a slap back to reality, Mitchell would poke his groomed head into her office with new ideas for the Whitney estate. "Do you like this gilded Louis XIV armoire? Or this King Louis bust replica. . . ?"

Send me. What did she think she was going to do out there in the Siberian wilderness—sew valances for her reindeer hut? Brilliant. She possessed even less evangelistic savvy than Paul did decorating skill. The thought of him hog-tied in beige grass cloth made her stifle a giggle as she tried to figure out how to hold onto the gorgeous missionary in front of her without letting her heart betray her.

Gingerly, she dug her hands into his sweatshirt. "This is fine. Where do I put my feet?"

"Brace your heels on those bars extending from the back wheel."

"Sounds like you've done this before."

He chuckled as he pushed off. "When I was a kid, my brother and I only had one bike so we took turns giving each other rides. My dad custom-made the footholds for us."

"You've had this bike since you were a kid?" She tried not to wobble as he gathered speed. The sense of being balanced by the man in front of her, her grip on his sweatshirt the only thing between her and an ugly scrape across the pavement, made her heart flutter in her chest.

"I've had it redone a few times. A new seat. A paint job. New handlebars. But the bike holds sentimental meaning for me. It's the only possession I dragged home from Papua New Guinea when I went to college."

"You grew up in Papua New Guinea?"

The wind lifted the hair from her neck, and the smells of fall perfumed the twilight breeze. Paul didn't even break a sweat as he pedaled them down Pecan Crossing and then onto a bike trail that rimmed the Brook's Country housing development. The low sun pushed out long block shadows as it sank behind the houses.

"Yep," he answered, and offered no more information.

Ellen hung on and pondered his words. Perhaps that was what made Paul willing to risk his life, to live out in the bush, to surrender the amenities of life. He'd never grown up surrounded by running water, refrigeration, or television. Cooking wild meat over an open fire probably seemed natural to Paul Stoneman.

Whereas, she'd probably starve.

The path meandered through the shadows, under the

embrace of golden oaks, crimson maples, and finally unfurled along Lake Holderman.

Ellen tried to suppress a giggle, but as they pedaled along the shore—she hanging on for dear life—she began to shake with glee.

"What's the matter back there? You okay?"

She bit her lip, trying desperately to swallow her laughter. Fat tears rolled down her cheeks. Paul finally stopped and turned around. The concern on his rugged face only made her laugh harder.

"What is it?"

She shook her head and slid off the bike, gasping for air, holding her sides. "Paul, is this your favorite place?"

His mouth raised in a half smile, tentative. "Well, yeah."

She shut her eyes tight and felt her mascara smear. Pressing her fingers under her lashes, she drew in a deep breath. "You probably didn't know, but we call this place Lake Hold-her-man." She looked at him and shook her head.

His smile dimmed, the silence between them suddenly making gooseflesh rise on her arm. Her words suddenly sounded so. . .hopeful. As if she were suggesting. . . Oh, no. So much for not betraying her heart. A lump the size of Montana rose in her throat, neatly cutting off her air. By the stricken look on Paul's face, he obviously had a similar lump. He'd just about turned white.

"I—didn't mean. . ." She grimaced and turned away, wishing the earth could open up and swallow her whole. *Right. Now. Please.*

"Ellen." His voice was so close, it raised the tiny hairs on the back of her neck. She could smell him, his masculine scent tinged with the right amount of soap. He never wore cologne, and she found that so. . .fresh.

Then he put his hands on her shoulders. The tenderness of his touch swept right through her sweatshirt and straight to her heart. She froze, listening to her heart pound.

"Ellen, can there be. . .I mean. . .is there. . .something going on between us?" His soft voice trembled.

She swallowed, knowing that if she shrugged, he'd probably back away faster than the speed of sound. She wanted, more than she even wanted her next breath, to turn and nestle her head into his wide, oh-so-muscular chest. She saw herself wrapping her arms around him and holding tight, feeling safe and alive and so very. . .

What? She could hardly admit to herself the emotions nesting in her heart.

Her eyes filled with tears as she stepped out of his grasp, away from him. Away from the feelings that threatened to bubble out into the purple twilight.

He sighed. "Okay. That's okay. I'm sorry."

He was sorry? She felt something dark and painful burrow into the center of her chest. She bit her lip and turned to look at him, fighting her common sense. Betraying tears welled in her eyes.

Paul's face twisted as if fighting a wave of emotion. "I'm sorry, Ellen. I didn't mean to offend you."

She began to shake her head, but he reached out and pulled her close. She dug her fist into his shirt, muted by a knot of emotions. She gritted her teeth. Why couldn't she just tell him that he'd crept inside her heart?

He rested his chin on her head. "I shouldn't have asked. Thank you for being my friend, Ellen. I know you're just doing the missions committee a favor, and I appreciate your help. Just forget what I said. Please."

Ellen ached at his words. "You don't understand, Paul." She broke away from him, wishing she could untangle the feelings in her chest. Oh, yes, she'd dreamed of this moment. . .too many times over the past week. She had her suspicions Mitchell had deduced her daydreams had more to do with an arctic missionary than the homey First Citizen's Bank interior or eighteenth-century French décor. But how could she tell him that for the first time—no, the second time—in her life, the missions desire burned in her heart? And that right in the center of that consuming fire stood Paul Stoneman, radiant green eyes fixed to hers?

What was she thinking? She had a life—not just a life, a thriving business. A condo with an incredible view. And she was doing her part for missions, just as Paul had said.

She felt ill. What a contribution to the lost. A natural palette and a couple of sage-painted walls. She'd throw in a patterned swag, maybe a couple tasseled pillows, and smack her hands, job well done. Thousands won for the Lord.

Poor Paul had only wanted to build a deck.

And she'd walked into his life and rearranged it.

The only problem was, he was the one rearranging hers. And if she didn't cut and run—right now—she might find herself baking bread over an open fire.

Somehow that thought made her wonder if she also

wouldn't be deliriously happy. Especially if she were doing it beside a man that made her feel gloriously alive.

"I'm sorry, Paul." Her voice sounded wispy in the night breeze. The rising moon had already begun to part the lake in a laser beam of light. Lake Hold-her-man. With the wind giving music to the dancing leaves and the hint of a wood fire in the air, the longing swept through her to adhere to the tradition, just once. To enjoy the embrace of a muscular missionary with a heart for God and just maybe dream of a future. . .

For Elegant Ellen and Grizzly Stoneman? The absurdity hit her like a cold slap.

Tears ringed her eyes. "You didn't offend me." She pressed her fingertips to her eyes. "Thank you for bringing me here, but I think I need to go home." She cleared her throat, feeling as if she had just kicked something spectacular in the teeth. "I'm sorry I invaded your life."

Chapter 6

"That went well, don't you think?" Mitchell sauntered out beside Ellen, cool and refined after their presentation before the First Citizen's Bank board.

She felt unraveled and trampled. Yes, they'd been polite, even when she'd tripped over her words. Again and again. Yes, they'd taken her recommendations and told her they'd consider them.

And then they'd invited in the next proposal—from a company straight off the cover of last month's *Decorating Today* magazine. They'd strutted past her, a troop of five, dressed to kill and armed with a multimedia extravaganza.

She felt like a carpetbagger, toting her wares in her shabby suitcase. Her little dog and pony show felt tawdry and uninspiring. "Yeah, sure," Ellen agreed and made a bee-line for her convertible.

So much for feeling like a spectacular future hovered on the horizon. She'd be lucky to decorate the local burger joint after today.

At least they had the Whitney account to keep macaroni

and cheese on her table. But Mitchell had landed that one—by himself, as he reminded her often. Partner. Maybe she needed him more than she realized.

"I'll meet you back at the office," he said, pulling up in his car and waving. She gave him a half smile and nodded.

She wasn't going back to Ellen's. Right now she needed her flannel pajamas, fuzzy slippers, and a big bowl of peanut butter popcorn.

She'd better get used to living on that.

The one person she longed to be with, to run to and bury her frustrated tears into his chest, was Paul Stoneman.

To him was the last place she could run. She'd burned that bridge Saturday night with her stinging freeze-out. She'd left the poor guy standing in the park, and she hiked, no jogged, okay, *ran* through the housing development, jumped in her car, and floored it.

That certainly left an indelible impression.

Ellen gripped the steering wheel, shivering in the cool October air. *Lord, I tried. I did. Why did it go so wrong? I just wanted to do something. . .important. Make a difference.* Her throat burned. She was making a real dent in the world by adding fringes to pillows. But hadn't God equipped her for this? She'd pulled a straight 4.0 at Oklahoma Evangelical University, the top in her home economics class. She could take a hunk of meat, a little flour and water, and turn it into beef Wellington that could bring a man to tears. She knew how to sew her own clothes. . .could even design them; and the one year she'd grown a garden, she had enough zucchini to feed a small nation. So why did she feel empty inside?

Maybe building campfires and telling Bible stories in the tundra was more suited for her than she realized.

The thought made her laugh. Right.

Then, suddenly, her throat tightened. *Right. Oh, no, please, Lord, really?* She saw herself, nails chipped, hair tangled in the wind, wrapped in a Khonba, smiling until her cheeks popped, and, all at once, like a divine breath, hope swept threw her. Gooseflesh rose on her arms.

No. Certainly that spectacular feeling of hope from God, the culmination of her dreams on the horizon didn't mean. . .

She shook her head. If she hadn't made it painfully clear Saturday, certainly her artful dodging of Paul on Sunday had sent a crystalline message to the man. *Keep away.*

And she couldn't, no, wouldn't, no, *shouldn't* roar up to his house, throw herself into his arms, and beg him to take her with him. The poor guy would drive her straight to the local loony bin. Not only would he be utterly confused, but the mere thought of Elegant Ellen chucking her fabric swatches and running off to join the Chukchi would reduce him to hysterics.

The image made her giggle. . .until she burst into tears.

That was exactly what she wanted to do. The desire burst into an inferno until all she could do was curl her hands around herself and sob.

God couldn't be serious, could He?

So she'd spent the last five years grooming her reputation, down to her manicured fingernails. What was it that Paul had said. . .*you never know what can happen when God gets ahold of your heart?* She bit her trembling lip. God had her heart, completely. And if He wanted to send her to the outskirts of the world, then she would do it. She took a deep breath, listening to her pounding heart hammer down her fears. *Okay, God. Fine.* The surrender swept peace through her like a healing wave, tears flooded her eyes, coursed down her cheeks. *I'll do it.*

I'll do it. The thought made her giddy. Hope, as light as helium, nearly lifted her out of the seat. Ellen White, a missionary?

Oh, yes.

The image of a little girl, braids down to her waist, praying that God would make her a missionary made her tremble. Some dreams were worth the wait.

Especially dreams that had glorious green eyes and wildly delicious hair. She tried not to let the memory of her screeching exit from Paul's life rake her thoughts.

But she couldn't deny the truth. She'd closed her account with Missionary Stoneman; and unless he managed to figure out where she lived and pound her door down, she'd only see him from a distance from her pew in the sanctuary.

Even that was close enough to break her heart.

Ellen's Elegant Design. He found her name etched into the brass plaque near the door. The lady had her own studio. In an upscale, three-story office complex with a concierge and a fountain in the center, no less. The place smelled posh; and as he walked across the marble floor to the elevator, he knew he should turn tail and sprint out of the building. And keep going until he hit the horizon.

Hadn't he gotten her message loud and clear yesterday? When she turned white and all but lined up blockers between them in the church lobby? Mitchell had either become her new bodyguard, or their relationship had soared to new heights the way Ellen stuck to him like glue.

But Cro-Magnon man Stoneman had blundered, and he knew it. The second he touched her shoulders at Lake Hold-her-man, she stiffened. He'd offended her. Then he'd rattled off some sort of apology and had made it a thousand times worse. She'd been embarrassed, and her tears made him want to cry too. She deserved so much more. She might have been doing a favor for the missions committee, but she'd done abundantly more than spruce up his house and help him keep his bargain. She'd added light and texture to his life. She'd made him laugh, reminded him that life didn't have to be a battle. It could be filled with a whimsy, with frills and decorations that made it magnificent. She might not be willing to trek with him to Siberia, but the memory of her smile would light the arctic winter landscape like an aurora borealis.

Ellen White was the extraordinary woman he'd been waiting for all his life. He spent the night staring at the ceiling, finally putting words to the explosive joy that filled his chest when she was around. He loved Ellen White.

She hadn't invaded his life.

She had invaded his heart.

And telling her that was more important than not looking like the fool he was, gripping a dozen pink long-stemmed roses, dressed like a country bumpkin in his rumpled corduroy sport coat and a flannel shirt. The clerk at the floral shop told him pink stood for appreciation. That seemed like a pretty good place to start. He smiled meekly at a man who looked like a lawyer and two women who smelled like a floral shop.

He watched the buttons light up, stop at three, then he gathered his courage and marched off the elevator. Suite 310. He followed the arrows and came to a halt outside Ellen's office. High-powered brass lettered the door.

He stopped, suddenly realizing his stupidity. Did he think that she'd be delighted that he'd tracked her down like a bounty hunter from the Wild West? He would open up his chest and give her his heart, and what was she supposed to do with it? Drop her future and snowshoe out to the frozen tundra with him?

He turned to hightail it down the hall.

The door opened. "Can I help you?"

Mitchell. Looking as refined as Paul did scraggly. "Hi. I, um. . .is Ellen in?"

Mitchell's gray gaze scanned him, turning cold and dark when it landed on the flowers. "Sorry, Pal. She's not here yet. Probably out shopping, celebrating with a new outfit." He left the words unspoken, but Paul could guess that Mitchell would love to add a comment about Paul's attire. Well, at least he didn't look like he couldn't change a tire or figure out which end of an ax to swing. No, he appeared completely barbarian next to Slick. "So you landed the bank account?"

Mitchell shrugged. "Probably. We won't know for awhile."

So Ellen's dreams had materialized. Which meant his recruiting tactics had netted exactly zip. She'd be better off if he'd just get out of the way. "Can you give her these?" He held out the flowers. "Just tell her they are from you. Congratulations and all." He managed a smile.

Mitchell angled his head, eyes narrowed. "Don't tell me you have. . .a thing for Ellen?" He chuckled, as if the very thought were preposterous.

Paul stared at him. Several inches taller than the man, Paul had no trouble giving him a look that would freeze a polar bear. "On second thought, maybe I'll give her the flowers in person."

Mitchell raised his eyebrows. "Suit yourself. I'll tell her to call you when she gets in." He eyed Paul like the man had just bathed in refuse. "Nice tie. I think those are coming back." He winked, then closed the door.

Paul bravely fought the animalistic urge to tie the flowers around Mitchell's scrawny neck, reminding himself he was a missionary. . .and his support might take a severe dip if he were found guilty of assault and battery.

Ellen White. Whatever non-future they had, he couldn't bear to think of her marrying Mitchell Frank. The thought made his flesh crawl.

He hadn't spent eight years in the backwoods for nothing. He could track with the best of the Chukchi.

Shopping. . .at which designer boutique?

Ellen cradled the bowl of popcorn on her lap while she dug into her sofa for the remote control. She'd closed the vertical blinds, but the afternoon sun filtered through them, striping the room mandarin orange. After a bubble bath, a

166

cup of hot cocoa, and a significant amount of time on her knees, reading the promises in Psalms and praying for God's guidance, she felt like she might be able to face life with her chin up. Well, maybe after a bowl of popcorn and an hour and a half with a romantic movie on DVD. Ellen still had some tears behind her eyes, begging to spill out.

Tomorrow she'd figure out a way to break the news to Mitchell. Yes, he'd be partner—well, not just partner. Owner. If she managed to find a mission board that would accept her and her home economics degree. The outrageous thought continued to stir her soul.

She pulled the afghan her mother had knitted over her knees, picked up Sylvester, her plump Persian cat, settled him on her lap, and pressed play on the remote. The DVD whirred and in a second the screen displayed her options.

She barely heard the knock on the door over the opening song.

Mitchell, probably wondering why she'd never returned to the office. He'd be holding a bottle of diet soda and a box of designer chocolates, offering to help her celebrate.

And she'd send him packing. Despite his friendship, she couldn't bear to spend the night talking about King Louis XIV and the palace of Versailles.

She displaced her fat feline, marched to the door, braced herself, and flung it open, a good-bye on her lips.

Paul Stoneman filled the hall, holding. . .a bouquet of roses? Her words died a quick death in her throat. He smiled, and she had to grip the door frame before her knees wobbled and sent her to the floor in a heap.

Paul, looking like a frontier hero, complete with flannel shirt, white smile, and—haircut? He'd shaved off that long mane to a high and tight crew cut.

And it made his green eyes stand out like gems in his rugged face. "Hiya, Ellen."

She opened her mouth, and a "Hi" squeaked out. Then she remembered she'd scrubbed her face clean of makeup and wore her ratty sweatpants and an old paint shirt. Lovely. And he'd caught her mid-junk-foodfest.

"These are for you." He held out the flowers. More than six. . .must be a dozen. Roses. Pink—for thank you, not red, declaring his undying love. She tried not to let that deflate her heart. Heartbreaker Stoneman stood in her doorway, looking like he held his heart in his hands. Perhaps she could forgive him for getting pink roses. . . .

"Come in, Paul. Please." She stepped back, held the door wider.

He stood there. "Um. . .well, okay." His movements seemed stilted. He looked around her apartment. . .as if searching for someone?

"You live here alone?"

She got down a vase and filled it with water. "Just me and Sylvester." She smiled at his look of complete horror. "My cat. I've never been a big roommate person." As if on cue, Sylvester wrapped around Paul's legs like they were old friends.

Paul nodded, as if agreeing with Ellen. Great pair they made. Loners. He, up there in the woods, she down in the urban jungle. Ellen cut the stems down, added the floral packet, then arranged the flowers in the vase. "They're beautiful. Thank you."

His smile didn't touch his eyes. He shifted from side to side as if poised to bolt. He ran his hand over his head, then stared at it, as if shocked by his new do.

"Did you want to. . .I mean. . ." Why was he here?

The movie played in the background. The romantic words of a love song filled the room like a purple elephant waiting to be acknowledged. And suddenly, as if the song had drummed it to the surface, she knew.

She loved this man. The truth took root in her heart and swelled through her entire body like a wave. *I love Paul Stoneman.* She loved his faith. Loved his vision. Loved his passion for his work, his idiotic attempts to help her wallpaper and paint. She loved his smile, his voice, even the way he touched her shoulders, so gently, as if she might break. She could see herself working beside him for the rest of her life, and more. The feeling nearly lifted her off the kitchen floor.

Somehow she stayed rooted, but she ached to blurt it out. *I love you!*

But what did she expect, that he would swoop her into his arms and beg her to run away to Siberia? Yes. She bit her lip, fighting the impulse to act on her desires.

He grimaced, as if trying dredge up some mysterious words. Then, in a voice she didn't recognize, "Please, Ellen. Don't marry Mitchell."

What? She blinked at him, not quite sure her ears were in tune. "Mitchell?"

Paul turned away from her. "No, I shouldn't have said

that. You can marry whomever you want. It's just. . .I. . ." He shook his head. "I should go."

He reached for the door handle.

"No!" She winced at the panic lacing her voice. How desperate could she get? "I mean. . .why would you think I would marry Mitchell?" She tried to keep her voice calm, but please, Mitchell? Mr. Beemer, who dreamed fabric swatches? Not when her heart belonged, one-hundred-and-fifty-percent, to a man who dreamed about serving God.

The kind of hero she'd longed for in the deepest places of her heart.

He turned to face her, and the expression in his beautiful eyes made her freeze. Longing. Raw and vulnerable. Her heart did a vault in her chest. Could he. . .did he. . . ?

"You two seem so. . .right together. I mean, at first. But Mitchell, he's—"

"Shallow, selfish, and materialistic?"

Paul blinked at her. "Well. . ."

"I know. Mitchell has his own particular charm, but he is completely self-absorbed." She rubbed her arms, suddenly comprehending his words. She and Mitchell. . .right for each other? Did that mean Paul thought she was shallow, selfish. . .materialistic?

She looked around her elite condo, replete with a white leather sofa, solid oak furniture, plush ivory carpet, velvet pillows, and a dried floral spray that had set her back two hundred dollars. Well, she swallowed hard, maybe.

But not anymore. She'd sell it all and donate it to missions. "Mitchell isn't for me. He might have been, once. But

170

I have other plans for my life. And, well. . .he doesn't fit into them." There, she'd said it. Practically plucked her heart out of her chest and held it out to him. *Please read between my words.*

"Other plans?" He frowned, eyes dark with confusion. "What do you mean?"

"I'm. . .I want to be a missionary." Could she speak any more plainly? *Please, Paul, don't make me flop down at your feet. Take me in your arms. Can you see God calling us together? Siberia, here I come!*

"A missionary?" He blinked at her, but the slightest smile tugged at his face. "A missionary?" he repeated, as if his hearing had cut out on him. She braced herself and waited for him to burst out into laughter.

Tears rimmed his eyes. "A missionary." The smile that broke out across his face lit up his eyes and went right to her pounding heart. He reached up and touched her hair. "I don't suppose that has anything to do with me?"

She wrinkled her nose at him. Somehow her voice emerged, soft, tiny. "It just might."

"I thought—"

"I know what you thought, Paul. But you were wrong." She touched his hand and leaned her cheek into it. "I did start out hoping to do my bit for missions. But. . .well, how could I resist your magnetic bohemian charm?"

He cupped her face in his strong hands. His touch sent a thousand ripples down her spine, and the way he looked at her threatened to turn her to pudding. "Ellen, I'm so crazy about you, it hurts. I think I started loving you the second you bulldozed into my kitchen, asking for a step stool."

She felt a blush start at her toes. "Paul, I'm in love with you. Completely. Utterly. Eternally."

His gaze traced her face like a caress, and when it landed on her lips, her mouth went dry. Then he kissed her. Impossibly tender, he tasted of sweet coffee and the promise of tomorrow. She wrapped her arms around his extraordinarily muscular shoulders and clung to him.

When he whispered her name, she buried her face in his chest and let tears run down her cheeks. He smoothed her hair. "Ellen. Are you sure? Do you know what you're giving up?"

She nodded into his shirt. Giving up and gaining.

"It won't be easy."

"I know. But if you're there, I'll make it."

He stiffened. She thought she heard him groan as he drew away. She looked at him, and a chill rippled through her. His eyes held darkness, a pain she didn't recognize. It tightened her chest. "What is it?"

He shook his head. "Oh, Honey, I'm sorry. I shouldn't have done this. This is my fault." He took another step away, and Ellen felt as if the Siberian winds had blown between them.

He looked at her one more time, his face twitching, as if on the verge of crumbling, then he flung open the door and fled.

Chapter 7

Paul paced the floor of his family room in the darkness, sweat dripping down his back. "I can do it with you by my side." He'd taken a two-hour bike ride, and still he couldn't outrun Ellen's sweet voice.

His worst nightmare. Ellen was going to the mission field because of him.

Her words bounced back to him. "I couldn't imagine you being anything else but a missionary. . . ." He groaned. She loved him. The fact that she was about to sacrifice her life, her job, her future because of that love made him sink to his knees and bury his face in his hands. He'd both dreamed of and feared this moment.

He'd found the woman of his dreams. . .someone with whom to share his life. And he had to leave her behind.

Not only was Ellen White woefully ill-equipped to be a missionary—something he was pretty sure God could deal with. But when life turned frigid, Ellen would blame him. He'd seen it before. Up close and in living color, complete with wails and the smells of death.

No, he'd never bring a woman to the mission field. Not unless she'd had her own, personal, inner sanctum experience. Without it, she'd shatter when the pressure hit.

Lord, please give me the strength I need to leave her.

Paul strode to the bathroom, ripped off his sweatpants and shirt, and stepped into the shower. He had obligations around the country, churches to speak in, and conferences to attend. He'd hit the road, tomorrow, and return in six months to collect his gear and hop a plane north.

He braced his hand against the shower wall and leaned into the spray, wishing he could wash away the shame of falling headlong in love with a woman he couldn't, wouldn't, commit to.

He felt like a wet, stinky dog.

The phone rang, and he closed his eyes. Ellen. Tracking him down. He'd noticed two messages on his machine when he returned, but nothing could make him press the button to listen. Not when he knew her voice, most likely filled with confusion and probably heart-wrenching tears, would play back in agonizing rebuttal. He'd turned off the machine.

The telephone rang. And rang. On the tenth ring, he decided she was the most persuasive person he'd ever met. On the twelfth, he turned off the shower, grabbed a towel, and dove for the extension in his bedroom, stubbing his little toe on the bed. "Hello!" Super. He sounded like an ogre.

Crackle. "Hello?" The voice sounded light years away. "Paul?"

His heart dropped as he recognized the voice. "Travis?" His replacement in Chukchotka. A young couple. MaryJo six months, or now eight months, pregnant.

"I finally found you." Relief tinged Travis's voice.

Paul hung his head, dread squeezing his chest. "Tell me everything is okay. Please." He squeezed the phone and pushed it into his ear, willing the connection clear.

"Congratulate me, Pal. I'm a dad." Travis's voice shook.

Paul swallowed, not sure what to say. "Is the baby, I mean. . .MaryJo?"

"She had a baby girl this morning. It was. . .dicey. We had to medevac her to Nome, and baby Nadia is in the neonatal unit, but she is breathing on her own and they think she'll pull through."

Paul leaned his head against the cool, sage-colored wall. "Praise the Lord, Trav. I'm so grateful."

It was hard to tell over the line, but he thought he heard Travis's voice catch. "Yeah, me too." He paused, and in it Paul felt his future begin to take shape. "We're not heading back. At least for awhile. MaryJo. . .well, it was rougher than she thought, and with the baby and all—"

"I understand. Absolutely."

He rubbed a hand over his stubbly hair, wishing he'd considered a second longer before he ducked into the barbershop. He'd need his mane for the winter. "You take care of yourself, okay? And give MaryJo a hug and my warmest congratulations."

"Thanks, Paul." Travis clicked off the line.

Paul held the dead telephone, grief snowballing in his chest.

What Travis hadn't said, but had clearly communicated

was, for a space of time, both his wife's life and his child's had hovered near death.

And Paul knew, better than he wanted to, how it felt to lose someone he loved.

He pushed back the desperate voices that rose from the past, the raw anguish of knowing the jungle pilots could never make it to their remote village before the snake's poison took effect. He closed his eyes, seeing his brother writhe, his mother mourn, his father pray. . . .

Yes, he knew exactly the cost of dragging a family to the outskirts of civilization.

And any man with all his brain synapses firing would quietly, politely, stay single.

Even if Ellen had her own private spiritual epiphany, he'd have to be knocked upside the head and hog-tied before he brought a woman he loved into the frozen night-mare of a Chukchi village.

Ellen had not an inkling of the type of life she wanted to dive into. Stories didn't do justice to the wind chill, the mountains of snow and ice, or the hunger that could eat a man, woman, or child alive.

No, she didn't have the foggiest idea of the realities of living on the back side of the world.

But he did.

He'd had no business loving her if he wasn't man enough to follow it through. And he was a regular coward of the county. He might not have a moment's compunction facing the perils of his missionary life, but the thought of losing Ellen to those perils—now was not too soon to pack his bags and hightail it back to Chukchotka, alone.

🏠

Ellen stood in his doorway, holding a take-out package of buffalo wings, horrified at the scene before her.

Clothing, strewn in piles, some clean, others—well, it was a bachelor pad. Paul's sleeping bag hung from the wrought iron curtain rod, clipped over the floral swag she'd talked him into. The blue fabric colored the room dark and ominous, and, coupled with the saggy, half full duffel bag on the floor, it created a sick feeling in Ellen's chest.

Paul was packing? "Paul, are you here?"

She heard movement in the bedroom, but stayed at the door, fighting the urge to cry.

He wasn't only slamming the door on their precious relationship. He was running back to Siberia. Without her.

"Paul?" Her voice sounded as if she'd forced it through a dark tunnel, scraped and bleeding. She tightened her jaw. She was not going to disintegrate into a mound of tears. If Paul Stoneman didn't want her, that wasn't going to keep her from letting the sudden fountain of joy in her heart sweep her all the way to the mission field. God had plans for her and they may or may not include Missionary Stoneman.

But oh, please, Lord, let me be wrong!

Paul emerged from the bedroom, carrying a handful of socks. He stopped and stared at her, his eyes betraying guilt and a horde of other unnamed emotions. He looked rough standing there, barefoot, in a wrinkled green army T-shirt and a pair of fraying Bermuda shorts. And, from the bags of exhaustion under his eyes, he'd probably slept as well as she did.

Obviously he hadn't heard her knock, enter, or call his name—twice. "Uh. . .hi," he said in a tone that didn't suggest he was happy to see her.

Ellen stared at the box of buffalo wings, suddenly wondering what idiotic impulse had possessed her to tramp over here like a desperate woman, hoping to bribe her man back into her life with a box of food. She attempted a smile and failed. "You're leaving?"

Oh, not only did she look desperate, she sounded it. She should leave. Now. Run from Heartbreaker Stoneman and his incredible eyes that turned her to cooked grits. Before he did any more irreparable damage to her heart.

He spared her the agony of looking in his eyes by turning away from her and cupping his hand behind his neck, a gesture she'd come to recognize as stress. "I got a call last night. My, uh, replacement had to fly out. His wife had an emergency—"

"Is she all right?"

"Yes, thank the Lord." He shook his head. "But I should have known it was no place for a woman. Especially a pregnant one."

In the weighty silence, rife with unspoken emotion, Ellen understood.

Paul was afraid. The wilderness might be his element, but Paul Stoneman wasn't about to bring a woman into his harsh world. She fought a rise of anger, not sure where it came from. Did he think she was ignorant? That she hadn't wrestled with sacrificing her condo, her car, her job, her life? She knew she would be completely out of her element and spend a significant time of her first term in tears, but he didn't hold a corner on the desire or ability to trust God. She was willing, and in her book that meant God could take her and turn her into fashion model or a forest maiden. It wasn't Paul's right to keep her from serving God or from experiencing the same joy of watching God equip and provide.

I'm thankful to be in a position to be forced to trust God, on a daily, hourly basis. Paul's words returned to her with a gusto that made her set the buffalo wings on the table and walk toward him. He flinched when she touched him, gently, on his arm. "I am leaving today, Ellen."

"And you're not taking me with you."

He shook his head. Slowly. Twisting her heart with the movement.

"I think that is about the most selfish thing I've ever heard."

He turned, his eyes wide.

"How dare you deny me the privilege of experiencing God like you do? Deny me the joy of trusting Him by living on the edge. And to think I thought this macho hunter image was charming!" She narrowed her eyes. "You're nothing but a self-righteous male chauvinist."

His jaw opened and fire sparked in those eyes.

"Let me quote you. 'You never know what will happen when God gets ahold of your heart.' Excuse me, was that limited to the male heart, or did you want to include every gender in that assessment?"

She had his attention now. A muscle in his jaw twitched.

"I guess you really didn't mean the words you spoke during

the missions conference, huh?"

His face actually flushed. "I don't know what you are talking about."

"You don't? Let's see, what verse was it you quoted? Isaiah, right?" She grabbed the Bible off his sofa and flipped to Isaiah 41:9. " 'I said, "You are my servant"; I have chosen you and have not rejected you. So do not fear, for I am with you; do not be dismayed, for I am your God. I will strengthen you and help you; I will uphold you with my righteous right hand' *but only if you are a man.*" She snapped the Bible shut and waggled her eyebrows at him.

He swallowed, then gently took the Bible from her. "Ellen, I know what you are trying to do. But you don't understand. What if something happens to me there? What if I die?"

The thought made her shudder, but she lifted her chin. "Then God is there, holding me up."

He blinked at her, then frowned. And it hit her like a blow that he thought that her sudden passion for missions was about him. That she so desperately needed him that she'd chuck her entire world to follow him into the bush. An incredulous laugh escaped her and she shook her head. "For all the conceited. . . Listen, Paul, I love you. But that's just a bonus here. If you don't want me in your life, I'm still following God's call. I'm not into hero worship, and I certainly wouldn't give up my world for anyone else but the Savior of my heart. And that, Paul Stoneman, isn't you."

He scowled, as if trying to digest her words.

"I'm willing to go with you, but only if you want me as

your partner. Not as a groupie and certainly not as excess baggage."

"Excess baggage?" A smirk lifted one side of his mouth. "Does that option come with your decorating satchel and a suitcase of wallpaper samples?"

Did he think this was funny? She'd all but bared her heart to him, and he laughed? She gritted her teeth, willing herself not to cry.

He obviously didn't love her enough to invite her into his life. She turned away, her chin up, wanting to drop to the floor, curl into a ball, and sob.

"Ellen." His soft voice pushed the tears out of her eyes.

"It's okay, Paul. I'm going home. And I'm surfing the Internet until I can find a mission organization that does want me."

"I want you."

She closed her eyes, bit her trembling lip.

He touched her shoulders, his work-worn hands so tender it nearly made her knees buckle. She silently flogged her rebellious heart for how it jumped to life in her chest.

"You're right," he said in a voice that felt like honey on her ravaged emotions. "I am afraid. And selfish. And a male chauvinist. But I also love you. And the only thing worse than not following God would be to know you went to Siberia because of me and died." His voice roughened. "I couldn't deal with that." He gently turned her, drew her close. She stiffened, but the smell of his T-shirt, clean and soft against his strong chest, shattered her defenses. His arms tightened around her as she dug her hand into the folds of his shirt.

Tears ran unhindered, betraying her completely.

"When I was a teenager in Papua New Guinea, my brother was bit by a taipan. It's one of the most poisonous snakes in the world, and he died within the hour. It crushed my parents, especially my mother. She spent two years in counseling, but I don't think she's ever really recovered."

"Do you expect her to?" Ellen leaned back and looked at him. "She lost a son. Even if she knew the risks, it didn't make it any easier. And the fact that she went into counseling isn't failure. It's life. They are back on the field, aren't they?"

He nodded.

"Do you seriously think that missionaries shouldn't crumble when life assaults them? Paul, if there is anything you've taught me, it is that missionaries are human. They struggle. They are afraid. Sometimes they fail. Life happens, in Papua New Guinea, in Oklahoma, and in Siberia. But God holds us. And that is the promise in Isaiah 41. We don't know what will happen in this life. Would it be any easier to handle the death of a child in America?" She shook her head. "We can't arrange our lives based on fear." She ran her hand down his rugged jawline. " 'So do not fear, for I am with you; do not be dismayed, for I am your God. I will strengthen you and help you.' Our only choice is to walk forward, through the doors He opens for us, trusting Him with each step." She poked her finger lightly into his chest. "You taught me that."

Paul nodded, then sent a wave of delight through her when he leaned into her touch. His eyes glistened, and a tear trailed down his cheek. "I knew when I met you that you were going to add beauty to my life." He wove his fingers into her hair.

"Ellen, I can't promise you a home or even an easy life. You know that. But I can promise you that I'll love and honor you. I'll respect you and do my best to provide for you." His voice thickened. Ellen saw a flood of delicious, heart-stopping emotions fill his eyes. "Marry me," he whispered. "Marry me and make my life as breathtaking as you made this home."

"Oh, Paul." She hooked her arms around his neck, rubbing her fingers into the stubble that had been his long, beautiful hair. "Yes. Without hesitation. Yes."

She could lose herself forever in the music of his smile. His incredible eyes glowed, and then he swooped her up into those lumberjack arms and swung her around the room.

"Paul! Put me down!"

But he only gave her a grin that betrayed his intentions a second before he lowered his mouth to hers and kissed her. It was impossibly tender, impossibly right, impossibly holy. She lost herself in the promise, the joy, the taste of his love. And all her dreams, the ones gathering on the distant horizon, materialized in glorious brilliance as they stepped forward, through love's open door.

SUSAN MAY WARREN

Susan has lived in Khabarovsk, Russia, the last eight years with her family working as a career missionary with SEND International. She has a deep love for the country and its people. When she's not teaching English or shopping at the open market, she homeschools her four children and writes their ministry newsletter. Find out more about Susan, her books, and her family's ministry at www.susanmaywarren.com.

Once Upon an Attic

by Tracey Victoria Bateman

Dedication

My brother and sister-in-law,
Bill and Kay Devine,
a loving example of how God intended
two individuals to complement each other.
Bill, the way you take care of your precious family
and love your wife as Christ loves the church,
blesses me more than you can know.
Kay, I'm in awe of your dedication to my brother
and the children God entrusted to you both.
Our family was truly enriched when you joined us.

Two are better than one,
because they have a good return for their work:
If one falls down, his friend can help him up.
But pity the man who falls and has no one to help him up!
ECCLESIASTES 4:9–10

Chapter 1

S*critch-scratch, scritch-scratch.*

Angela Cooper flopped onto her back and glared through the darkened room at the ceiling above her four-poster, mahogany bed.

Scritch-scratch, scritch-scratch.

With a growl, she snatched her gym shoe from the braided rug beside her bed and took aim. She chucked it toward the unseen robber of sleep, then ducked out of the way as gravity brought it crashing back to the bed.

What Angela could only surmise to be rodents scurried about in the attic above her bedroom. How many of those creatures were up there, anyway? It sounded like an army of—whatever they were.

"Ugh," she huffed, rolling to her side and closing her eyes in a valiant attempt to catch three. . . She opened one eye and glanced at the digital clock on her nightstand. A sigh escaped. Make that two and one-half hours of sleep before the alarm went off.

Imagining the bags rising beneath her eyes, Angela felt a

growing panic inside. She didn't do well with lack of sleep, and tomorrow she had to be at her best. Four classes of freshman and sophomore college students were counting on her to impart pearls of biological wisdom into their spongy little brains.

Scritch-scratch, scritch-scratch.

With a cry of despair, she grabbed the extra pillow next to her and pressed it over her face. Whom did she speak with at the university about donating lab specimens?

Scritch-scratch.

"That does it!" Flinging back the covers, she propelled herself from the bed and stomped barefoot through the living room and into the kitchen. She grabbed the broom from the utility closet and moved with determination to the spare bedroom. In the corner, she rose on her toes and snatched at the rope latch on the attic door, pulling until the steps unfolded and touched the floor. She carefully made her way to the top, holding on to the broom with one hand and the ladder with the other.

"All right, you pesky vermin. This house ain't big enough for the both of us," she said, putting on the Oklahoma drawl she had become enchanted with. "And since I'm the one who pays the bills, you all can just mosey on outta here."

This was what she'd been reduced to? Dueling with rats at three-thirty in the morning? She pulled herself up into the attic and groaned at the pitch-black room. "You'd think someone afraid of the dark would remember to bring a flashlight," she chided herself. And since she hadn't a clue where a flashlight might actually be, Angela decided to go back to bed—but not before placing a very important phone call.

In the kitchen, she switched on the light, pulled out the phone book, and perused the yellow pages until she found "exterminator."

She was not losing one more night of sleep!

Predictably, she reached an answering machine. She rolled her eyes at the gravelly drawl on the other end of the line. "Bob's Extermination, specializing in roaches, rats, and termites. Leave a message, and we'll call as soon as possible."

Beep.

Angela paused and grimaced in the awkward silence. She could never quite think of anything to say even though she knew the beep was coming up. "Uh—yeah, I have something in my attic—rats, I think. I—um. I won't be home tomorrow, but please feel free to call my office at the university, or just come by and pick up the key to my house. Oh, yeah, my name is Angela Cooper, and I'm in the biology department. Thanks."

After giving both her home and office numbers, she hung up the phone with a sense of grim satisfaction. Let those scratching vermin have their fun. "Eat, drink, and be merry, you little pests," she said to the ceiling, "because tomorrow you die!"

Back in her bedroom, she sank into the pillow-top mattress and closed her weary eyes.

Scritch-scratch.

"Argh!" Flopping onto her stomach, she gathered the pillow in her arms and brought it around the back of her head and over her ears.

The alarm went off ten minutes after Angela fell

asleep—or that's what it felt like, anyway. A flick of her finger halted the offending screech.

Gotta love that snooze button.

Light splashed mercilessly into Angela's eyes as she squinted awake, the offending brightness muted only by the jade green walls. "Ugh. Snooze never lasts long enough."

In that moment between fuzzy sleep and fully awake, a sense of panic began deep in the pit of Angela's stomach. She widened her eyes and jerked upright, twisting her torso around. The truth of the matter screamed into her brain as she saw three red numbers taunting her from the bedside clock: 8:26! Her first class was scheduled to start at nine!

"Oh, no. Oh, no!" She tossed back the comforter and swung her legs over the side of the bed. Late for her very first day. Thankfully she'd showered last night and laid her clothes out for today. She grabbed the navy blue suit from the hook on the inside of her closet door and slung it, hanger and all, onto the disheveled bed. Dressing in record time, she ran to the bathroom, washed her face, brushed her hair and teeth, and bolted from the house.

Fifteen minutes later, she pulled into the parking lot across the busy street from the college campus, searching frantically for a space to pull her ten-year-old sedan into. She circled the lot three times and was close to tears when she spotted a blue SUV backing out of a space near the back of the lot. At the same time a gold luxury car entered the parking lot and headed toward the SUV. "Oh, no, you don't, Buddy." Ramming her foot on the gas, she made it just in time to whip her car into the lone space. The man inside the luxury car scowled, but Angela paid him no mind. After all, she'd been in the lot longer than he had and, besides, all was fair in late-night rodent war and parking spaces!

Kendall fought back the irritation rising inside of him as he watched the attractive thirty-something woman hurry across the parking lot toward the underpass that would take her to the main campus.

He circled the lot for ten more minutes, then finally gave up and pulled his car into metered parking. Making a mental note to come out after each class and deposit coins, he hurried to catch the shuttle to the science building.

He noted the time as he headed straight to his first class. Before he reached the door, the sounds of laughter, mingled with screams, reached his ears, causing his feet to pick up the pace. A groan escaped his lips at the sight of water spewing from the sink in the middle of the room.

He rushed across the wet floor as the students roared with laughter. And someone began a chorus of "Singin' in the Rain." He opened the cabinet beneath the sink and tried desperately to turn off the water to the faucet, all the while being sprayed in the back and legs. Finally the geyser stopped, but not before barely an inch of his clothing remained dry.

In defeat, he sat on the floor, soaked and feeling like an idiot. So much for changing his image from the Nerdy Professor to Dr. Smooth. But it looked like this was destined to be another year of his being the subject of half the campus wisecracks.

Knowing he needed to face his new students, he slowly stood and greeted the still-chuckling group of college seniors—who Kendall personally felt should be above such petty pranks.

"As you might have guessed," he said, "I'm Professor Tyler. And this is Bioethics and Advanced Anatomy 410. We'll be focusing on bioethics in this course, so if that's not what you signed up for, I suggest you go see your counselor to straighten out your schedule. Otherwise, I'll expect you here at nine A.M. every Monday, Wednesday, and Friday, for the next four months." He cleared his throat and swiped at a drop of water making its way from his forehead downward. "For today, however, I need to find something dry to put on. So be back on Wednesday. I'll pass out the syllabus then. In the meantime read the first twenty pages of your text and come prepared to discuss it in class."

Chairs scraped against the floor and the distinct sounds of low laughter filled the room as students filed past his desk. Kendall looked down at his soaked clothes and sighed. All he had in his office to change into was a pair of coveralls he'd borrowed from maintenance last winter when his car stalled in the lot.

"Professor Tyler?"

Kendall glanced toward the small voice coming from a very pretty, pixielike face. "Yes?"

The blond-haired girl gave him a shy smile. "I'm sorry. I turned on the faucet to wash my hands. I. . .I didn't know the handle would come off."

"Think nothing of it. These things happen." He intended

to discuss the inconvenience of using a lab room for his bioethics lectures with the head of the biology department at the next available opportunity.

"Thanks for understanding. I'll see you Wednesday." She beamed at him and walked toward the door.

"Same old Professor Tyler. And I really hoped you'd be able to make it through one class without a disaster."

Inwardly, Kendall groaned at the taunting voice. Robert Amesley. Last year, Kendall had been forced to flunk him, after giving the student every chance to make a passing grade. He knew bioethics was necessary for Robert's chosen major, but he had hoped the young man would choose another professor when he tried the class again. Obviously the kid chose him again just to taunt and intimidate him. Kendall hated to admit even to himself how well Robert's plan had worked. What the kid possessed in confidence and brawn, he lacked in mental effort. At least Kendall could one-up him in the brain department and witty sarcasm. "Back again, I see. This is beginning to become a habit. Maybe we can actually get you out of here with a C average, this time. Otherwise, we might have to give you frequent flyer miles, eh?"

Robert's eyes narrowed and a red flush shadowed his face. "Let's hope." He gave a sneer and slapped the handle to the faucet in Kendall's palm. "It was supposed to be you that turned it on. But I guess you got a pretty good dousing anyway."

Sucking in a cool breath, Kendall watched the six-foot-two-inch jock stride from the room. He sent a silent plea toward heaven. *Lord, please let him feel vindicated by soaking me. I don't think I can handle an entire semester of his pranks.*

Sloshing across the room and down the hall, he stopped at his office, quickly changed into the coveralls, wrote a note canceling his next class, and headed down the hall, feeling ridiculous in a pair of coveralls.

"I heard what Robert did," Sarah Kingsley, a promising pre-med student said as she passed him in the hall. "Don't you worry. We'll get that rat!"

Warmed by the support, Kendall couldn't resist a smile. He was still smiling a moment later when a hand grasped his arm and pulled him toward an open door.

"I'm so glad you're here," the woman said breathlessly. "I'm late to my next class. When I start the day out late, I never seem to catch up. Those lousy rats kept me up all night and then I overslept. . .ugh. Who has time for a long story?"

Kendall listened in bewildered silence as the woman rambled.

"Anyway, I've written my name and address on this paper and here is my house key. Just leave it under the welcome mat when you leave. I know that's not original and probably just invites robbers to break in, but I'd forget it if I told you someplace else."

Trying to get a word in edgewise, Kendall opened and closed his mouth three times before he finally got an opening.

"I'm afraid there's been a mistake."

"Oh, no! Don't tell me you're only here to give an estimate." The woman's lips began to tremble. "I'm sorry, I don't mean to cry, but those rodents kept me awake all night. And this wasn't the first time, either. If I don't get some sleep tonight, I'll be worthless to teach anything. Please. You have to help me."

For some reason and against all that could be classified rational, Kendall smiled at the disheveled woman. . .who looked strikingly familiar. Her enormous blue eyes pleaded, and he was powerless to say no.

"So you say you have rats in your attic? You're in luck. I have lots of experience dealing with rats." The two-legged, dim-witted variety.

She seemed to wilt in relief. "Oh, thank you so much. Just leave a bill on the counter when you leave, and I'll mail you a check. Or should I pay you up front?"

He couldn't resist a grin. "I'll bill you."

For the first time she seemed to notice him as she paused to run long, slender fingers through her chestnut hair. Her gaze lingered upon his face a beat before she shook her head, grabbed a briefcase from her desk, and dashed toward the door.

"Thank you so much," she called over her shoulder. "You're a real lifesaver. . .well, I guess the rats won't think so." She giggled, and Kendall felt like giggling along with her. Thankfully she sprinted down the hall before he could make a complete fool of himself.

Now. . . How did one rid an attic of rats?

Chapter 2

Kendall moved carefully across the wooden attic floor, sidestepping evidence that some sort of animal had taken up residence. In his bag were six rattraps, peanut butter to bait the traps, and poison just in case the creatures weren't interested in peanut butter.

Kneeling in one corner, he baited a trap, set it, and moved to the next corner. A shudder crept through him. He hated rodents. Just the thought that one might be lurking behind boxes of Christmas decorations or the old foot-locker against the wall—watching him—gave him the willies. He should have just told the new professor he was a colleague instead of standing like an idiot watching her lovely face while she rambled.

Once she caught on to the deception, she'd probably never go out to dinner with him. And surprisingly enough, he found her interesting to the point that an evening with her stimulated his imagination. No woman had done that in quite some time. So how did he tell her the truth and still convince her he wasn't a half-bad guy?

A slow grin spread across his face. Get rid of the rats, of course.

His victory imminent, Kendall filled the rest of the traps, laid out the poison for added insurance, and tiptoed across the room. A flash of movement caught the corner of his eye, and he wheeled around just in time to spy a plush, furry tail slip through an opening in the wall just below the window. Furry?

Kendall strode back for a closer look. Sure enough, a hole the size of a softball glared back at him. Outside the window, a two-story pecan tree hosted the animal that had just escaped from the attic.

He groaned softly. Those weren't rats playing in the attic. They were squirrels. Nut-eating, furry little animals, cute enough to be pets. No decent human being could kill a squirrel. That would be like killing a bunny rabbit or a puppy.

Even as he retraced his steps to the traps and set them off with a drop of his hammer, Kendall's mind played a video of the new professor's lovely face as she thanked him for freeing her from the rodents. He pictured her desperation when she spoke of needing a decent night's rest and begged him to come to the house today. What was he going to do? No matter how cute the furry little beasts were, the fact remained, they couldn't share a home with a sleep-deprived professor of biology.

The only way to ensure they didn't bother Professor Cooper was to keep them out of the attic altogether. And the only way to accomplish that was to fix the hole in the wall.

A sigh escaped Kendall's lips. Fixing walls wasn't exactly

part of the course study for a biology professor. He rested his thumbs in the belt loops of the old jeans he'd changed into before driving to Professor Cooper's house.

Still, he had to at least give it a shot. A promise was a promise, and Professor Cooper expected rodent-free living conditions upon her return from the university.

After packing all the traps and poison back into his duffel bag, Kendall climbed down the ladder and headed for his car. It appeared a call to the university canceling his last two classes of the day and a trip to the lumberyard were in order.

Angela breathed a sigh of relief as she drove down Pecan Crossing Street and turned into her driveway. She'd started the day running late and had kept the momentum going hour after hour, never quite catching up. Now, all she needed was a thirty-minute soak in a warm bubble bath—and maybe with a few candles around the bathroom to help her relax. Dinner would be a warm bowl of soup, then she'd go to bed early and hopefully catch up on last night's missed sleep.

If only the exterminator had gotten the job done.

She trudged up the walk until something nudged her calf. A half scream escaped her lips, and she jumped.

"Sorry!"

Angela turned toward the voice. A boy—young man really—in his early twenties jogged from the two-story frame home across the street. "I missed that shot by a mile." He flashed her a knee-weakening, movie star grin.

"Huh?" Angela inwardly cringed. The kid was half her age, and she had to force herself not to bat her lashes and giggle like a cheerleader.

"My basketball rolled over here."

"Oh! Yes, of course it did." Angel grabbed the ball and handed it over.

"Thanks." He stuck out his hand. "Robert Amesley. I saw you at the university today."

Accepting the proffered hand, Angela smiled. "Professor Cooper. You're a student?"

He gave her another cocky grin. "Yep. A senior. I'm pre-med."

"Congratulations. Since we're neighbors, just let me know if there's anything I can help you with."

An uncomfortable twinge inched through Angela's stomach as he slowly lowered his gaze from her eyes and swept the length of her. He gave her a bold stare and raised his eyebrow. "Thanks, I'll do that." After another grin and a wave, he jogged away, leaving Angela feeling a little undressed. Clearly, he thought there was more to her offer than a teacher offering to help with challenging upper division work.

She sighed. When a girl was in her twenties, finding a decent guy wasn't too difficult. If one turned out to be a jerk—like Robert Amesley—there was always another one who had been brought up properly.

But once a woman reached her mid to late thirties, the prospects narrowed by the year. Her choices had slimmed to widowers, divorcés, and men who either lived with their mothers or men no one in her right mind would marry in the first place. The last types, especially, seemed to come out of the woodwork from time to time.

Angela gave a rueful grin as she climbed the steps to the porch. They probably figured a forty-year-old woman with a clanging biological clock wasn't going to be too choosy.

But they were wrong. Angela had every intention of staying single until the man God intended for her to marry came along. From the foundation of the earth God had planned for her future, and she refused to settle for less than fulfilling that perfect plan.

For now, however, she had only her immediate future in mind, and that warm bath was looking better with every step.

She lifted an edge of the welcome mat and glanced underneath. At the sight of the bare concrete, her stomach dropped like Newton's apple. No key? She raised the mat higher until it cleared the porch. There had to be a key! Hours had passed since she'd spoken with Bob, the exterminator. He should have de-vermined her house and been long gone by now.

After a second of despair, she tried the door. She blew the pent-up air from her lungs. It was open. Relief mingled with alarm.

Was the man crazy? How could he just leave a person's door unlocked? Anyone could have waltzed in and stolen anything they wanted.

With a huff, she pushed through the door, kicked off her shoes, and dropped her briefcase onto the coffee table. She walked into the bathroom and sat on the edge of the tub. Grabbing a bottle of aromatherapy bubble bath, she turned on the water and let it run over her hand until it reached the right temperature—somewhere between really warm and too hot.

The bubbles began to foam into the water and, with a smile, she walked back to her bedroom, peeled off her clothes, and grabbed a clean pair of comfy sweats from her chest of drawers. Back in the bathroom, Angela stepped into the water, sucking in a cool breath as she lowered into the steamy, scented bubbles.

"Take me away," she said with a smile and leaned back on her yellow bath pillow, closing her eyes. In moments like this, she realized life wasn't all that bad, after all.

Th–thud. Th–thud. Th–thud.

Angela's eyes popped open. Her stomach turned somersaults and her breath picked up at the fear rising inside of her. That sound most definitely didn't come from the unwanted houseguests living in her attic. Only a monster rat could have made a sound like that. Besides, the exterminator had. . .

She gasped. The exterminator had left the door open. Someone had been lurking ever since she had gotten home, and she hadn't even known!

Slowly, very slowly, Angela sat up. Shaking from head to toe, she grabbed at the towel next to the tub and wrapped it around her as she stood. As quickly as she could, she dressed, not bothering to dry off first.

Her heart slammed against her chest as she tiptoed across the bathroom. At the doorway, she glanced first one direction, then the other, and stepped cautiously over the threshold.

A moan caught her attention, and she stopped short.

A moaning thief?

The sound came from the spare room. Against all logic she headed in that direction, first tiptoeing into her bedroom to grab a bat from the closet. She sent a hasty prayer of thanks that she'd actually played on the church softball team for the past ten years and owned the handy weapon in the first place.

Somehow, her shaking legs held her up while she walked stealthily to the spare room. She peeked around the corner and stopped short in surprise. On the floor at the bottom of the attic stairs sat the exterminator, rubbing his ankle.

"Hey!" Angela jumped into the room, wielding the bat like a sword.

A yell loud enough to scare away any rat resounded in the room as the startled man jumped to his feet, lost his footing, and fell hard back to the floor.

"What are you doing in my house?"

"You asked me to get rid of your rats, remember?" He growled and alternated rubbing his knee, then his ankle.

"Y—you should have been done long ago."

A sheepish expression crossed his features. "Yes, and I would have except that there are no rats in the attic."

"What do you mean? Did you get rid of them?"

"No." He eyed the bat warily. "They were squirrels."

"Squirrels?" Cute, cartoon character squirrels flitted to Angela's mind. She gasped. "You didn't kill them, did you?"

A smile curved the corners of his lips. "No. I couldn't do it."

"Good."

"That's why I'm here so late. I saw one of the little creatures hightail it out of a hole, so I drove to the lumberyard and got some wood to fix it. I assumed if I boarded up the hole, they wouldn't be able to get in."

"Wonderful idea!" Angela was so relieved, she set the bat down and hurried to help him get up.

"Actually, it's not that wonderful. . . ." He labored to his feet and leaned against her for support.

"What do you mean?" Angela grunted under his weight.

"To tell you the truth, the reason I fell down the ladder is that a squirrel shot out from the corner just when I was starting down."

"Oh, no!"

"I'm afraid so."

They hobbled into the family room.

"But I already closed up the hole, so the squirrel can't get out."

Angela was unable to contain a weary sigh. Why couldn't anything be simple?

"Here, sit on the couch and put your foot up on the coffee table. I'll get some ice."

In the kitchen, she filled a plastic bag with ice, sealed it, and took it back to the living room. "Put this on that swelling, and let's see if we can get it to go down."

"I don't want to inconvenience you." His smile was much too attractive to belong to a bug killer. Angela's pulse picked up a bit as his gaze captured hers. His eyes were nearly the color of the comforting beige wallpaper and framed by thick, black eyelashes, which Angela thought no man had a right to come by naturally—especially when she had to use two coats of mascara just to make her eyelashes visible.

"Don't be silly." The shrill crack in her voice made her inwardly cringe. A telltale sign of nerves that anyone acquainted with her could spot a mile away. She cleared her throat and squared her shoulders in an attempt to gain her composure. How was she ever going to wait out that swollen ankle without making a big fat fool of herself?

She tried to shake off the sudden spurt of anxiety. That smile was too good to be true. It just had to be! Besides, it would be just her luck that the reason he wasn't wearing a wedding ring was because he didn't want to get bug spray on it. And if he wasn't married, he probably still lived with his mom.

Angela grabbed the phone and shoved it toward him.

His brow raised in alarm.

"Do you need to call your wife to let her know you'll be a little late?"

"Huh?" Then his face registered understanding. "Oh! I'm not married."

"Your mother?"

"My mother? She lives in Kansas."

That was the best news she'd heard in awhile. The thought of dating an exterminator had never crossed her mind, but then again, Angela had never met the right exterminator before. This one had black hair, slightly graying at the temples, and a square jaw with an alluring cleft in his chin. And he was too gentle to kill an innocent little squirrel.

She enjoyed mulling over the possibilities, but first things first. She had to do something about the creature or creatures still hiding in her attic.

"So what do you suggest I do about the squirrels still running around in my attic?"

"I wish I knew." He gave her an apologetic smile, the

corners of his light brown eyes crinkling. "I suggest a good pair of earplugs if you want to get any rest, though."

"What do you mean you don't know? You're an exterminator, aren't you? Who else would know?"

A flush covered his cheeks. "To tell you the truth, Professor Cooper—"

"Angela, please."

He smiled again. "Angela, I need to tell you something."

Angela's heart sped up. Those seven little words. Inevitable words. Only they didn't usually come until she'd at least had one date. And they were usually followed by, "It's me, not you." She proceeded with caution. "What do you need to tell me? Is. . .is there more than one squirrel?"

"Possibly, but—"

A heavy sigh escaped her. "Figures. How do you go about getting them out of the attic without killing them?"

He gathered a breath. "To be perfectly honest, Angela—which I probably should have been in the first place—I don't have any idea how to get rats or squirrels or anything else out of someone's attic."

"What do you mean? Your ad says you kill rats, roaches, and termites."

"I could have handled the rats with the traps and poison, but roaches make me queasy."

Laughter bubbled to Angela's lips. "Boy, did you ever pick the wrong career if you can't take the sight of a roach!"

"The truth is, I'm not an exterminator."

The laughter died on her lips, and she gave him an incredulous stare. "What?"

205

"I'm a professor of biology over at the university."

"No, you're not. I am."

He chuckled. "We both are. I'm Professor Kendall Tyler. I teach Bioethics and Advanced Anatomy."

There was no doubt as to his sincerity. What Angela couldn't understand was why he had claimed to be an exterminator.

"I can tell by the look on your face you'd like to know why I—"

"Yeah, it's kind of an odd thing to do, Professor." *Figures, the first decent guy I meet in ages, and he turns out to be an exterminator impersonator.*

"Please, call me Kendall. And the explanation to my odd behavior is that you looked so flustered and distraught, I couldn't help myself."

A hero.

A sigh rose up, and Angela narrowly escaped the urge to allow it release. Instead, she cleared her throat.

"Well, I suppose I should thank you for coming to my rescue." Feeling like an utter fool, Angela rose from the chair. "I'm going to order a pizza. The least I can do is feed you supper after you got rid of one squirrel. And let me know what I owe you for the materials it took to board up the hole in the wall."

"Please, those are on me. And you don't owe me any pizza. If you're angry or uncomfortable, I'd be happy to leave immediately."

"Don't be silly. How could I be angry when you were just being helpful? Is cheese pizza okay?"

He nodded.

Angela glanced at the phone number scribbled on a scrap of notebook paper and stuck to her refrigerator with a magnet. After ordering a cheese pizza, she headed back into the living room. "I guess that's your car parked on the street?" she asked. She'd assumed it belonged to one of the neighbors.

"Yes."

"I beat you to a parking space this morning."

He grinned. "So that's where I've seen you before. I thought you looked familiar earlier today."

She jerked her chin. "I'm not going to apologize. I was in that lot for ten minutes before you got there."

"Oh, I know. Parking is terrible on campus. I ended up in the metered lot."

"Well, Professor—"

"Kendall."

Angela's heart skipped a beat. "Kendall, then. It looks like our meetings are just one disaster after another, doesn't it?"

"I wouldn't exactly say that."

"At any rate. You'll be limping to class tomorrow, and I'll be dead on my feet from another night of squirrels dancing in my attic."

"I'll call an exterminator tomorrow for advice on how to get rid of the ones left behind."

"Oh, don't worry about it. It's not your problem."

"Just the same, I feel responsible."

"One more thing I'm not quite clear on."

"What's that?"

"The reason I thought you were the exterminator is

because I heard someone say 'we'll get that rat.' You were also wearing coveralls. That's not exactly typical wardrobe for a professor of biology."

A deep laugh rumbled from his chest. A pleasant sound, even if it was at her expense. "I have a bully in my class who loves to try to fluster me. I had to flunk him last semester, and he took my class again possibly to try to intimidate me so I'd pass him this time. Today he removed the handle from the faucet so I'd get soaked. And of course it worked. Another student heard about it and called him a rat."

Angela joined his pleasant-sounding laughter. She had learned long ago to laugh at herself to set people at ease. But inwardly she wanted to sink under the floor. When would disaster stop following her?

Chapter 3

"Are you serious, Lady?"

Angela glared into the incredulous, lined face of Bob, the exterminator. He'd finally returned her call, five days after her frantic, middle-of-the-night plea for help. From the looks of his beady eyes and weak chin, killing a few squirrels wouldn't be a problem. But Angela had been trying frantically to come up with a lifesaving alternative.

Clearly, Bob thought she was crazy.

"Well, I just thought if we could get them out of the attic without actually killing them—"

"Uh-huh, so let me get this straight." With a skeptical lift of his brow, Bob shifted the majority of his considerable body weight onto his right leg and shot his thumb toward the attic window. "You want me to catch the squirrels without killing them—"

"Or hurting them."

He gave her a withering glance. "Right. Then you're suggesting I let them go into the tree?"

"Well, yes. I think that's a reasonable solution." Heat

suffused her cheeks, but Angela nevertheless squared her shoulders, determined not to let this killer see that he could reduce her to feeling like an uncertain little girl. "D—don't you?"

An exasperated sigh escaped him, and he rubbed the back of his neck as though seriously contemplating tossing her out the window along with the squirrels. "Look, Lady, I'm an exterminator. A smart girl like you should know what that means. I exterminate. I'm not on the squirrel's side. I'm the enemy. I search them out and use whatever means necessary to get rid of them."

Am I supposed to be impressed? Still smarting from being called a girl, Angela arranged her face into the fiercest scowl possible.

Bob grabbed his bag of death and headed toward the hole in the attic floor.

Panic twisted inside of Angela as she watched him start down the steps. "W—wait."

He hesitated. "Yeah?"

"What am I supposed to do about these squirrels?"

"You want my help?" His smirk indicated he would not be inclined to accept her mission of mercy.

"Well, I guess not. But can you recommend anyone who might consider removing them unharmed?"

A wicked chuckle left his throat. "Call the humane society."

She wanted to growl but restrained herself as she heard him chuckling and mumbling about women as he tromped heavily down the steps. Although she knew it was bad taste not to accompany him to the door, Angela decided Bob could find his own way out as far as she was concerned. The door slammed a second later, and Angela sank wearily to the dusty attic floor.

Lord, what am I going to do?

A *scritch-scratch* caught her attention, and her heart sped up. It was one thing to be safely in her bed listening as her guests moved around above her. It was another thing entirely to be on the same level with the little beasts. She hopped to her feet and headed for the steps. She was almost to the bottom when the phone rang. Skipping the last three steps, she hopped to the ground and sprinted to the living room. She snatched up the cordless phone from the coffee table, stubbing her little toe in the process.

"Hello?" The word came out with a heaviness that was evident even to her own ears.

"Hello? Angela? Are you all right?" Kendall Tyler. Even through excruciating pain, Angela couldn't mistake the smooth, soft-spoken voice on the other end of the line.

"Yes." Sinking into the overstuffed, forest green recliner, she winced and rubbed her throbbing toe. "I just hit my toe."

"Oh."

What else do you say in that situation? Angela had to smile. She'd only seen Kendall for brief moments of greeting since having pizza on Monday. She was relieved to note that he wasn't avoiding her.

"Should I call back when you feel better?"

"No. The pain is already beginning to ebb." Ebb? Angela inwardly groaned, then she realized this man was an intellectual. She certainly didn't have to pretend stupidity to keep from intimidating him. "What can I do for you, Kendall?"

"I wondered how things are going with the squirrels. Did you manage to get rid of them?"

A deep sigh escaped Angela's lips. "No. The exterminator didn't like the idea of returning the little creatures to the pecan tree. I'm beginning to think I might just let them live up there. I guess I'm getting used to the scratching because I slept straight through the noise last night."

"I see. . . ."

The hesitance in his voice piqued Angela's curiosity. "What?"

"It's just that the squirrels probably went into the tree for food. Without a way to get out of the attic, I wonder how long they'll be alive, anyway."

Angela gasped as her mind conjured the image of the poor animals slowly starving to death. That was worse than a quick, painless extermination as far as she was concerned. "What should I do?"

"I think the best thing for now is to remove the board and let them leave."

"And let the rest of the family back inside?"

"Given the alternative, I see no other solution."

Angela released a sigh. "I suppose you're right."

"Are you busy tomorrow?"

Was he asking her out? Angela swallowed past the sudden lump in her throat. "I planned to grade some papers." Ack! Could she change her answer?

"I see. Think you might be finished around four?"

Whew! Granted a second chance. "I think so. Why?"

"I thought I'd come over and remove the board."

Instantly deflated, Angela tried not to let her disappointment show. "Oh. Well, that will be fine. Thank you."

He hesitated again. "How about getting a bite to eat afterward? We could have an early supper. Or late lunch—whichever you prefer."

Embarrassed beyond belief by her transparency, Angela was on the verge of refusing when he continued.

"That was the second reason I wanted to call, anyway. I've been trying to drum up the nerve to ask you out all week; but after I pretended to be the exterminator, I wasn't sure you'd say yes."

The corners of Angela's lips lifted in a smile. "You were only trying to help."

"So, I'll take off the board, and then we'll get a bite? And maybe take in a movie if there's one playing we both like?"

Dinner and a movie? Yes!

Straightening her shoulders, Angela willed her composure to return. She wouldn't get her hopes up until after Kendall dropped her off. If he asked for a second date, she could be optimistic.

"Sure," she said, so impressed with her poise and confidence that she dared to add, "I'll be looking forward to it."

They ended the call a moment later, and Angela couldn't resist hugging a pillow to her stomach and giggling like a girl. Kendall Tyler wanted to date her.

Don't let me mess this up, God. Please. If Kendall's the man for me, help me not make a total fool of myself and scare him away.

Of all the days of the week, Saturday was Kendall's least

favorite. He had no one to share in the cleaning of the garage or painting shutters. He'd always dreamed of raking fall leaves into piles and then falling into them. Without a kid around, that would just look ridiculous, so the dream had slowly faded into nice, neat rows of leaf-filled bags each year. As he strode up Angela Cooper's walk and noted the red and gold leaves on the ground, suddenly he was transported to an imaginary life where he and Angela were married with two children—one boy, one girl—who loved falling into piles of leaves and thought it just wonderful to see their daddy do the same.

Daddy.

He felt the stupid grin split his face just as Angela opened the door.

"You look happy," she said, her own smile lifting Kendall's heart even higher.

"I like fall." He stepped inside. "Something smells good. Are you baking?"

A pretty blush covered her cheeks. "It's a pumpkin candle. I like to burn them while I clean on Saturdays."

He glanced about appreciatively at the tidy house. "It looks nice in here."

"Thank you."

Kendall stood, unsure what to say next and not wanting to assume he was free to head to the attic without an invitation to do so.

Angela seemed equally ill at ease.

"So," Kendall finally said, "did the squirrels keep you awake last night?"

214

She smiled, obviously relieved for another topic of conversation. "You know, I think I might be used to the noise. I didn't hear a thing." Then her eyes widened in horror. "Oh, Kendall. You don't think they're dead, do you?"

"I don't know."

She stared, dread written across her face.

"Should I go on up and remove the board?" he asked. "I could look around while I'm up there—just in case."

"Thank you."

Kendall's tool belt clanked in his hand as he followed Angela to the spare bedroom. She pulled down the ladder and stepped aside. "I'll wait here."

A smile tugged at Kendall's lips. "All right. I'll be back."

He reached the top of the steps and slung the belt onto the attic floor as he lifted himself into the attic. Glancing around, he noted evidence of an intruder. He walked around, peeking behind boxes and bags, furniture, Christmas decorations, anywhere a dead squirrel might turn up.

Sufficiently convinced the squirrel still lived, Kendall grabbed his hammer from the tool belt and went to work. He wedged the claw on the underside and pulled until the board loosened. Just as he gave a yank, the squirrel darted from its hiding place in the corner and crossed over Kendall's legs. With a yelp, he jumped to his feet, flinging the hammer in an involuntary moment of panic.

In helpless dread, he watched as it flew through the window, shattering the glass.

"Is everything okay up there?"

Kendall's hair fluffed in the breeze blowing in. "The

window broke. But don't worry, I'll get another one."

"It broke?"

Hearing Angela's footsteps climbing the ladder, Kendall winced and tried to compose himself into some semblance of a dignified, mature man.

"Are you hurt?" she asked as she climbed into the attic.

"No, but I'm happy to report your squirrel isn't dead." He gave her a sheepish grin. "And I got the board off."

"That's a relief." Her eyes widened. "Oh, boy. That's some whole in the wall, isn't it?"

"I'm so sorry. I'll take care of this. The squirrel ran across my legs, and I guess I overreacted."

She grinned and joined him at the window, where he stood looking out at the pecan tree. "Are you kidding? I would have jumped into the tree."

He chuckled, then laughed out loud as her pleasant giggle twittered through the room. "I'll get this glass cleaned up and cover the window. I'm afraid there's no place open to get the glass to replace it today. I can pick it up after class on Monday. Will that work for you?"

"No problem."

Angela found an old quilt with which to cover the broken window and within half an hour, all the glass was cleaned up, the window was covered, and the two of them left the house in the twilight. They moved down the walk toward Kendall's car, parked at the side of the road.

"Professor Cooper!"

Angela looked up to find Robert Amesley jogging toward

her from across the street. She felt Kendall's grip tighten around her elbow and tension clouded the air between the three of them.

"What are you doing?" Robert stared at Kendall as though sizing him up. A sneer marred Robert's otherwise perfect face.

Angela's defenses rose. "Well, Robert. I think it's pretty obvious I'm headed out for the evening. Did you need something?" she asked pointedly, moving closer to Kendall.

All traces of animosity left Robert's face in an instant and he flashed her that movie star grin. "I thought I might take you up on your offer to help me with Dr. Tyler's bioethics class."

Before she could reply, Kendall spoke up. "If you're having trouble with my class, I'd be happy to help you, Robert. All you have to do is make an appointment with me. There's no need to bother Professor Cooper. She has her own students to teach."

A warm glow moved slowly over Angela, leaving her feeling cozy and blanketed.

"She offered to help, Tyler. So maybe you should mind your own business."

In an effort to defuse the quickly deteriorating situation, Angela placed her hand on Kendall's arm. "It's all right." She leveled her gaze at Robert. "I am willing to help you if you will make an appointment and meet me in my office."

"Oh, come on. We're neighbors. Couldn't we just study in your living room?" His gaze slid over her, a slow smile spreading across his lips. "Or another room if you prefer?"

Angela's cheeks warmed at his inference. "My office or nowhere," she said firmly.

He gave a short laugh. "No, thanks. I'll find my own help." He sauntered away.

Kendall opened the passenger side door. He blew out a breath. Angela sat on the cool leather seats and waited for him to walk around and slide beneath the steering wheel.

"I take it Robert is the 'rat'?"

"Huh?" he asked distractedly as he turned the key and started the car. Then nodded. "Oh, yeah."

"Has he pulled any more pranks since the first day?"

"No, thankfully." He shifted the car into gear, then pulled cautiously into the street. "The sad thing is that his father, Samuel Amesley, doesn't bother to hold him accountable for any of his grades or his actions."

Angela stared in disbelief. "You mean Robert is Dr. Amesley's son? The president of the university?"

"The one and only."

"And he lives on my street? They must not pay presidents very well."

Kendall chuckled. "Robert's parents have been divorced for many years. Dr. Amesley has been married twice since, as a matter of fact. Robert's mother attends First Church, which is where I go."

"Oh, you know her?"

"Not really. The church is huge. I've seen her in Sunday school class."

"Maybe I should make a point to get to know her. I

haven't met any women since moving here."

"What about a church? Are you a Christian?"

"Yes, I am. I hated leaving my church back home in Springfield, Missouri. But I knew God was leading me here."

A smile curved his lips. "I'm glad He did." The look he gave her sparked of intimacy, but in no way evoked the uncomfortable feeling she encountered so often with men. He looked her briefly in the eye—and nowhere else—before returning his attention to the road.

That feeling of warmth spread over Angela again. Definitely a feeling she could become used to. She gave him a shy smile in return. "So am I."

"Would you be interested in attending services with me tomorrow?"

"Yes, I would love to."

"Great! What if we go to the park for a picnic afterward?"

Angela hesitated. He was asking her for a second date before this one was even over? Either this man really liked her, or he was more desperate than she was.

"Did I come on too strong? We don't have to have the picnic. I don't mean to sound desperate. But I haven't been interested in a woman in a very long time."

"Why is that?" Angela knew she was transparently looking for a little flattery, but after all the years of being completely resistible to men, she couldn't help but wonder what the attraction was from his perspective.

He pulled into the restaurant parking lot and maneuvered the car into a space close to the door. "Most of the women close to my age are married. Others are widowed or divorced with kids to raise. As much as I like kids, I don't want to start with teenagers—not that I have anything against teenagers or women who have them."

He was being so careful in his explanation, Angela couldn't resist the temptation to tease him. "So I should make sure my twin fourteen year olds stay scarce when you're around?"

Kendall gave her a sharp glance, then laughed out loud. "I guess I deserved that. I suppose if the right woman came along and she had a few teenagers, it wouldn't matter. But to answer your question. . ."

Angela's heart went into a tizzy as Kendall took her hand from her lap and encased it with both of his. "It's an amazing and unbelievable bit of blessing to find a lovely woman who has never been married or had children and happens to be close to my age. Add to that the fact that you're a Christian and a biology teacher, and I feel like I've been given a Christmas present three months early. And you have a great sense of humor—which is a necessary quality for anyone dating me."

"Why's that?"

"So far, I've trapped squirrels in your attic, twisted my ankle falling down your stairs, and broken your window. All within one week of meeting you."

He had a point. "You haven't seen me in action yet," she admitted. "I'm usually a disaster waiting to happen."

"Come on, let's go in. Maybe together we can stay composed."

Angela grinned optimistically, but her optimism faded

when she snagged her heeled boot on her pant leg while getting out of the car and nearly plunged headfirst onto the parking lot. As if she'd staged it, she fell instead into Kendall's arms.

"Then again," he said, his voice husky, his breath fanning her burning cheeks, "composure may be overrated. I think I could get used to coming to your rescue this way."

Chapter 4

"So you understand, Professor Tyler, how this situation could be misconstrued?"

Kendall leveled his gaze at Dr. Amesley. The man's elbows rested on his desk, his fingertips steepled in an obvious attempt at intimidation.

"No, I don't. Professor Cooper is a colleague, not a student. The university has no rule forbidding professors from fraternizing."

The university president narrowed his gaze and leaned slightly forward. "Of course it doesn't. But your actions could reflect poorly on this university. Surely you understand that as an evangelical institution, we have to have our standards."

Kendall forced himself not to roll his eyes that this man could speak of standards.

"My actions, Dr. Amesley?" Irritation rose inside of Kendall, and he fought back the swelling tide of words designed to put an unfit parent in his place.

Amesley lifted his eyebrow. "My son says you're a frequent visitor at Miss Cooper's home."

"Yes, I am a frequent guest of Professor Cooper's. It's all innocent, I assure you. But even if it weren't, I again must refer you to university rules."

"Granted, but when your association with another faculty member hinders the education of a student, I feel it's my duty to step in."

"What do you mean?"

"My son tells me Professor Cooper was going to tutor him weeks ago until you made it clear you were displeased with the arrangement."

Remembering Robert's insolence toward Angela ignited Kendall's ire. "As I recall the incident you are referring to, your son was flirting and looking for attention from an attractive, single professor. That's all. He made Professor Cooper uncomfortable, so I stepped in and assured him I would be more than happy to go over the material he's struggling with during office hours. If he really wanted help, he would have taken me up on the offer."

Dr. Amesley gave a condescending chuckle. "I hardly think Robert needs to flirt with a woman twice his age. The boy has more dates than he knows what to do with."

The obvious pride in the man's voice increased Kendall's irritation. "It might not be a bad idea for him to spend a little less time dating and a little more time studying. I'd hate to have to flunk him again, but so far he's not doing any better than he did last semester."

"Are you threatening to fail my son?"

"Of course not. I'm merely informing you that his grades are in jeopardy again this semester. He has to be held accountable for his own grades. If he is truly struggling with the information presented in class, it might not hurt for you to encourage him to come see me during office hours."

He stood, leaving Kendall no choice but to do the same. "I see. Thank you for coming in, Dr. Tyler."

A feeling of unease swept Kendall, and he left the president's office with a prayer on his lips.

The past few weeks had been the happiest of his life. He and Angela had been out every Saturday night and attended services together each Sunday. He still hadn't quite drummed up the courage to kiss her, but he had the feeling she'd be receptive to it when the time seemed right.

Unwilling to risk another mishap, he'd called on Handy Dan, a friend and professional handyman from church, to replace the glass in the attic window; but the squirrels still ran in and out, at will, through the hole in the wall.

Angela didn't have the heart to risk having them killed. He wasn't sure how reasonable that decision was, but he couldn't help the swell of tenderness her soft heart caused inside of him. At forty-two, Kendall had never even come close to caring about a woman the way he cared for Angela.

"What are you smiling about?"

He glanced up to find her standing at the door of her office, a grin firmly planted on her full lips.

"I'll give you three guesses."

A blush crept over her cheeks. "Want a cup of coffee?"

He glanced at his watch.

"You have fifteen minutes before your next class," Angela supplied for him.

"Then I'd love a cup." He followed her into her office and took a seat while she handed him a mug of black coffee, then replaced the decanter on the hot plate.

Angela hopped onto her desk. "So what did Dr. Amesley want to see you about?"

"It seems Robert Amesley feels our relationship is hindering his academic growth."

"Yours and mine?"

Kendall nodded.

Angela gave him an incredulous frown. "How so?"

The indignation lacing her voice mirrored Kendall's feelings. He relayed the conversation.

When he was finished, Angela sniffed. "I should sue the little brat for sexual harassment. I can hardly walk out of my house without having him jog over like I invited him or something. He's reduced ogling to a fine art."

"Do you think I should speak to him?" Kendall didn't consider himself the jealous type, but he didn't like the thought of Angela being made to feel uncomfortable or unsafe in her own yard.

She waved his suggestion aside. "He's just a pest. And I honestly think he does it more to get a rise out of you than because he's irresistibly attracted to me." Her smile drew him, and he stood. She raised her chin to meet his gaze, and only the fact that he had coffee breath kept him from taking her into his arms right then and there. He didn't want her memory of their first kiss to be anything other than perfect and sweet.

"I'd better head to class," he said.

"Don't forget you're coming to dinner at my house tomorrow night."

He reached out and traced a line down her cheek with his forefinger. "How could I? I'm counting the minutes."

She covered his hand and smiled until Kendall thought his heart might burst. "Me too."

Kendall whistled softly as he walked to his classroom. His mind wandered back to his meeting with Dr. Amesley, and the feeling of unease descended over him again. Surely he wouldn't be punished for giving Robert a fair grade. Besides, there was nothing Robert and his father could do to him. He was a tenured professor, after all.

A sense of impending doom followed him into class and wrapped tight fingers around his gut each time he caught Robert's secretive gaze. Kendall wasn't a bit sure he wanted to find out what the boy was up to, but he had the feeling he was going to find out whether he liked it or not.

Billows of black smoke rose ominously from a skillet of what was supposed to be shrimp fried rice. With a cry, Angela grabbed the handle and tossed the entire mess into a sink of soapy water. While it sizzled, she hurried to open every window in the house. Poor Kendall. He'd been counting the minutes for this? She groaned. Kendall might be a disaster with tools, but she was definitely a disaster in the kitchen. How could a match between them ever work? It was ceasing to be funny and just becoming worrisome.

A loud knock at the door pulled her away from fanning smoke through the kitchen window. "Come in!" she called, assuming Kendall had arrived early.

"Should I call the fire department?"

Angela started and turned. Could things get worse? Instead of Kendall, Robert stood in her kitchen, a mocking grin planted on his face.

She glared and resumed her fanning. "No need to call the fire department. How about grabbing a towel and helping me out?" At the moment she wasn't going to quibble over who helped her.

"Not much of a cook, eh?"

Tears pricked Angela's eyes. "Kendall loves shrimp. I was trying to fix him some shrimp fried rice."

"Hey, don't cry about it." His voice sounded alarmed. "Ol' Tyler won't care about this."

With a sniff, Angela glanced suspiciously through the haze and studied his face. "Why are you being so nice?"

"I can be nice when I want to be." He cast her a sideways glance and grinned while he fanned. "Besides, Tyler's been almost bearable since he started spending time with you."

"Is that so?" Angela barely contained her gleeful smile. "Is that why you told your daddy about us?"

He ducked his head. "Oh, come on. Don't hold that against me. I told him weeks ago. Can I help it if he does everything on his own schedule? You have no idea how many late birthday gifts I've gotten over the years."

A twinge of pity stirred inside Angela. "All right. I'll give you the benefit of the doubt. This time. Thanks for the help. Now how about taking a hike so I can get ready? Kendall will be here any second, and I'm a mess."

"I don't think you're a mess," he said softly and stepped closer.

"What are you doing?" Angela croaked out.

"Something we've both wanted since we met."

Before Angela could respond, he pulled her to him. She turned her head just in time to avoid his lips making contact with hers. His cool mouth found her cheek, instead.

"Am I interrupting?" Kendall's steely voice gave Angela the diversion she needed to detach herself from Robert's embrace. "The door was open."

Angela gasped. "Kendall! This is not what it looks like."

"I'm sure it's not." His glare found Robert. Eyes steely and fixed, he raised a brow. "I think you'd better go."

A short laugh left Robert's sneering lips. "Maybe the lady would prefer you to leave."

"Robert. . . ." Angela appealed to the softer side of Robert she had briefly witnessed.

"Okay, okay, I'm going." He tossed the towel onto the counter and took long strides through the living room. At the door, he turned and regarded Kendall with a grin. "Hey, Professor, don't forget to pick up a copy of the campus newspaper tomorrow." The door banged shut as he took his leave.

Angela turned to Kendall. "What do you think he meant by that?"

"No telling. But I'm not going to let him ruin our evening."

Warmth flooded Angela's cheeks. "I'm afraid I already did that, Kendall." She waved toward the mess in the sink.

"Nonsense. Let's go out."

"But I wanted to surprise you with a dish you love. I guess I should have ordered in and pretended I cooked it."

His brow raised.

She grinned. "Just kidding. Still, I wish I could cook as well as I imagine I cook. Meals just never turn out the way I think they're going to. You might as well get used to either doing the cooking or eating out most of the time." Realizing what she'd just insinuated, Angela felt her eyes grow wide. "Oh, Kendall, I didn't mean to imply. . ."

He took her hands and pulled her closer. "I'm glad you're thinking long-term for us, Angela. I admit I've been dreaming of the white picket fence, two kids, a two-car garage, and jumping into a pile of leaves, myself."

"Jumping into a pile of leaves?" Angela's heart nearly pounded from her chest as his cologne filled her senses, making it difficult for her to concentrate.

"Long story." He smiled down at her. "The point is, I believe God brought us together, and I am happy and honored that you can envision a future for us that might include my cooking our meals or taking you to dinner after a long day in class. . .before we come home together."

Angela couldn't resist the happy smile that spread its way across her face. "I guess we've both waited long enough for the right person, that it's only natural for this to feel comfortable and right so soon."

He squeezed her hands and tugged her closer, his head descending until Angela could feel his warm breath. "I'd almost given up."

"Me too," Angela whispered, just before his mouth covered hers, removing all logical thought from her mind. He released her hands and encircled her waist as Angela's arms went about his neck. His lips were warm and soft, just like she'd known they would be, his kiss urgent, yet tender. She sighed in contentment when he pulled away—just far enough to gaze deeply into her eyes.

"I care a great deal for you, Angela. I know we've only been seeing each other for a few weeks, but this is real."

"I feel the same way." She waited for him to resume their kiss and felt a startling disappointment when he dropped his arms from her waist and stepped back.

"This brings up a whole new dilemma, doesn't it?" he asked.

"What do you mean?" She was a bit rusty at kissing, but surely she wasn't that bad.

Kendall smiled and reached for her hand. She gave it willingly and followed as he guided her through the living room, picked up her purse from the coffee table and handed it to her, led her to the door, lifted her coat from the rack and helped her on with it. Then he ushered her out the door. On the front step he stopped to button her coat for her. "Our relationship is at a new level," he said huskily. "We'll have to be more careful, not only so that we don't fall into sin, but also to avoid the very appearance of evil."

Angela's love for Kendall reached a new level as she witnessed his strength of character. *Thank You for this man, Lord. Make me worthy of him.*

Chapter 5

K endall slammed the new issue of *Campus Tornado*, the university newspaper, on his cluttered desk and seethed inwardly, trying to gain control of his raging emotions. One name ran over and over in his mind. Robert. The reporter hadn't named his source, but it didn't take a professor to figure out who had initiated this ridiculous article.

The phone jangled. Kendall snatched it up without waiting for a second ring. "Yes?"

"By your tone, I assume you saw the paper?" Angela's grim voice drifted through the receiver.

"Unfortunately."

"Well, we both know it's a lie, so there's no way they can prove anything."

"They didn't intend to prove anything, Angela. This is harassment, plain and simple. It casts a shadow over both of us as professors, not to mention besmirching our reputations as Christians."

Kendall picked up the paper. The headline assaulted

his sensibilities. Investigation Looming into Allegations of Professor's Incompetence.

His gaze skimmed the words of the bogus article. "An unnamed source states, 'Professor Tyler is so busy romancing the new biology professor that he's completely unavailable to his students.' According to the same source the accusations don't stop there. 'He discourages his students from trying to get help from anyone other than himself. Almost like he's jealous or something.' "

Jealous. Obviously, Robert was taunting him.

"Oh, Kendall. We'll get through this. Let's just ignore it."

"I've taught for twenty years, and I've never had a single mark against my reputation. Now this kid gets a crush on my girlfriend and suddenly my character is in question."

"Am I your girlfriend?" The lilt in Angela's voice lightened Kendall's mood.

"I'd say you could safely call yourself that. Any objections?"

"None whatsoever."

Kendall's heart picked up a beat and, for a moment, he almost forgot about the defaming article.

"You still feel like going to the game tonight?" Angela asked quietly.

Releasing a heavy sigh, Kendall leaned back in his chair. "I don't know."

"You shouldn't hide out like you're guilty of something. Let's go watch the game and prove to Robert and his father that you can't be bullied."

"All right." Kendall nodded to no one in particular. "I should be finished with my guest lecture around six."

"Good. Pick me up at six-thirty?"

Before Kendall could answer, the line went dead. He frowned, pressed the button to get a dial-tone, and dialed Angela's number. A busy signal greeted him. He tried again, got the same busy signal, then glanced at his watch. He had ten minutes to get to class.

Angela stared at the chewed-through phone line along the attic wall. The squirrels had to go. That's all there was to it. Even if she had to resort to calling "Bob, the exterminator" in order to accomplish it.

With a huff, she climbed down the ladder and stomped out the front door. She knocked on three different doors but no one was home. Beginning to despair, she headed across the street to the Amesley residence. She stopped at the edge of the walkway leading to the front steps. What if Robert was the only one home? Could she really go in and use a student's phone? Weighing her options, Angela decided to chance it. And if Robert was the only one home, she'd keep trying her other neighbors, even if she had to hop the privacy fence separating her yard from the neighbor behind her house. She breathed a relieved sigh when Mrs. Amesley answered her firm rap.

"Yes?"

"I'm sorry to bother you," Angela said breathlessly, "but I have squirrels in my house and they chewed through my phone line, and I wondered if I could use your phone to call the telephone company."

"Squirrels! Of course you can come in and use the phone."

The youngish blond smiled pleasantly and moved back from the entrance. "I've noticed you at church and have been meaning to come over and introduce myself."

Angela immediately felt at ease and smiled warmly as she stepped inside. "I've been meaning to come over and get to know you as well."

"Well, I'm glad you did," the other woman replied. "I only wish it hadn't taken an inconvenience like this to get us together."

The woman was beautiful. It was easy to see where Robert had gotten his good looks. Too bad he hadn't inherited a bit of his mother's sincerity and goodness as well.

As if summoned by her thoughts, Robert appeared just as his mother escorted Angela into the kitchen. His arms were laden with books, and he dropped them onto the table with a grunt.

"Hello, Professor Cooper," he said with more respect than Angela had ever observed from him.

"Hi, Robert." Mindful of the newspaper article, Angela fought to remain civil to the young man.

"Professor Cooper is here to use the phone," his mother explained. She motioned toward the wall and smiled warmly. "Go ahead."

"Aren't they paying you enough?" Robert asked, his tone sarcastic.

"Don't be smart," his mother scolded. "The professor has squirrels in her attic, and they bit through the cord. She's here to call the phone company."

"Squirrels?"

"Long story." Angela turned to his mother and smiled. "Thank you, Mrs. Amesley. I'll be out of your hair as soon as possible."

"No trouble at all and please, call me Jennifer."

"Jennifer, then. You can call me Angela." They exchanged a smile, and Angela had a feeling, Robert notwithstanding, that she and Jennifer would be good friends.

Fifteen minutes later, Angela said good-bye to Robert and his mother and headed back home with the phone company's promise that a maintenance man would be there to replace the phone line by Monday or Tuesday—definitely Wednesday at the latest.

She climbed the steps to her porch and was about to unlock her door when the sound of Robert's voice calling to her brought a groan to her lips. Had she not just met his mother, Angela might have been tempted to pretend she hadn't heard him. As it was, she turned with a long-suffering sigh. Hands on her hips, she waited for him to reach her.

"Uh-oh, I can tell by your body language you're mad at me." His expression was anything but remorseful.

"After that stunt you pulled with the newspaper, of course I'm angry."

"Don't hold that against me." He gave her a sheepish smile and glanced at his high-priced sneakers. "It was mainly a prank."

"It wasn't a very funny one."

"Well, I guess that depends on whose perspective you're looking from."

Refusing to play his game, Angela leveled her gaze at him. "What can I do for you, Robert?"

He cocked his head to one side like a puppy. "It's what I can do for you that brings me over."

She eyed him warily. "And what's that?"

An infectious grin split his lips, and Angela almost smiled back before she caught herself.

"I know how to get rid of those squirrels in your attic."

"Forget it. I'm not killing them."

"Of course not! Who could kill Rocky?"

"Rocky?"

He gave her an exasperated sigh. "Bullwinkle and Rocky?"

"I thought Rocky was a beaver."

"No. Anyway, in my poor misguided youth, some friends and I built a trap to catch baby rabbits in my backyard."

Angela gave him an indignant frown.

He held up his hand. "Don't worry, my mom made us let them go."

"That's a relief."

"It just so happens I still have the trap, and I'd be willing to help you out for a small fee."

"Fee? How much?"

"Not much. How about you tutor me and help me pass this semester?"

"Are you kidding me? After that article today, you honestly expect me to help you?"

His face grew instantly devoid of all traces of humor, and he gave her a look of earnest appeal. "Professor, I'm going to fail all but two of my classes if I don't get some real help. Tyler's class isn't the only one I'm having trouble in. I don't know what's wrong with me, but I only need these classes, and I can graduate at the end of the semester. I've already been accepted to medical school for next semester, but I have to pass every class first. I need help."

Angela was almost certain he was being honest and her heart went out to him, especially now that she'd met his mother. "Why not go and talk with your professors? They'd be willing to help."

"This is hard for me to admit, but I need more help than they have time to give me."

"You don't think I'm busy?"

"Yes, I know you are. But just think. . .no more squirrels in your attic. And I'll go back and get Toni to print a retraction of today's article."

"Toni?"

"Toni Blackwell, the editor." He gave her a cocky grin. "She has a thing for me."

Rolling her eyes, Angela turned back to her door and slipped the key in the lock. "All right. Be over here tomorrow morning at nine, and we'll get started. I'm going to trust you to do what you say and get rid of the squirrels, but the main reason I'm agreeing is because you promised to get Toni to retract the story. I want Kendall apologized to as well."

"You're willing to start tutoring me before I keep my end of the bargain?"

"Of course. As annoying as you are, I can see your mother raised you right, so you'll keep your word. Besides, there's nothing you can do about the paper until Monday. Tomorrow is Saturday and I have some time. There's no point in wasting a perfectly good day. Don't forget your books and notes."

She tossed a glance over her shoulder before stepping inside. "And be on time."

Noting the relief wash over his face and a spark of joy leap to his eyes, Angela softened. She felt good about this decision; she only hoped Kendall wouldn't have any objections.

Two hours later, she had reason to regret her decision, and all traces of sympathy for Robert flew out of her heart. She and Kendall grabbed cups of hot chocolate on their way to the bleachers where they would sit to watch the football game. On the way down the steep steps to an available seat, Angela noticed Robert and his group of friends. She returned Robert's wave as she passed and focused her attention on finding a seat when Kendall slammed into her from behind. Both cups of warm hot chocolate soaked the back of her sweater.

Robert's cronies hooted as Angela caught her footing just in time to avoid tumbling down the rest of the bleacher steps.

"Are you all right, Angela?" Kendall asked, his face red, eyes flashing anger.

"What happened?"

"I was tripped," he said grimly.

A gasp escaped Angela's lips, and she turned sharply to Robert. His eyes sparked amusement, but he shook his head and put up his hands, palms forward. "I'm innocent," he said.

Angela could see that he was far enough away from the aisle that he hadn't actually tripped Kendall, but she suspected he'd somehow been involved.

"Which one of you did this?" Her gaze roved the group.

One by one they looked away. She gave a self-righteous sniff. "Good. You're ashamed. You should be." She waved at the twenty steps below them. "Do you see how far Professor Tyler and I could have fallen? We might have been seriously hurt or even killed if we'd broken our necks." She gathered a deep breath and leveled the full force of her glare at Robert. "You're all old enough to stop behaving like children and take a little responsibility for yourselves."

Kendall cupped her elbow. "Come on. Let's get you home so you can change that sweater."

"Oh, I don't want to ruin our evening."

"You didn't. Robert did." A muscle in Kendall's jaw twitched. Angela hadn't seen him angry before, but there was no doubt that he'd just about had his fill of Robert Amesley and his shenanigans.

Now probably wouldn't be the best time to tell him that she was tutoring Robert, so against her conscience, she kept the information to herself and enjoyed the feel of his fingers intertwined with hers as they walked hand in hand back to his car.

Chapter 6

Listen, Robert, if you don't concentrate, you're never going to pass this midterm. You're at least three weeks behind on information, as it is."

For the last two hours, they'd been going over text readings and borrowed notes for Kendall's class. Little by little Robert was getting the information. But Angela could see that anything requiring original thought was difficult for him.

With a heavy sigh, he leaned his chair back on two legs and scowled. "This is stupid. Who cares about whether or not a human clone has a soul? I hate those kinds of questions."

"The point isn't to know the answer with certainty," Angela said, trying to remain calm. "You simply come up with a reasonable opinion and do your best to support it."

He groaned. "I never pass philosophy-type classes." He stared in front of him, his voice reflective. "My dad's going to kill me if Tyler flunks me again."

Angela's stomach jumped at his vulnerability. "Robert. You can do this."

"I'm not so sure. You give me statistics and information

I can memorize, and I'll ace a test every time. That's why my GPA is as high as it is. But what does my being a good doctor have to do with these philosophical questions? These types of classes should be elective," he groused. "They shouldn't be required for graduation."

"I don't know. Personally, I feel better knowing that my doctor can think intelligently if a situation arises where he has to make a decision based on his morals. There are many instances where medical opinions differ. I want a doctor with the ability to question cut-and-dried medical decisions if they go against ethical, moral, or spiritual convictions."

Robert snorted. "You sound like my mom."

"I knew I liked her." Angela couldn't resist a teasing grin.

"My dad's all about the money." His expression grew dark as his eyes narrowed. "Son," he lowered his voice, obviously mimicking his father, "you go into a field where you can rake in the dough. Don't you dare go into family practice and work on snot-nosed babies or underprivileged parents. Be a surgeon. Preferably a plastic surgeon."

He glanced at her with a sad smile. "So guess what? I'm going to be a plastic surgeon."

Compassion rose inside of Angela, pushing away the memories of Robert's insolence over the past few weeks. "Is that what you want?" she asked softly.

As if realizing he'd revealed more about himself than he'd intended, Robert flashed her his grin and dropped the chair back to all four legs. "Sure it is. What greater ambition could there be than to remove the wrinkles and fat from the rich and famous?"

"Ha, I could think of a few." Angela tapped the text in front of her. "If we're finished soul-searching, let's get back to work."

Thankfully, Robert behaved himself for the next hour. When Angela's stomach began to growl, she suggested a break for lunch. She fixed them each a sandwich and they moved to the backyard to enjoy the crisp, sunny fall day. Sliding into the bench attached to the picnic table, she motioned for Robert to sit across from her.

"You know I didn't trip Tyler last night," Robert launched as though they had been discussing the matter. "Right?"

Angela felt her defenses rising. "I thought we'd do better not to bring that up."

"I figured. I just want you to know I had nothing to do with it. I didn't even tell Mike to stick out his foot. But, come on, my friends know what a hard time the professor gives me. They're just looking out for my best interests."

"So you think practically breaking Professor Tyler's neck and dousing me with hot chocolate is looking out for your interests? Really, Robert. That's pretty childish. You should get some grown-up friends."

His face reddened, but he gave a nonchalant lift of his shoulders.

Spurred on by his obvious discomfort, Angela decided to press the issue. "Furthermore, I think you owe Kendall an apology."

He gave her a snort. "Like that's going to happen. I'm apologizing to you, isn't that enough? You got the worst end of it."

"I'm not the one who was humiliated. Everyone knew Kendall was the target of your friend's little prank. I honestly don't see how anyone can be deliberately thoughtless."

He grinned. "So, you're saying I'm unethical?"

"I'd say you're thoughtless and will do anything for attention." Angela noted that despite his frozen grin, his eyes took on a hard glint, but she went on anyway, heedless of his anger. "I wonder why a young man your age would feel the need to humiliate another human being. Is it to make yourself look better?"

"I don't need anyone to make me look better." He flashed her that saucy grin. "In case you haven't noticed—and I know you have—I look pretty good already."

Now it was Angela's turn to blush. "I'm not talking about outward looks, and you know it. What does your dad think of your inability to pass Kendall's class?"

He sneered. "What does Tyler think of your tutoring me?"

He had her there. Angela lowered her gaze, her confidence gone. She studied her soda can and clamped her lips tight.

"I see." Triumph laced Robert's tone. "You didn't tell him."

A sigh of defeat left Angela's lips. "All right. I didn't tell him. Yet," she said pointedly.

"So how come you didn't tell your boyfriend about us? Afraid he'd be jealous of your spending so much time with a great-looking, younger guy with a definite attraction to you?"

"First of all, there is no us. I see only a student who needs help and a professor with squirrels in her attic. It's a trade-off, not a relationship."

He held up his hands in surrender. "Okay, okay. I get it. That still doesn't answer why you didn't tell him about our little arrangement. Which takes me back to his being jealous. You know, you should be really careful about getting involved with the jealous type. I've dated a few and it's no fun, believe me."

"Kendall is not the jealous type. And even if he were, there would be no reason for him to be jealous."

"Whatever you say." He gave her a knowing grin, then drained his can of soda. "How about if I go up and check on the trap?"

"Sure, you do that while I clean this stuff up, and then we'll get back to work. But no more talk about Professor Tyler. Deal?"

"No more trying to get to the bottom of my deep-seated issues. Deal?"

Angela accepted his proffered hand with a smile. "Deal."

Kendall walked up to Angela's porch with a little apprehension gnawing at him. Something felt wrong. Maybe it was just that he hadn't called first. He'd never just dropped by before, but surely a man could stop by and see his girlfriend while he was out for the day without making an appointment. Besides, her phone wasn't working, so how could he? He'd picked up Chinese food for lunch. Hopefully she was hungry and would welcome the interruption of whatever she was doing.

He rapped firmly with his knuckles.

In a moment, Angela appeared. Her hair was up in a

ponytail, her face scrubbed and just a bit pink.

"Kendall! This is a surprise," she said through the screen door. "I wasn't expecting you today, was I?"

He smiled, his spirits suddenly lifted by the mere sight of her lovely face. "I was picking up groceries and got a sudden urge to see you. Do you mind?"

"Of course not."

She glanced behind her.

"Is everything okay?" Kendall asked.

"Huh? Oh, of course."

"Can I come in?"

"I. . .I thought you didn't want to give people a reason to talk. Remember, avoiding the appearance of evil?"

Kendall chuckled. "I think a little lunch during broad daylight pretty much takes care of that. Don't you?"

"I guess so."

"I don't have to come in if it makes you uncomfortable," Kendall said with a frown. "We can eat at the picnic table or even here on the porch. I only care about spending a little time with you. But if now isn't a good time—"

"Oh, Kendall, I'm sorry for being so rude." She opened the screen door for him. "Come in."

Relief filled Kendall. "For a second I thought maybe you were trying to brush me off."

"Never." The look she gave him snatched Kendall's breath from his lungs.

"If my arms weren't filled with egg rolls and chicken chow mein, I'd take you in my arms and kiss you right now."

Pink tinged her cheeks. "Then maybe it's a good thing your arms are full."

"No maybe about it." He followed her through the living room and into the kitchen. Setting the bags on the table, he frowned as a familiar book caught his eye. He picked up the text from his bioethics class. "Did I leave this here?"

Angela cleared her throat as though to speak, but instead, an irritatingly familiar voice broke the silence.

"We got one, Angela!"

Kendall spun around as Angela gasped. Robert Amesley stood proudly displaying a cage containing a squirrel.

Disbelief flooded Kendall, along with a painful sense of betrayal. "Robert is getting rid of your squirrels?" That was Kendall's job. He should have done that for her, not some smart-aleck kid.

"I can explain," Angela said breathlessly.

"So Robert is the reason you weren't going to let me in?"

"It's not what it looks like. Really. Robert heard about my squirrel problem and offered to use a trap he had at his house. You know I couldn't bear to see the little squirrels hurt." She was rambling, a sure sign she had something to hide. "But after the little monsters chewed through my phone cord, I knew I was going to have to get rid of them one way or another. Robert's plan seemed to make the most sense. And in return. . .well, I'm tutoring him."

She gathered a deep breath and glanced at him, worry clouding her eyes.

Kendall couldn't think of anything except that she'd gone to his nemesis for help instead of coming to him. He could have done something, but she'd decided to let it go. . .to share her home with the creatures rather than take a chance on killing them. Now, Robert was a hero, and Kendall looked like an idiot once again.

"Don't forget to do something about that hole," he said to Robert. "Otherwise they'll just come back in."

"Already taken care of. I tipped that old foot locker and wedged it in front of the hole for now. Next week I'm going to replace the board." His look of victory went through Kendall like an electric current. A painful jolt and a reminder that there would always be a "Robert" in his path to over-shadow him.

"Well, let's hope Professor Cooper's end of the bargain is as profitable to you as yours obviously is to her. I'll let you two finish what you're doing."

"Kendall, please, you don't have to go. Robert and I can work later."

"I thought we were going to dinner later."

She stopped short, her eyes widening. After spending a morning with "super jock," she'd obviously forgotten all about their standing Saturday night plans.

"Don't worry about it," he said shortly. "I have some papers to grade anyway."

He turned and headed for the door.

"Bye, Professor Tyler. I'll keep her company." Robert's amused voice followed him.

"Robert, shut up," Angela growled. Her shoes clacked against the wood floor as she trailed behind him to the door. "Kendall, don't go. You haven't eaten your lunch."

"Put it in the fridge, and you can have it later for dinner."

On the porch, she placed her hand on his arm. "I'm sorry I didn't tell you."

He leveled his gaze at her. "Why didn't you? Actually, a better question is, why didn't you ask me to trap the squirrels? Instead you make a bargain with that kid who's been nothing but trouble to us for weeks?"

She shrugged. "I just thought Robert's idea was a good one. And honestly, he's more orneriness than maliciousness."

"You don't call that article malicious?"

"Well, yes, I suppose it was. But he's agreed to talk to the editor and have them print a retraction."

"A retraction doesn't undo the damage to my reputation."

Angela's eyes narrowed and she scowled. "Honestly, Kendall. You're being as childish as Robert. Do you really think anyone cares about our relationship or whether or not I tutor Robert? This was nothing more than a stunt to get on your nerves. And you are playing right into his hands by showing him how jealous you are that he's the one getting rid of my squirrels. Have you ever even considered that maybe God keeps Robert in your face for a reason? What if you need to be the one to help him? Don't bother to pick me up tonight. I have plenty to eat here." With that she spun around and went inside, slamming the door behind her.

Anger burned in Kendall as he headed for his car with quick, clipped steps, and remained his companion during the drive through town. Only while sitting through midday, Saturday shopper traffic at a light did the anger slowly subside.

Maybe God keeps Robert in your face for a reason.

Kendall's mind began replaying the last year's association with Robert. The kid had been a troublemaker from the first day of last semester. He was the type that had intimidated Kendall all of his life. The handsome, cocky, athletic guy who always put down brainy types as though they were some breed apart. Kendall had never been able to understand why one group thought they were so superior to the other. Especially high school boys and girls. They were all plagued with the same raging hormones, the same dreams for the future, the desire for marriage or successful careers or both. The difference was that guys like Robert made it their life's pleasure to humiliate those like Kendall. And apparently they never outgrew the tendency.

If Angela wanted to allow this kid to dupe her into helping him study, so be it. It wouldn't do him any good. Kids like Robert were too shallow to understand ethics. He'd be lucky to eke by with a D. And Robert knew he needed a C in the class to graduate and go on to medical school. A troubling sense of satisfaction wormed its way through Robert until a blaring horn informed him the light had changed to green.

He breathed a heavy sigh as he sat at his desk and started grading papers. There had always been and always would be "Roberts" in his life to remind him he'd never quite measure up.

He was like Clark Kent. . .without Superman. He would never be anyone's hero.

Chapter 7

K endall stroked his chin and reread the thoughtful answer on Robert's page. If this had been the type of question a student could cheat on, Kendall would have been tempted to believe Robert had stolen the answer from someone else. But that wasn't the case.

The topic of discussion: If regenerative medicine turns out to be possible, but the destruction of human embryos is necessary to create new organs for transplant patients, would it be morally appropriate to use existing embryos that, for numerous reasons, are destined to be destroyed anyway? Might the answer be different if science advances to the point of cloning stable human embryos for such use? If you were on the President's Advisory Council for Bioethics and Human Dignity, what questions would have to be raised by the council in order to come to a satisfactory recommendation?

Surprisingly, Robert had deviated from his typical, flippant answers and had come to an honest, thought-provoking conclusion. And though Kendall saw flaws in his logic, the discussion merited a high mark.

This brings us to the moral question raised by Charles Dickens in his novel, *A Tale of Two Cities.* Do the needs of many outweigh the needs of one? In this case, the question translates to: Do the rights of an already formed human being outweigh the rights of one embryo, cloned or otherwise, which, if allowed to develop, would grow into a human? Does the saving of one life justify the destruction of another? Would the answer be any different if a thousand lives could be saved by the destruction of the same embryo?

Society is too diverse to conclude on any of these questions to the satisfaction of all. It is the same argument pro-life and pro-choice opponents have debated for years. When does life occur? Conception? Delivery? When the heart beats for the first time? At what point in human development does God breathe the proverbial breath of life into a mass of tissue? Since science has yet to give a satisfactory answer, then as flawed as we are, we must decide to the best of our ability at what stage do we destroy an embryo. Two days? Twenty? Why not a four-month fetus?

What is life? I am not wise enough to answer that question with moral certainty. Any medical professional or scientist who believes in God should quake at the very thought of presuming to know the answer. Will a God of justice allow man to advance to the point that we are able to create life asexually through cloning and then destroy that life for the sake of medical advancement?

Therefore, my recommendation to the president would be to fund research and development to find a less morally questionable alternative to regenerative medicine. Why take a chance that in the interest of medical advancement, we destroy something God holds precious?

Kendall read over the other five essay answers. All in all, equally well thought-out and intelligently conveyed. He marked his comments, determined to give credit where it was due. When he finished grading the midterm test, he discovered Robert had actually gotten an A. Since the midterm made up 80 percent of his grade so far, Robert was passing his class with a C average, despite the low grades he'd received on pop quizzes.

A grin spread across his face and he reached for the phone, then dropped the receiver back into the cradle. The temptation to call Angela and congratulate her on her work with Robert was strong. But he realized he couldn't share a student's grades. Not to mention the fact that Angela hadn't spoken to him in two weeks.

Admittedly, he hadn't tried to call her either; but until today, Kendall had considered himself the wronged party. Angela was tutoring Robert behind his back, after all. But he knew he couldn't hold that against her. In retrospect, he had come to realize she was only trying to help them both. Her squirrels were back outside safe and sound where they belonged, which he'd discovered in passing from Robert; and a nice front-page retraction had graced Tuesday's edition of the *Campus Tornado*. Robert had kept his end of the bargain, and Kendall was surprised to find himself rooting for the young man to complete the rest of the semester with equal success.

It was obvious to Kendall that he'd failed to look beyond how intimidated he was by the school jock. He hadn't given Robert the kind of support he needed to successfully complete the class. Angela had seen through the young man's arrogance and had tapped into his intelligence and the character that lay beneath the seeming lack of such. Kendall knew he owed her an apology.

With a sigh, he picked up the phone once more and dialed Angela's office number.

She answered on the first ring.

"Hello?"

"Hi, Angela. It's me."

A brief hesitation carried through the phone line with a clear message: He'd blown it. The best thing that had ever happened to him was out of his life because of his own lack of self-esteem. He wouldn't add insult to injury by running after a woman who was finished with him.

He cleared his throat. "I'm sorry I bothered you. It was a bad idea. I'll let you go."

Before he could straighten his elbow to hang up the receiver, Angela interjected. "Wait, Kendall."

Kendall's heart slammed against his chest. "Yes?"

"How are you? I've missed you."

"Then why didn't you call?" He winced. *Why did you say that, Stupid?*

"I don't know. I should have. I guess I just let my pride get the better of me." Tears thickened her words.

"Don't cry, Honey. Everything is going to work out." The desire to hold her in his arms and press her head against his shoulder was so strong, he could almost feel her soft warmth and silky hair between his fingers. "We need to see each other. Are you busy tonight?"

"Oh, Kendall, I'm sorry. I'm having dinner with Robert and his mother. She invited me several days ago. She seems so lonely, I don't have the heart to cancel—although I'd rather see you."

The regret in her voice was so heavy, Kendall had no doubt she meant every word of it. "No, that's all right." Disappointment hit Kendall hard, but he knew she was trying to consider his feelings by letting him know she'd rather be with him.

"Tomorrow?" she suggested. "If I get all my midterms graded after dinner tonight, I'll have the entire day free."

"Sounds great. Channel 4 weather says tomorrow is supposed to be unseasonably warm. Do you want to take advantage of it and go to Tiger Springs Park for a picnic and maybe take a rowboat across the pond?"

"Sounds wonderful." The relief in her voice told Kendall all he needed to know. She still loved him and had missed him as much as he'd missed her the last two weeks.

"I'm sorry, Angela," he said suddenly, surprising even himself. He'd intended to wait until they were together to clear the air between them. But once the words were out, they had a profound effect on the very connection between them.

"I am too, Kendall. I should have been honest about Robert. I was going to tell you the night of the game, until his friends pulled that stupid stunt. I was afraid you'd blow a gasket."

"I would have. You read me pretty well."

"But I should have trusted you to consider it and come to a rational compromise."

Kendall wasn't sure there would have been a rational compromise at the time, but he appreciated that she was giving him the benefit of the doubt.

When he hung up the phone, he felt infinitely better than he had since their argument. A giddy sense of expectancy permeated him as he passed out papers in his bioethics class a few minutes later. He tried not to watch Robert, but found himself helpless to keep his gaze from the young man's face. When he dismissed his class, he wasn't surprised to find Robert standing over his desk as the other students exited the room.

"Was this just a ploy to get Professor Cooper back?"

Unprepared for such an accusation, Kendall frowned. "What do you mean?"

"You gave me an A. I've never gotten higher than a D in your class." He tossed the test onto Kendall's desk. "Don't you think it's a little odd it happened when you and the professor aren't speaking?"

"Are you accusing me of unethical behavior?" The ridiculous irony hit like a sledgehammer. "I teach ethics!"

A sarcastic grin tipped Robert's lips. "When it comes to a woman as special as Angela, it would be pretty easy to forget ethics and do whatever it takes to win her back—including giving me a good grade because she's the one helping me."

Kendall released a long breath. "I admit that would have been an easy solution. And I'm surprised at your grade. But no one can teach you the kinds of responses you gave. Professor Cooper might have encouraged you to look deeper inside yourself to discover your true opinions about certain ethical and moral questions, but she didn't earn your A for you. You earned it. You gave some thought-provoking answers, and I was impressed."

Disbelief shone on Robert's face. "You honestly mean that?"

"I do. And I'll let you in on a little something else. Angela and I made up."

Suspicion mingled with a knowing sneer covered Robert's countenance. "So, you used my grade to your advantage."

"She doesn't know about your grade. I didn't think it would be ethical to discuss a student's grade with another professor. I imagine you'll want to tell her about it at dinner tonight and give her a chance to congratulate you."

Robert shook his head. "I don't get you, Man."

"Let's just say, our mutual friend reminded me that I'm not in high school anymore," he said wryly. "And I need to stop feeling like the skinny, nerdy kid that guys like you pick on."

Was that a sheepish look on Robert's face? He cleared his throat. "Well, maybe she's made me realize that I'm not in high school anymore either and maybe it's time to stop feeling intimidated by 'brainiacs' like you and start thinking for myself."

A revelatory silence fell between them as Kendall tried to summon the proper response. Finally he glanced at Robert and shrugged. The small gesture seemed to clear the air and Robert laughed. "Who would have thought you and I would ever have anything in common?"

"Certainly not I. God has a way of working things out that way, I suppose."

"I guess." Robert snatched up his test. "See you Monday."

A song of praise rose to Kendall's lips as he watched him go. If God hadn't brought Angela into his life, there was no telling what might have happened with Robert.

Suddenly, he knew what he had to do. He glanced at the clock. He'd have to hurry before the shop closed. But he was a man on a mission and wouldn't fail.

Chapter 8

October may not have been the smartest time for a row across the water, but the advantage was that Angela and Kendall were the only two in sight. The sun, which had seemed so warm and friendly while they sat at the little picnic table on the bank of the pond, now served as nothing more than a romantic movie effect. Beautiful, but useless.

Kendall was just glad they'd each dressed warmly enough to offset the chill rising from the water.

He felt like a kid at Christmas as he waited not so patiently while Angela cooed over the new and improved Robert. He barely heard her words as he watched the sunlight dance across her hair. Her eyes seemed to glow from the reflection.

"Did you hear what I said?"

Angela's voice arrested his attention, and Kendall snapped to in order to give her full consideration.

"I'm sorry. I was focused on your beautiful face. Do you know that one of your dimples is higher than the other one?

I've never noticed that before."

A pretty blush washed over her cheeks. "Kendall. . ."

Ardor rose in his chest, and Kendall knew for the first time what it meant to love someone with every fiber of his being. He'd gladly give up his books and his luxury car for this woman. His most precious possessions. That was saying a lot for a forty-two-year-old bachelor set in his ways and, until he met Angela, happily single.

"I've been starved for the sight and sound of you the past two weeks." He pulled the oars into the small boat and took both of her hands, scooting them both closer to the center of the boat so that their knees touched. "Promise it'll never happen again. I've felt like only half a man without you."

Her eyes sparkled with unshed tears. "I haven't felt whole either. I'm so sorry I held on to my anger for so long. I. . .I guess I just never believed I'd find a man for me, as if I've been waiting for a bomb to drop, instead of trusting God that you didn't just seem like the answer to all of my prayers. You really are the man for me."

Elation and relief swelled in Kendall's heart. He reached into his jacket pocket and retrieved a small velvet box.

Angela's eyes grew wide, then filled with tears as she glanced from his hand, then caught his gaze. Kendall sucked in a cool breath as her expression softened with love and tenderness. For him.

He fought back his own tears as he squeezed the hand he still held and extended the box.

"Oh, Kendall. It's just beautiful," Angela breathed.

Kendall slid off the seat and onto one knee in the bottom

of the boat. "Angela, I've been waiting all of my life to fall in love. When it happened, I was completely thrown for a loop. But I know I want to spend the rest of my life with you. If you'll have me."

He caught his breath and waited, then released it when her lips spread to a lovely smile. She pulled her hand from his and set the ring box in her lap. Looking down at him, she cupped his face in her hands. "There's nothing I'd rather do with the rest of my life than to spend it as your wife."

Kendall reached up and cupped the back of her head, drawing her face down until his lips met hers for a timeless kiss, soft and tender. As passion rose inside of Kendall, deepening the kiss, he felt his better judgment prick him and reluctantly he pulled away.

"I'm so glad you're a godly man," Angela whispered, her sweet breath warm against his skin. "I know I can remain true to God while we wait to be married."

"It's not going to be easy," he drawled. "But we both love God enough to be strong for each other."

"Yes."

Kendall couldn't resist a teasing grin. "You don't believe in long engagements, do you?"

She blushed again and dropped her gaze, then looked back up. "Kendall?"

"Yes?"

"Will you put the ring on my finger?"

The ring! He'd forgotten all about it. She held the box out to him.

He lifted the sparkling token out and slid it onto the

third finger of her left hand. "It's a little loose."

"Not enough to fall off. I like it just like it is." She stretched her arm out in front of her and admired the ring. Kendall took that as a cue to get back in his seat. He started to rise and felt a lump under his foot as he put his full weight down.

"Ow!"

With his mind registering that the "lump" beneath his foot was actually Angela's foot, Kendall instinctively shifted his weight to the other foot—too quickly. He lost his balance and tipped the boat. He heard the sound of Angela's screams before they both splashed into the chilly water. Angela's head bobbed out of the pond a second after his. Treading water, Kendall spat out a mouthful. "Are you okay?"

Angela nodded. "Let's just get back in the boat."

Moments later, dripping and shivering in the rowboat, they sat helplessly looking about for the oars, which had apparently either floated away or sunk to the bottom of the pond.

"I'm sorry, Angela."

A shrug lifted her shoulders. "It's all right. You didn't do it on purpose."

"Hey! You two need any help?"

From the bank, the owner of the boat rental called through cupped hands.

"Yeah!" Kendall called back, relieved beyond words that someone had seen their accident. "We lost the oars."

"Be there in a jiffy!"

"There, no harm done." Kendall's voice sounded much

more cheerful than he felt. Angela barely spoke beyond giving cursory responses to his attempts at conversation. Awhile later, armed with a new pair of oars, Kendall got them safely to the bank, soaked to the skin, but otherwise fine.

"I'll just be a minute," Kendall said as he offered his hand and assisted her from the rowboat. "I need to settle up with the guy who owns the boat."

"Listen, Kendall," Angela said through chattering teeth, "since I have my car, I'm going to drive home. But first. . ."

As though suddenly in a nightmare, Kendall watched her remove the engagement ring and hold it out to him. "What are you doing?" he choked out.

"I'm sorry. This was a big mistake. It just won't work."

"You won't marry me because I tipped the boat? Isn't that setting your standards a bit high?"

"That's not it." Her lips trembled, and from the tears trailing down her cheeks, Kendall knew it was only because she was cold and wet. "Don't you see? One disaster after another has followed us since we started dating."

"You just said I was the man for you! Did God suddenly change His mind just because we're both a little clumsy?"

"I'm sorry, Kendall. I just don't want to live constantly wondering what's going to happen next. I just—please, I have to go."

Kendall watched with disbelief as she sloshed to her car and drove away from the park.

How are You going to fix this one, Lord?

Tears coursed down Angela's face as she drove away from

the park, soaked and miserable. Whose dumb idea had it been to get into a rowboat in October anyway? It would serve them both right if they came down with pneumonia.

Today had started out as perfect as any day could be and as usual had ended with a disaster. How could they live their life together this way? They were just a major disaster waiting to happen.

Fresh tears of despair coursed down Angela's cheeks until she was barely able to drive. She was just beginning to gather herself together when she pulled onto Pecan Crossing and headed her car toward her little house. For an instant her spirits rose. The little family of squirrels had made their way to the front yard.

A smiled tipped her lips, a welcome relief from the tears. She pulled into her drive, thanking God for the tiny lift in spirits. The squirrels scattered at the movement of her car, disturbing their frolicking.

Thumpity-thump. Thumpity-thump.

Angela gasped, horror filling her entire being like a vicious fist clenching her stomach. She put the car in park. Paralyzed with dread, she couldn't summon the initiative to open the door and leave the car. She couldn't bear the thought of what she might find. Resting her head against the steering wheel, she sobbed.

Her poor little squirrels! Why couldn't she do anything right?

She wept out her misery over Kendall, over the squirrels, over her poor pathetic life, until a knock at her car window startled her. She glanced up to find Kendall standing next to the car, a concerned frown creasing his brow.

With a glad cry, she opened the door and practically flew into his arms. He held her until she was able to compose herself enough to blubber the entire story.

"Oh, Honey," he said, pulling her close. "I'm so sorry. I know how much you love those squirrels." He held her at arm's length. "Go inside and let me take care of it, okay?"

"I'm so glad you're here," she whispered. "I don't know what I'd have done if you hadn't shown up."

"Did you really think I'd let you go that easily?" He smoothed her hair back from her face. "We may be clumsy, but so far we've never messed up at the same time. When I fell down the attic stairs, you were there to help me to the living room? Remember? When you burned the dinner, I was there to take you out."

Angela sniffed and smiled sadly. "And now, when I kill a poor, innocent squirrel, you're here to protect me from the sight of his little furry body squished like a bug."

Kendall winced, and his face drained of color. He swallowed hard. "That's what people do when they love each other." He cleared his throat. "Now go on and let me get it over with, okay?"

"I. . .I can't leave you to take care of this alone."

"Are you sure?"

She nodded, hoping she appeared braver than she felt.

Kendall squeezed her hand and nodded. "All right." With a deep breath, he knelt down and looked under the car, then reached for something.

Angela's lips trembled, and her stomach turned with

dread as she waited for him to retrieve the dead animal. She noticed he was pulling back, and she squeezed her eyes shut.

When he chuckled, she opened her eyes in surprise, ready to demand what he thought was funny about a mangled little beast. When her eyes lit on the object he held in his hand, she couldn't resist a smile of her own. Kendall held out Robert's basketball, now flattened beyond saving.

"Oh, thank You, Jesus." Nearly weak with relief, Angela shook her head. "That's one of the most traumatic things that has ever happened to me. I just don't know what I'd have done without you."

"You'll never have to find out," he said, dropping the dead ball onto the ground and stepping close. "Because I'm always going to be there for you. Is that all right with you?"

"Oh, Kendall. Of course. I'm so sorry I let my fear get the better of me." She smiled at him. "And you're right. We never seem to have a clumsy moment at the same time. Maybe God's mercies will always cover us that way."

"And even if we have occasional times of simultaneous disasters, that's okay too. We'll get through them together." He reached into his soggy jacket pocket and produced the ring. "I'm afraid the box is somewhere at the bottom of the pond. I'm glad you were wearing the ring when we got dumped out."

She didn't protest when he took her hand and, for the second time, slipped the ring on her finger. "Please don't take it off again," he whispered, before wrapping her in his arms and pulling her to him.

"I won't," she promised against his lips. He kissed her, leaving them both breathless by the time he released her.

A grin curved his mouth. "This is one thing we definitely don't mess up."

Angela gave him a playful shove. But when he kissed her again, sealing their commitment to spending the rest of their lives together, she had to agree. A happy contentment swelled inside her.

Kendall placed his arms around her shoulders and turned her toward the house. "I'll walk you to the door so you can get cleaned up and into some dry clothes."

Angela nodded, suddenly exhausted from the myriad emotions she'd gone through.

They approached the steps and Kendall laughed. "Just think of the story we'll have to tell our children when they asked how we met," he said. "A few squirrels, an obnoxious student, and a late first day of school all contributed to God's plan to get us together."

Angela slipped her arm around his waist as they climbed the steps together. "I guess it just goes to show you that God will use whatever He wants to accomplish His purpose in our lives."

At the door, Kendall took her hands in his, his look of love nearly snatching Angela's breath away. "I love you," he said.

"I love you too." Angela's voice barely rose above a whisper.

He kissed her and not one doubt remained in Angela's heart. Kendall would always be there to steady her. And she would always be there to steady him.

Together, they would stand strong forever.

TRACEY VICTORIA BATEMAN

Tracey lives in Missouri with her husband and their four children. She counts on her relationship with God to bring balance to her busy life. Grateful for God's many blessings, Tracey believes she is living proof that "all things are possible to them that believe," and she happily encourages anyone who will listen to dream big and see where God will take them. E-mail address: tvbateman@aol.com Web site: www.traceyvictoriabateman.homestead.com/index.html.

Mending Fences

by Susan Downs

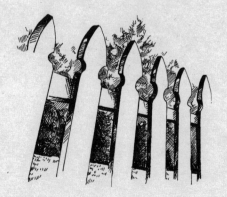

Chapter 1

Winnie Wainwright pulled a toaster from the depths of the cardboard box and set the appliance beside a teetering stack of pots and pans. The fifty-year-old wedding gift had shorted out soon after Bill's death, and she could almost hear her daughter asking why on earth she had bothered to pack and lug this piece of junk all the way to Oklahoma. Still, she couldn't bear to throw it out. The apparatus had made much more than toast over the years. When she looked at the toaster's dull and dented stainless casing, Winnie saw five decades of shared-breakfast memories reflected back at her. She planned to display it, with pride, on the plant shelf over the kitchen sink; and if Carla asked her about it, she'd tell her it was a part of her "primitive" collection. These days, the more beat-up and rusty the item, the more chic.

An ol' antique like me must be the height of fashion. A chuckle escaped Winnie's lips at the thought.

The muggy air and tedious work sent a flash of heat sweeping over her. She swiped away the perspiration from her forehead and started to bend over the box to remove another item when the dog began to bark. "Whatever possessed me to tell Carla I would dog-sit her worthless little mutt while I'm trying to unpack?" Winnie shook her head in mock disgust at the yipping sheltie.

She relished the idea of baby-sitting her first grandchild when he or she made an appearance in five months or so. In fact, the prospect of being less than a mile away from family, as opposed to hundreds, had played a big part in Winnie's decision to move into this vacant house, which her daughter had originally built for herself before she married Jack. Still, she hadn't reckoned that her grandmotherly duties would include looking after a dog Carla pampered like a child.

She crooked her arms at her waist. "Skipper, what's gotten into you? I let you out not five minutes ago, now you want out again? Enough! Hush up now!" Winnie tried to keep a stern tone, but the corners of her mouth twitched upward at the sight of the gyrating mass of fur. With one final whine, the dog ceased his kinetic frenzy just long enough to meet Winnie's gaze. Then, he skittered across the kitchen's vinyl floor through the maze of moving boxes and began to jump up and down in front of the cluttered counter, punctuating each leap with a short bark.

A faint jingle wafted from behind a stack of clean tea towels.

"Oh, corn and cabbage! The phone!" Winnie stumbled her way around the cardboard-box obstacle course as she went in search of the ringing's source. "Even with the volume turned up full-tilt, that cordless contraption is impossible to find." She riffled for the receiver amid a pile of crumpled newsprint she had discarded after unpacking her everyday dishes. All the while, she chided herself for not returning the phone to its base after calling to start newspaper delivery. "Never had trouble locating the silly thing when a cord was attached," she muttered to the dog. He answered with a woof.

The mountain of tea towels pitched into the sink when Winnie finally found the receiver, but she ignored the mess, knowing she would have to race to answer the phone before the incoming call rolled over to voice mail. She mashed the talk button in mid ring.

"Um, hello. Wainwright's." Winnie nodded and smiled at the little dog when he quieted and heeled at her feet.

"Mom?" A crackle of static all but drowned out the word.

"Carla, is that you?" Winnie pressed the phone closer to her ear. "You'll have to speak up, Honey. I can barely hear you."

"This cell phone. . .bad signal. I'll walk. . .windows. . .if that helps. . ." Her daughter's voice flickered out and back in, but Winnie had gotten pretty good at guessing at missing words. "If I lose you, I'll call right back. . . . Wanted you to know. . .made it to Los Angeles okay." Either Carla had moved to a better spot or a satellite had shifted or some such technical thing, because Winnie could now make out most of what her daughter was saying. "Not much time to talk. Our connecting flight was delayed leaving Dallas. They're already boarding the first-class passengers for the flight to Hawaii. Is Skipper behaving himself?"

"Skipper is fine." Winnie watched the dog's tail swish in

double-time and wondered if the animal's hearing was so keen as to recognize Carla's voice coming through the phone. "We'll get along splendidly. How 'bout you? You feeling all right, Honey? I know you're pretty much over the morning sickness, but flying always makes me a little queasy even without being pregnant."

"Physically, I've never been better, Mom, but I still feel absolutely awful for running out on you at a time like this and leaving you alone to do all your own unpacking."

"Nonsense. You had no way of knowing when you booked those flights that the farm would sell lickety-split. I'm not helpless, you know. And I wouldn't hear of you canceling the trip of a lifetime just to help me empty a few boxes. You two did more than your fair share before you left."

She surveyed the bungalow from her kitchen vantage point. Yesterday, Carla and Jack refused to let Winnie lift a finger in the loading and unloading of the moving van, even though she was perfectly capable of carrying a few boxes. And when it came time to arrange the furniture, she'd not been allowed to do anything other than direct traffic. The very idea of selling the family farm and moving into Carla's rental house had been theirs. In the four years since Bill's death, Winnie had resisted her daughter's urgings to move to Milltown to be near her. Not until she learned she would soon be a first-time grandmother did Winnie seriously consider the idea.

"When it comes to putting all this stuff away, I really need to do the job myself or I'd never be able to find anything. By the time you return from your getaway, I'll have this place looking all cozy and feeling like home." Winnie glanced at the stacks and piles and heaps of kitchen things that covered every square inch of counter space, then she let her gaze rest on the boxes waiting to be opened and unpacked. Skepticism shadowed her wishful thinking and spoken words.

"Without a doubt, when we arrive back home in three weeks and swing by your place for a visit, you'll have every-thing spic-and-span and one of your famous buttermilk pies cooling on the windowsill. . . . Oh, hey, Mom, I've got to go. They just announced the boarding of our row. But I meant to tell you. If you run into any trouble, any trouble at all, there's a list. . . . Of course, dial 9-1-1 for fire or police emer-gencies, but the insurance company, the electric company, gas, telephone, their numbers are all written down—taped to the pansy floor. There should even be a number for a good handyman that our last tenant used when she had a problem with squirrels in the attic."

"Pansy floor? What's a pansy floor?" The question slipped out before Winnie realized she had, once again, admitted to misunderstanding Carla's soft voice. She could almost see her daughter rolling her eyes. If they had been together, they would have probably shared a laugh. However, Winnie didn't think her poor hearing was all that funny. Ever since she'd suffered a bad ear infection last winter, she found she some-times had trouble hearing out of her right ear. She kept hop-ing that, given time, her hearing would return to normal, but she hadn't noticed much improvement yet. So, even though Skipper sat quietly at her feet and the house was silent, Winnie pushed her index finger to cover her right ear and block out any noise. Then she pressed the phone closer to her left ear and wedged it tight against her shoulder.

"Not *pansy floor*, Mother. Listen. P-a-n-t-r-y d-o-o-r." Carla said the words slow and so loud that Winnie winced and pulled the phone away from her ear.

"Oh, I see it. Yes, here it is, taped to the inside of the pantry door. The number for Handy Dan the Fix-It Man is listed right at the top and highlighted with a yellow marker. But, Dear, there won't be any trouble. You just have fun and don't worry a smidgen over me. Since your father's passing, I've done pretty well at taking care of myself out in the middle of Boondocks, Kansas. I'm sure I can handle whatever comes my way here in Milltown."

"All right. I've really got to go now. They'll make me shut my cell phone off while I'm on the plane, but leave a message if you need me, and I'll get back to you as soon as I can. Make Skipper behave himself."

"Don't worry about a thing, Sweetie. We're going to be fine. Just fine." The steady hum of a dial tone answered Winnie's consolations, and she pushed the *end* button to disconnect the open line.

She scanned the kitchen for the phone's base and sighed, unable to dislodge the ballast of gloom growing in her chest. "Oh, Bill. What have I done?" From force of habit, Winnie spoke to her deceased husband as though he stood nearby. For the life of her, at this moment she couldn't recall whatever logic had convinced her to move into this little place of her daughter's and out of the rambling farmhouse where she had lived with her husband for forty-six years, then alone for the past four. She had held both a yard and a barn sale and then given several truckloads full of donations to the Salvation Army. Yet, after whittling down her possessions to those things she felt she couldn't do without, her accumulation of worldly goods still amounted to more than she could possibly squeeze into this small house. She hated the thought of her pickup leaving oil spots all over the driveway, but the single-car garage held so many boxes, she figured it might be months before she could park it inside—if ever.

Even so, her despair went deeper than the problem of where she was going to put all this stuff. A woman her age had no business starting over in a new town. In a new state. With a new circle of friends. She looked at the phone in her hand, half tempted to call Ruth at the rest home back in Junction City. Maybe today she would be having one of her good days, and maybe Ruth would recognize Winnie's voice or remember her best friend's name.

Winnie shook her head and placed the phone on top of the refrigerator so she'd know where to find it the next time it rang. From the inside looking out, she still felt like a thirty year old—until she passed a mirror or saw a lifelong friend like Ruth. Poor Ruth's good days were few and far between of late, and Winnie didn't think she could deal with any more sad reminders today of her own advancing age.

"Skipper, what would you say to a walk? This mess will still be here when we return. I believe it would do us both good to get out of this stuffy kitchen and breathe a little fresh air." The dog answered with two shrill barks. His toe-nails click-clacked on the vinyl when he scampered over to the open pantry door and waited for Winnie to retrieve his leash from a hook.

Winnie overlooked Skipper's forgotten obedience training when he strained at his leash and pulled her onto the front porch, but she stood her ground when he tried to scamper down the steps. Roiling dark clouds rumbled across the May sky and a scrim of Oklahoma red clay dust curtained the unfamiliar neighborhood. The air weighed heavy with the scent of rain. According to this morning's farm report, hours yet remained until time for official sunset. However, while Winnie watched, the streetlight across the way flickered on as though signaling a beacon of approaching danger. "Looks like a storm's abrewin', my four-legged friend, so I'm cutting this adventure short." A swoosh of wind confirmed her decision to stay close to home. "You hurry up now and just tend to your business here in the yard." She hitched up the collar of her all-weather jacket and cinched the tie of the crisscrossed opening tighter around her waist.

The loud *whomp-whomp-whomp* of a weather advisory alert pulled Dan Parker's attentions away from his woodworking project and toward the small television that kept him company in his converted-garage workshop. He'd been working to the background accompaniments of thunder and lightning, wind, and rain all afternoon, but he hadn't paid it any mind until now.

"We interrupt our regularly scheduled programming to bring you a special weather bulletin," a computer-generated voice broke in as the image of the local meteorologist from the evening news replaced that of a syndicated game-show host.

"Yes, this is Kyle Bixler with your Channel 6 Weather Team. Well, folks, looks like we have some nasty weather coming our way. This word just in—the National Weather Service has issued a tornado warning for several counties within our viewing area." The young whippersnapper of a man with plastic-looking blond hair positioned himself in front of a satellite-image map while a list of counties began to scroll across the bottom of the screen. "If you are within this range. . ." He used his finger to circle the place on the map where a large red blotch extended across several county lines. ". . .We suggest you seek emergency shelter immediately and take all necessary precautions to ensure your safety. . . ." Dan pressed mute on the remote to silence the annoying voice of the broadcaster.

He walked to the door that led out onto the back patio and looked out. Sure enough, an eerie shade of green tinged the ash-gray clouds, and sheets of rain sent the trees in his yard dipping and swaying and do-si-doing like square dancers at a barnyard shindig. He had been intent on building the birdhouses he'd promised for the church's mission society to sell at their upcoming bazaar, so he hadn't paid much attention to what was happening outside.

The tornado siren on the street corner began to blow with an escalating blare until the noise reached an earsplitting crescendo.

He studied the igloo-shaped mound of earth that rose from the middle of the backyard and considered making a dash for its hatch door. Back in the sixties, during the Cold War days, his wife had insisted on him installing the shelter to protect their family from a Soviet nuclear attack—an apocalyptic horror that had, thankfully, never materialized. Instead, the cellar had become their refuge against Oklahoma's fierce storms and the perfect storage place for his wife's home-canned jams, jellies, and vegetables.

If Esther were still alive, at the first thunderclap, she would have hustled into his workshop with her fat black cat, Rhett, under one arm and her emergency bag slung over the other, prodding Dan to join her out back in the "fraidy hole." But Esther was gone and, after calculating the distance and wetness factor, he talked himself out of the idea. He preferred to take his chances here in the dry comforts of his workshop.

Dan watched the rain collect in puddles around Esther's rosebushes alongside the house. His cheeks puffed and deflated in an involuntary sigh. Counting the six months after the last stroke had left his sweetheart totally incapacitated, he'd been without her for close to three years now.

He turned away from the yardful of bittersweet reminders and moved back to his workbench. For a split second, the lights flickered; and, even though there was not a complete loss of electricity, Dan figured he ought to unplug all of his power tools and computer equipment. Another sigh of loneliness escaped as he reached for his electric drill. He paused and washed his palm over his chin's evening stubble. While it had been true what everyone said about his grief subsiding over time, the loneliness left in mourning's wake was almost as hard to bear. He'd learned to stay busy in order to keep his mind on other things besides his inner angst. But after three years, he was getting mighty tired of jigsawing plywood lawn figures for the endless stream of Milltown community and church fund-raising events.

He might be lonely, but he wasn't desperate. So he'd gotten to where he never mentioned anything about female companionship—and his lack thereof—to the folks around town or at church. Every time he did, he'd been snookered into a blind date with the latest eligible blue-haired member of the Keenager's Sunday school class or forced to play bingo at the senior citizen center alongside geezers who had a good twenty years on him.

From the looks of the radar map on the TV screen, the squall line of thunderstorms appeared to be rapidly moving out of the area and the neighborhood sirens ceased their wail. *Wonder if the aftermath of this storm will bring me some business?* The thought had no sooner crossed his mind than he scolded himself for his callousness. He didn't really want to profit from another's misfortune, but it had been awhile since he'd had *real* work to do. He'd stayed busier than a coon in a cornfield over his forty-year career as a carpenter specializing in interior remodeling and home repairs. But after taking so many months off to sit by Esther's side at the rehabilitation center, the only time his phone rang now was when his kids called to check on him. The last couple of times the phone bill came, he'd been half-tempted to drop the second line he'd kept for his business calls.

A jangle from the very object of his thoughts gave him a

start. He answered before it let out another ring.

"Hello." As Dan waited for the caller to respond, he heard her rake in a jagged breath. Somewhere close by, a dog's bark rang out in a steady, shrieking trill.

"Is this Handy Dan. . . ?" The woman's voice on the other end of the line held a definite tremor. "The repairman?"

"Yes, Ma'am. Name's Dan Parker, but folks call me Handy Dan. 'If it's broke, I'll fix it,' that's my motto and my guarantee. How can I be of serv—"

"Pickles and parsley! I can hardly hear a word you're saying. That dog! Can you hang on for just a moment please. . ." Her next words sounded muffled, and Dan suspected she'd covered the receiver with her hand, although he could still make out every word she said.

"Stop that racket immediately, or I'll have to shut you up in the bathroom so I can hear." The barking ceased, and the voice returned to its previous ungarbled state, although an undercurrent of trembling still remained.

"I need help. Now. Can you come?"

For a second, Dan tried to conjure up a face to match the frantic speech. Then the voice shrilled, "I'm wet. It's raining. And a tree just came through my roof!"

Chapter 2

A *tree through her roof?* "Give me just long enough to take down your address, and I'll be right over." Dan poised the nub of a carpenter's pencil over a piece of plywood so he could scribble down the information.

"Give you time to get dressed, you say?" She sounded as though she were about to lose a battle with tears. "Listen, I don't have time to wait for you to change clothes. This is an emergency!"

"No, Ma'am. You didn't hear me right. I'm ready to run out the door this very second. I just need an address. You know, tell me where you live. How can I find you?"

"An address. Of course you need an address. . . . Dear me, I know the road is called Pecan Crossing. You turn right, heading north, off of Main at the Sonic Drive-in. That'll put you onto Mistletoe Lane. Take that till it dead ends onto this street and turn left. I think it's the fourth, maybe fifth house on the right. I've only been here a day. Haven't memorized the number yet. I'll have to go outside—see if I can find it posted anywhere—"

"Whoa! Wait!" He imagined how his Esther would have reacted had she been in this lady's shoes, and he figured she would have been bawling her eyes out by now. He winged a quick prayer heavenward that he might squelch the woman's fears before real panic set in. "You've given me all I need to find you. I'm pretty sure I did some work on that very house not too many months back. Shouldn't take me more than three minutes to get there."

"Okay. I'll be watching for you out the window." Her relief traveled through the phone line as Dan hung up. However, the moment the dial tone began, he remembered he hadn't asked the woman's name. He could only hope and pray he was right about her location.

He donned his rain suit and clapped on his tattered *89ers* baseball cap. Then he grabbed a couple of blue plastic tarps from his paint supply closet and threw them into the cab of his Chevy F-10. After he'd settled behind the wheel, Dan turned over the ignition and backed the truck out of his carport. He pulled onto the rain-slicked street with his windshield wipers set on their fastest speed.

Dead tree limbs, garbage cans, and other light debris littered the yards he passed by, but Dan didn't see any evidence of serious devastation when he drove down a near-deserted Main Street. The town's two traffic lights were blinking yellow instead of the normal stop-and-go pattern, and he made record time as he traveled the several blocks to where he hoped to find the right house.

When he topped the rise in the road, a low whistle escaped through his teeth. No wonder the woman caller had sounded so distraught. Whether a tornado had swept through or straight winds, he couldn't say for sure, but some brutal force had twisted the trunk of a massive pecan tree like a hay straw and peeled back the bark to expose its creamy white insides. The leafy branches disappeared into the roof of the house.

Dan steered his truck into the driveway and parked behind a red pickup that looked to be the same year and model as his own, only this one sported a Kansas license plate. He slung his tool belt over his shoulder and gathered up the tarps. The door of his pickup emitted a fingernail-on-chalkboard squeal when he nudged it open with his knee. He'd no sooner bumped the door shut with his back-side and started down the walk when a woman, clad in a water-splotched denim shirt and blue jeans, stepped out onto the front porch. A yippy little dog that looked to be a teacup version of a collie trailed behind her.

Since his arms were full, Dan nodded a greeting to the lady. She mirrored the gesture. From this distance, she appeared to be about his Esther's age, which would make her about five years younger than his own sixty-nine, but the similarities between his deceased wife and this woman ended there.

His sweet, freckle-faced Esther had always been rather stout. She used to laugh and refer to herself as "a woman of substance"—until the effects of her stroke peeled away the excess weight and left in its place folds of jiggly skin. When-ever they kissed, Esther, at five-feet-no-inches tall, always had to stand on tiptoe and tilt her head back while he bent down to meet her lips. This straight-as-a-post, thin-as-a-rail lady could likely look him dead in the eye without any effort whatsoever. And he stood just shy of six feet.

Although Dan always thought Esther's hair looked just fine, she had felt it necessary to hide what she called her "mousy gray" with bottled brown coloring, and then she'd frizz it up with a permanent wave. The tanned woman on the porch, however, had short, smooth hair the color of polished chrome. He could imagine how it would glint and sparkle if the sun decided to shine.

"You must be Dan Parker," the woman shouted over the dog's raucous barks as Dan ascended the steps and found shelter from the rain under the porch's overhang. She snapped her fingers and the pup gave one more whine, spun around in a circle, then heeled. "I can't thank you enough for hurrying over here so fast. I don't know what on earth I would have done if you hadn't. As you'll soon see, I've got quite a mess on my hands. . . . Oh, and just so you're aware, right after I talked to you, I called the insurance agent—a Mr. King, I think his name was—to see about making a claim. Thankfully, before I moved in, my daughter possessed the foresight to add coverage for my things to her existing property insurance. . . ."

Dan smiled and nodded, figuring he couldn't get a word in edgewise if he tried. She was obviously one of those women who rambled when they were nervous.

"Anyway, all that's beside the point. . . ." She waved a hand in the air as if to dismiss herself. "When I told the agent I'd called you, he recommended your work highly and said you'd charge a fair price. He was certain he'd have no problem approving your estimate—said you could start right to work."

The lady paused. "Okra and onions! Here I've rattled on and on and never even introduced myself. Please excuse my bad manners. I'm Winnie. Winnie Wainwright, but just plain ol' Winnie is fine. I realized after I hung up that I forgot to give you my name. I'd offer to shake your hand, but I can see your arms are full." She reached out and, with uplifted palms, waggled her fingers at him. He only got a quick look because he didn't want her to catch him staring, but he didn't see any signs of a wedding ring. "Let me take that for you," she said in a loud voice, "and then tell me what I can do to help so we can get you home at a decent hour on such a dreary night. I'm afraid my pulling you away at dinnertime like this has spoiled your wife's supper plans. Shall I take you around to show you where the tree went through the roof?" She smiled just enough to expose the cutest little dimple in her right cheek. Suddenly, Dan wished he had taken the time to shave this morning—or had at least worn a shirt without paint splatters down the front.

"No, Ma'am, that won't be necessary. I could see the damage when I drove up. No sense in getting yourself drenched. And don't you worry about interrupting my supper. The only one waiting for me at home is my wife's old cat—and my dinner plans amounted to peanut butter and crackers. If you don't mind, I'll just drop this stuff here on the porch, then run back to the truck and get my chainsaw and ladder. The faster I get to work, the less water damage this rain will cause inside your home. Am I right to assume the tree came all the way through the ceiling as well as the roof?"

He waited for her to respond, but she simply stared at him, unseeing, with her brow furrowed and her lips pursed. He wasn't at all sure she had heard what he'd said. Following an extended pause, that far-off look left her eyes, and she met his gaze. "I'm so sorry," she said, shaking her head. "Did you ask me something? My mind is racing in a thousand different directions at the moment."

"Quite understandable." Dan raised his volume to increase his odds of being heard over the wind and rain. At the same time, she leaned toward him with her head cocked toward her right shoulder. "Listen, Miz Wainwright— Winnie. Don't you worry about a thing. You take your little dog back inside and try to stay dry and warm." He tipped his head toward the front door. "I'll tend to things out here. I don't expect I can do much more than cut away the tree limbs and tarp the hole in your roof before darkness sets in. When I've patched things up the best I can, I'll come back around, and we can discuss an estimate for the full extent of the repairs."

The woman maintained her regal bearing even when she crouched to scoop up the dog. "Well, then, I'll leave you to your work. But don't hesitate to ring the bell if you need anything at all. Until yesterday, I lived on a farm so I'm accustomed to hard work and, despite what my dear departed husband used to think, I'm not made of sugar and I won't melt in the rain."

She excused herself and slipped inside; but while he

gathered his things from the truck and set to work, he couldn't keep his thoughts from wandering to the stately Miz Wainwright.

Racing against impinging darkness, Dan set to work cutting away the tangled limbs and clearing all the storm rubble from the gaping hole in the roof. The rain slackened, but even so, water dripped from his cap and down his neck. A chill wind whipped at both his rain suit and the billowing tarp and rattled the ladder beneath his feet. Despite the uncomfortable working conditions, however, a praise chorus echoed through his mind: *God is so good. God is so good. God is so good, He's so good to me!* And Dan realized for the first time in fifty years, another woman besides Esther occupied his thoughts.

Winnie coaxed Skipper into the laundry room, where she shooed him into his carrier and latched it closed. She simply couldn't cope with a mollycoddled pet on top of all the other things weighing on her mind. With a doggy sigh, the hound sank onto his blanket and nested his head atop his front paws. Winnie rewarded his quiet compliance by leaving the light on when she walked out and shut the door.

"Bill, what should I do now?" She lifted her gaze heavenward as she spoke, swallowing hard against the rising knot of emotion that threatened to clog her throat. Her hands shook too much to proceed with unpacking anything breakable. And, judging from the pops, snaps, creaks, and saw-buzzings that resonated over the back portion of the house, for safety's sake she needed to steer clear of her bedroom with its yawning hole in the roof.

She wasn't in any hurry to return to the epicenter of disaster anyway. She shuddered to think how close she had come to serious injury—or worse. After coming back inside from her rain-interrupted walk with Skipper, she had left the dog dozing in front of the TV and gone back to her bedroom to unpack her prized collectibles and souvenirs of overseas travel. She had unwrapped the last of the box's contents—a delicate Korean figurine, which Bill had carried home from the war—and was reaching to arrange it on an étagère shelf, when a tree came crashing through the ceiling with a tsunami-force blast of rain and leaves. She suffered only scratches as a leafy branch swept past her. The limb knocked the statuary from her hand on its demolition course with her remaining treasures. She had screamed, dashed out of the room, and slammed the door behind her. From the looks of things, it would be some time before she'd be able to sleep in her own bed again.

At least she had gotten hold of a man who could help her. Someone up above must surely be watching out for her. She didn't know what she would have done if this Mr. "Handy Dan" hadn't been available.

Just by looking at him, she sensed him to be a nice man. A kind man. A salt-of-the-earth type of man she could trust. Deep laugh lines traveled from the corners of his eyes, and only years of smiles could etch the path his wrinkles took around his lips. Even in the middle of total chaos, something in Handy Dan's face and soft-spoken demeanor put her at ease and assured her that all would be well.

She wondered where *Mrs.* Handy Dan was on a rainy night like tonight. He had referred to his wife's cat, so he must surely be married. *Wherever she is, I hope his wife realizes what a gem she's got in a husband like Dan.*

Something else he had said niggled at the back of Winnie's mind. Peanut butter on crackers. . .what kind of a supper was that? She might not be able to accomplish much in the way of unpacking with all this commotion going on overhead, but there was one thing she could do to make herself useful while she waited for the repairman to patch things up for the night. She could fix him some real food to eat.

Winnie went through the steps of brewing a pot of decaf, all the while thankful that she'd unpacked her coffeepot first thing this morning. Then she shuffled around and through the labyrinth of boxes to the other side of the kitchen and opened the fridge. Carla had left it stocked with sandwich fixin's, along with a pot of beef stew made from Winnie's mother's recipe.

"He looks like the kind of guy who'd go for your favorite— pimento cheese on rye with a slice of pickle loaf. Don't you think so, Bi—" The name faltered on her tongue. For the first time since her husband's death, Winnie felt silly and awkward talking aloud into thin air.

An hour later, Winnie opened the front door and looked outside. To her surprise, she found the sopping-wet handyman scraping his muddy shoes on the doormat. He held the bill of his ball cap curled between both hands and had obviously tried to get his unruly wisps of salt-and-pepper hair to lie flat. She had no idea how long he'd been standing there or if he had rung the bell.

"Won't you come in, Mr. Parker?" Winnie swung the door open wide and stepped aside to allow him a wide enough berth to enter the room. When she did, Skipper began to growl and bark from his laundry room confines, making the difficult task of understanding the soft-spoken man next to impossible. She strained to hear him without appearing too obvious at her attempts.

"Thanks, but I'd really better not, Miz Wainwright. Removing the tree from your roof took longer than I expected and it's getting mighty late." He glanced at his wristwatch.

"As long as no more tornadoes pass through tonight, those tarps should keep the water out, but I'll be back first thing in the morning to start working on repairs." He looked over his shoulder, then down at his feet, forcing Winnie to lean closer toward him to catch his words. "Would you mind if we waited until then to sit down and discuss an estimate? I'd be able to tell more about the extent of the damage to the trusses by daylight anyway."

Winnie nodded her consent, and Dan responded with a chuckle.

"My kids are sure to be calling me when they hear about the severe weather that's passed through this neck of the woods." He shuffled his muddy shoes across the doormat while he spoke. "Especially my daughter, Patty. She'll be driving up from Dallas to check on me if I don't answer my phone. Beginning back when my wife had a stroke that left her paralyzed and unable to talk, that daughter of mine seemed to think it was her duty to assume the role of mother hen."

"So your wife—is she still in ill health?" Winnie wished he would look up when he spoke to her, but this wasn't exactly an appropriate time to ask him as much.

"She's been a-bed now for close to three years after suffering a series of strokes that had left her comatose. Her wish was to be entered in the Angel's Haven rest home down in Dallas where she and I grew up. Just so happens it's not far from where Patty and her family live, so she goes by every so often and takes flowers and such. I miss Esther something fierce, but I watched her suffer for so long here in Milltown General, I know she's far better off where she is."

His wan smile cut right to Winnie's heart.

"How very sad for you all. I can relate a little to what you're going through. Four years ago now, my husband suffered a heart attack while he was plowing the field for spring planting and was in the hospital for a month before he went into full cardiac arrest and died." For a brief moment, she was transported back to that sad and awful day. Yet, the look of empathy and compassion in Handy Dan's eyes soothed her like a healing balm.

"Well, I won't keep you. Come as early as you like in the morning. I'll rise with the rooster, especially since I've got all this unpacking to do." She glanced over at the kitchen table, which she had cleared of unpacking clutter and set with a place setting of one. "Sweet butter beans! Wait! I almost forgot. I fixed you up a bit of supper while you were on the roof. I know you need to get on home, and I won't keep you, but if you'll stay here just a minute, I'll wrap up these sandwiches for you to take along with you as you go."

When Winnie left Dan alone on the porch to wrap up his supper, he washed his hand over his face, then shook his head from side to side, berating himself. Why had he blabbed on and on about how and when his wife had died? He'd even gone so far as to tell her where Esther's body was interred. What had gotten into him? All he could think was he'd been nervous in the presence of such a beautiful woman. He must have sounded like a pathetic and lonely old man. One of the numerous reasons he steered clear of the senior citizen's center was because so many of the old-timers there felt it necessary to give an "organ recital" and expound on their latest ailments. Now here he was rambling on and on about Esther's stroke and her passing just like the best of them. He'd been so consumed with his own tale of woe that he hadn't even bothered to ask Winnie about her children and if she had grandchildren or find out what brought her to Milltown.

Well, starting tomorrow, he'd stop with all the gloom and despair and focus on getting better acquainted with Winnie. Tomorrow he'd pull into Winnie Wainwright's drive when the rooster crowed.

Chapter 3

In that ethereal mist between sleep and waking, Dan thought he smelled coffee percolating. He anticipated the give on the mattress when Esther would sit on the bed and offer him the morning's first cup of brew. A contented sigh lifted his chest. All was right with the world. . . until reality barged in, unwelcomed. If he wanted to wake up and smell the coffee, he should have set the timer on his coffeemaker before he went to bed so that it would start brewing at five o'clock.

He certainly needed a jolt of caffeine. Last night, after listening to his daughter's bellyaching on the phone for the better part of an hour, he'd found it nearly impossible to fall asleep.

All through his predawn quiet time, Dan prayed about his attitude toward Patty. Even so, he stewed and fumed all the way across Milltown during his drive to the Wainwright house. That daughter of his! To listen to her, one would wonder how he ever managed to survive without her telling him what to do.

"But, Dad-dy," Patty had whined into the phone when he told her about the repair job he'd taken on. "I don't think I approve of your climbing around on a steep roof or high ladders at your age. You're liable to fall and break your neck. Besides, I thought you were staying busy making all those cute little lawn ornaments."

Her acquired Texas drawl raised the hackles on the back of Dan's neck, but he held his tongue and let her speak her piece.

"You need to tell this Wainwright woman she'll have to find someone else to do her repairs. It was nice of you to help her out in an emergency and all, but I'm sure she can find a professional company to finish the job. I know this may come as a surprise to you, but you're not a young buck anymore. It's high time you learned the meaning of the word *retired*. If Mama were still with us, she'd put her foot down, and that's for sure."

Coming from anyone other than his own daughter, such demeaning implications of his helpless state might have been fighting words. Nevertheless, he knew Patty loved him and meant well. She had his best interests at heart and wouldn't intentionally hurt him for the world. But to listen to her talk, one would think he was eighty instead of sixty-nine. He felt far from ready to join the rocking chair set.

"I appreciate your concern, Pumpkin—" When the term of endearment slipped from his lips, he thought of Winnie Wainwright's propensity for vegetable exclamations and smiled to himself. "However, I've already given my word, and I'm not about to back out now. Don't worry. I'll be fine.

Looking forward to the job, in fact." *But I don't dare tell her the full reason why.* If Patty suspected there was even a remote possibility that another woman had caught his eye and might someday vie to take her mother's place as his wife, there would be no closing the floodgates of her tears.

He'd given Patty some lame excuse for needing to say good-bye and cut her off before she could wheedle him down with a fresh batch of protests. Yet, all through the night and into the dawn, her words trailed him like a bloodhound, determined to spoil his day.

When he pulled into the driveway behind Winnie Wainwright's pickup, he shoved all thoughts of his daughter aside. By the light of day, it only took one look at the devastation in the yard and to the house to convince him he had other, more urgent matters in need of his attentions. He had a job to do for a fair lady in distress.

"Come on in!" Winnie swung the front door open as he reached out to ring the doorbell. Her dog snarled and growled at Dan from behind Winnie's red bandanna-print skirt. With her tall, thin figure, shimmering silver hair, and stylish outfit, she looked as though she stepped off the cover of a *Today's Country Woman* magazine.

"I've got the coffeepot on," she said over the dog's clamor, "but you'll have to excuse the mess."

"You've got a mighty ferocious guard dog there—"

"What's that you say?" Confusion blanketed Winnie's features. "You've got a mind to do what to the dog's hair?"

"No." Dan smiled. "The dog. . ." He took careful pains to raise his voice and enunciate his words. In a motion Dan was coming to recognize as a course of habit with Winnie, she inclined her left ear toward him. "He isn't going to attack me if I come inside, is he?"

He attempted to keep a lighthearted tone, but he meant the question more than he let on. He'd heard that the half-pint varieties of these fancy breeds were often meaner than the big ones.

"I don't think he's ever been known to inflict physical harm." She followed Dan's line of sight down to the dog. "He is definitely a prime example of the old adage, 'his bark is worse than his bite.' But I'll shut him in the laundry room for the time being. That'll give you a chance to inspect the interior damage without him nipping at your heels." She lifted the dog into her arms and motioned with her head for Dan to come inside. The animal's growls faded to a low rumble, then stilled.

"I wouldn't be surprised but what he can smell cat on my clothes and that's got him all riled up." Dan pushed the front door closed behind him. "What's your pup's name?"

"His name is Skipper—but, hominy grits!—" Winnie shook her head and laughed. When she did, Dan caught a glimpse of the dimple in her right cheek. "This mangy critter isn't mine! He belongs to my daughter, Carla. I'm just dog-sitting while she and her husband Jack are in Hawaii. I'm actually more of a cat person myself, like your wife. Still, I'm not one to keep inside pets. I left all my animals in the country where they belong."

She sidestepped a hodgepodge of storage boxes and crossed the living room, opening a side door just long enough to shoo the dog into what Dan presumed to be the laundry room. A *scratch-scratch-scratch* and pitiful whine filtered from the other side of the laundry room door, but neither Dan nor Winnie acknowledged the sounds. After a few more canine moans, a hush settled over the house.

"Jack and Carla, hmm?" He let the names rattle around in his memory bank while Winnie poured two cups of coffee. "You wouldn't by any chance be referring to Jack and Carla Dugan, would you? The ones who built this place?" As he spoke, he leaned against the kitchen island that jutted into the open living space. The cord to an old toaster dangled off the countertop. Dan noted the frayed wires poking out from the plug when he picked it up and began to roll it between his fingers.

"Why, yes. How do you know my Carla?"

Dan waved off her offer of creamer or sugar, and she reached across a stack of place mats and tablecloths to hand him a man-sized coffee mug.

"I attend First Church, same as your daughter and son-in-law." He looked Winnie straight in the eye, then smiled. "You've got reason to be proud of Carla and Jack. They're quality folks, through and through." Winnie nodded her agreement to his assessment as he continued. "It's refreshing to see young people like those two following the Lord. Jack and I serve on the buildings and properties committee together." Dan looked down and shook his head. "Poor guy. Whenever he's got a free Wednesday night, I also call on him to help me with the group of fifth-grade boys I teach in the Christian scouting program that meets at the church.

He's always happy to help. And he's great with kids. I declare, that young man has the patience of Job!"

When he lifted his gaze back to Winnie, she flashed him another dimpled smile. "My son-in-law proved he's a man of infinite patience when he married that daughter of mine. She's an only child—a miracle baby who came along when Bill and I were, um, shall I say, past our prime. As a result, I fear Carla can be. . .well, to put it politely, determined. Strong-willed, if you know what I mean."

"I know exactly what you're saying. My daughter, Patty, came from that same stubborn mold. I think her younger brother Peter joined the air force mainly to get some relief from Patty's ironfisted rule. She is a great mom to my eight-year-old twin grandsons, though, and her husband's personality is the perfect complement to hers. God knew what He was doing when He placed those two wild urchins in Patty and Brian's care." Dan took a sip of his coffee and set the mug back down on the corner of counter space Winnie had cleared.

"Twins? Brussels sprouts and broccoli spears! Did I hear you say twin grandsons? Wouldn't that be nice!"

Dan popped the heel of his open hand on his forehead. "Ah, sure, I'm getting it now." He bobbed his head slowly up and down. "The thought just occurred to me why you've moved to town. I don't suppose the fact that your only child is expecting her first baby had anything to do with you relocating, now did it?"

"That had everything to do with it." The sheer delight of being a new grandmother sparkled in Winnie's dark sable eyes. "I can't think of anything else but my first grandchild that would convince me to pick up roots at this stage in my life."

"Grandkids are the one great compensation for growing old. You're blessed to have the opportunity to live close by. You'll see to it, I'm sure, that Jack and Carla's little one will be spoiled royally." He paused and scrubbed at his chin.

"You know, now that you told me you're Carla's mother, I can see the family resemblance. Carla has your eyes."

Winnie's cheeks blushed a dark shade of pink at his words, which, in turn, set off a heart-pounding, palm-sweating chain reaction within him. Without forethought or warning, he winked at her. When he did, Winnie's eyes grew round. He felt his face flame. He'd not been so openly flirtatious since his unmarried, army days and couldn't imagine what had come over him to do such a thing now. He cleared his throat, fighting for words—any words—that might relieve the tension crackling between them.

The last thing he wanted was for her to think he had designs altogether unrelated to her roof and home repairs. . . for the time being, anyway.

While he knew some widows and widowers rushed into another marriage soon after the loss of a spouse, Winnie had been without her mate for a year longer than he had been without Esther. Like him, she was probably one to want to take things slow. Any future romantic relationship he might enter into, whether with Winnie or another, would need to be built first on friendship and then allowed to develop into something deeper over time. No one, not even someone as lovely as the lady standing before him now, could fully capture the special place Esther occupied in his heart for so many years. But he could see how a woman like Winnie might add a delightful dimension to this autumn season of his life.

He swallowed around the knot in his throat and somehow found his voice.

"Here I am standing around lollygagging, and that's sure not what you're paying me to do. Daylight's aburnin'. Let me take a gander at that hole in your roof from the inside, here. Then I'll get down to the business of repairs." He took a final swig of coffee and stretched across the island to deposit his mug in the sink.

"There's no need for you to trouble yourself with showing me around. I think I can manage to find the damage on my own." He tried to make eye contact with her, hoping to offer a smile and ease the tension he'd caused between them by his thoughtless act; but whether on purpose or not, she didn't seem to be listening to him.

Did he just wink at me? Winnie's pulse pounded in her ears with such force, she couldn't hear a word of Dan's last remarks. *Bill, I do believe this man winked at me.* Even though she addressed her late husband in her thoughts, for once she was almost glad Bill wasn't there to witness this little interchange between her and another man or observe her response. *Candied yams! Don't tell me my eyesight is playing tricks on me. It's bad enough my hearing is out of whack of late.* She turned away from Dan and feigned an intense preoccupation with washing out their coffee cups. *No, surely I'm mistaken. He seems like such a nice, church-going fella. He couldn't have. Wouldn't have. Could he?*

Would he? Even though his wife may be in a coma and bedfast in Texas, he's still a married man!

She glanced up to see Dan walking away, toward the master bedroom and the area of the house where the lion's share of the storm damage had occurred. The recollection of his pain-filled eyes last night as he spoke of his wife's strokes and resulting long-term illness dispelled Winnie's suspicions that he had been making a flirtatious overture. She didn't think anyone who spoke of his wife in such tender, loving terms would entertain adulterous thoughts, no matter how hopeless his spouse's prognosis for recovery or how lonely he must be. Besides, he spoke as if he had a personal relationship with Christ. Perhaps her own loneliness and vulnerability had tricked her mind into seeing things, misinterpreting his friendly demeanor.

She wondered if she would ever be able to share her home, her life, her love with another man. No one could replace Bill. What they'd shared had taken a lifetime to build. But as she watched Dan's broad back disappear into the other room, a distant remembrance of sharing a man's companionship swept over her, and she wondered if she would ever know such pleasant comforts again.

Skipper barked and whined from his laundry-room prison, and Winnie knew from the urgent tone he needed to go outside. Any other time, she would have let him out in the backyard to run free and tend to his business. However, she knew the fence had been damaged in the wake of the pecan tree's demise, and she didn't dare risk losing her daughter's precious little darling. She retrieved Skipper's leash; but before she opened the laundry room door to let him out, she trailed the path Dan had just taken to the master bedroom. He stood with his head tipped back, scratching his jaw and gawking at the hole where the ceiling fan belonged. Rainwater had soaked the area in sufficient quantities before the tarps were nailed in place so that waterlogged plaster still dripped from the hole's periphery and coated the room like snow. Carpet, furniture, open wardrobe boxes, the shattered remains of her prized curios from the étagère shelf—a shroud of gloppy white goo covered them all. The ceiling fan, minus a couple of blades, had landed half on, half off her bed.

"I'm heading outside to take the dog for a little walk. I won't be gone long. Since you say you've worked on this place before, you probably know your way around here better than I do. But if you need to get up into the attic, I believe there's a pull-down ladder in the second bedroom that I'm converting into a den. You can get onto the deck and to the backyard from there too. I'll try to set that room straight today, since it appears that I'll be sleeping on the sofa bed for awhile. In the meantime, feel free to shove the moving boxes around to make yourself a path."

"Sure thing." He held her gaze for a long moment. Then he opened and closed his mouth, evidently rethinking the wisdom of what he was about to say. Winnie could not read his thoughts; but when his mouth turned up at one corner in a lopsided smile, her heart jumped a beat.

Skipper yelped.

"Sweet corn on the cob! The dog's sounding desperate now. I'll be back soon."

Throughout the course of her brief excursion with Skipper, she chastised herself for her reaction to Handy Dan. What had gotten into her? First, she imagined him winking at her, and then a mere smile from him sent her pulse racing. Not since she had fallen in love with Bill some fifty-plus years ago had she so much as given another man a second look. Now, a married man had turned her head in a most disconcerting way.

She finally decided the events of the past few days had left her feeling more vulnerable than she fully realized. Dan didn't look much like Bill, but something about that sparkle in his eyes and that crooked smile of his hinted at the inner qualities her husband and the handyman shared in common. She must be reacting on a subconscious level to this kind fellow's ability to resurrect those same desires for comfort and protection that Bill used to meet in her life. Now that she was aware of this area of susceptibility, she would simply have to take extra care to keep her guard up around Dan.

When she walked in her front door after escorting Skipper around the block, the dog started in with his low-throated, growling undertones. Dan stood hunched over the island countertop in her small kitchen, writing in a small notebook. He nodded a greeting.

Considering Skipper's disdain for the handyman, Winnie thought it wise to deposit the dog in the laundry room for the time being, so she sidled past the kitchen on her way to accomplish the task. She kept the leash taut and steered Skipper as far away from Dan as possible. "No need to stow the pup away on my account." She turned back to Dan as he spoke. "I think little Skipper and I need to make peace with one another if I'm going to be around for the next few weeks." He stooped and held his hand out flat. Skipper, emitting a low rumble, took a tentative step toward Dan and sniffed. "Judging by my damage estimate, I'm probably looking at close to a month to finish up this project right—that's assuming weather's permitting when I'm needing to work outside." He knelt down on one knee and began to chuck the dog under its chin. Skipper nuzzled closer and allowed the man to scratch him between his ears.

Dan looked up at Winnie. Triumph gleamed in his pewter gray eyes.

She sloughed off the feathery tickles that rippled up and down her spine and tried to concentrate on what he was telling her. "A month? Did I hear you right?" She glanced at the page in his notebook to see if she could find out why he would need so much time. His chicken scratches and cipherings filled the page. "Do you really think it will take that long to set everything right again? Or are you thinking it's better to err on the side of caution in your guesstimate of how long it'll take to finish the job?"

"I know it sounds strange, but sometimes repairs can take as long, or longer, than the original construction. Let me show you how I'm figuring things." When he stood, he lifted the dog into his arms and continued patting and stroking its fur. Skipper leaned into Dan's hand, looking more like a Cheshire cat than a persnickety sheltie. "I'm not real fast, especially since I work alone, but I'm thorough, and

I'll do it right the first go 'round. Still, maybe you can help me find a way to trim off some more time."

A faint scent of aftershave wafted past Winnie as Dan set Skipper down and reached for his notebook. The fragrance sent a whirlpool of sentiment swirling through her. Despite Carla's teasing that her father liked a grandpappy's cologne, Bill used to slap on the same spicy cologne every morning following his shave. For weeks, months, after his death, Winnie would take her husband's bathrobe to bed with her, burying her nose in the terry cloth to recapture his essence and ease her loneliness. The night she realized his masculine aroma had forever faded away, she had crumpled with an anguish every bit as overwhelming as the day Bill had died. She had lost another piece of him, never to be retrieved. The finality of his death hit her anew, and she had cried herself to sleep.

Winnie closed her eyes and breathed deeply to savor the cherished musky smell. But now, she no longer felt the crushing pain of grief or even a pang of sadness. Instead, a pleasant warmth swept over her and sent a smile playing on her lips.

"When the tree hit your roof, she busted one truss clean in two, cracked a couple others." Dan interrupted Winnie's brief reverie and brought her back to the crisis at hand. "That'll need fixin' first thing, before I can do much else."

He used checkmarks to tick off the items on his long list of repairs as he read them aloud. "Inside, you'll need new insulation in the attic, and I'll have to replace the particle-board flooring up there if you hope to use it for storage. The window

I repaired for the last tenant busted out too, so it will need new glass. Your master bedroom will require a total remodel—new carpet and padding installed; ceiling repaired and retextured; a new ceiling fan and light fixture put in; then the walls need patched and repainted. The force of the impact caused what I call 'nail pops' and cracks in the ceiling plaster throughout the rest of the house as well, so those will all need to be spackled and repaired. Outside, we're looking at a whole new roof—decking, shingles, and all. You've got a couple of broken boards on your deck, and the tree took out a whole section of fencing on the south side of the house. Chopping the tree into firewood will take me a good part of a day as well."

Although Winnie tried to give her undivided attention to Dan and concentrate on the job details, her mind kept wandering. She envisioned Carla and Jack returning from Hawaii to find her home—the house they had built with their own hands—torn to smithereens. She knew they would both be more than a little upset with her if she didn't tell them the extent of the damage right away; but if she called and told them now, they'd be on the next plane home from Hawaii. Winnie would forever feel guilty for interrupting the honeymoon they had waited more than two years to take.

"I was really hoping to have everything back in tip-top shape before Carla and Jack arrive back home." She pursed her lips as she pondered her dilemma. If she waited until all the repairs were done, then she could break the news to them slowly. On her own terms. At her own speed. Under just the right circumstances. But if things were still in disrepair when they returned, she'd never see the end of Carla's smothering. Winnie wanted to establish her independence and show her daughter right off the bat that she was capable of managing things on her own. She felt it important to set her ground rules for living so close to her daughter before Carla tightened the screws of her protective nature and smothered Winnie to death. She wasn't ready for the role reversal she'd heard of folks her age having to endure, and she refused to let her daughter start mothering her.

"Tell you what. I don't have much else to do, so I'll plan on working every day, save Sundays. With a little help from above, maybe I can wrap everything up in three weeks instead of four." Dan nodded in agreement to his own revised plans. "In fact, that'd work best for me too. My daughter's been nagging me to come down to Dallas for a visit over Memorial Day weekend. That'll give me a chance to take some flowers out to Esther and tend to things there at Angel's Haven. Then, when the twins' school lets out for the summer and I've overstayed my welcome at Patty's place, I'm hoping to bring the boys back up here to Milltown for a little visit. They've been planning for a year on us camping out at Red Rock Canyon. I'd be a pretty lousy granddad if I backed out on them now."

"My, yes! You need to do that." Winnie didn't want to be responsible in any way for tarnishing Dan's image in the eyes of those twin boys. Although Dan looked like the perfect grandfather to her—old enough to teach them a lesson or two that he'd learned from the school of hard knocks, yet still young and strong enough to go on all those rugged, outdoorsy adventures boys love.

She let her gaze wander around the room while she thought of ways she might help him finish the job as soon as possible. "I wouldn't be much good to you on the roof, but once I've gotten things a little more under control on the unpacking front, I'll do all I can to help you inside. I'll have you know I wield a mean paintbrush."

"Winnie?" Bewilderment crinkled Dan's features when she turned her full attention back to him. Skipper punctuated his inquiry with a bark.

"Yes?"

"Aren't you going to answer your phone?"

Chapter 4

Two weeks later, Winnie wondered just how many phone calls she'd missed due to her faulty hearing. She figured out that, rather than scolding Skipper when the dog went into a yipping frenzy, she ought to first check to see if the phone was ringing. With a sigh, she admitted that perhaps the time had come for her to see a hearing specialist.

This time, however, she could blame her failure to hear the phone on the racket created by Dan's sander in the other room. Thankfully, Skipper, once again, sounded an alert.

Winnie cupped her hand around the phone's mouthpiece and hoped the sound of the ongoing repairs didn't transmit all the way to the South Pacific. "Carla, you're spending an awful lot of money calling all the way from Hawaii like this. You could pay for several nice outfits for the baby for what this one phone call is costing you."

The day after the storm, when Carla called to say they'd arrived at the resort safe and sound, Winnie managed to avoid going into detail about the extent of injury to the house. She made light of the fact that she had hired Handy Dan, saying strong winds blew down a tree limb and she'd ask him to come in and fix the damaged fence as well as a place on the roof in need of repair.

While everything she'd said had been entirely true, her deliberate downplay of the situation pricked at her conscience. During the next week's phone conversations that followed, Winnie found it increasingly difficult to maintain her ruse. She didn't know if she could keep from spilling the beans about the catastrophe if Carla were to call again.

"It's sweet of you to keep checking on me, but you really don't need to call again since you'll be flying home a week from tomorrow. I'll just see you when you get back, and you can tell me all about your trip then. I can't wait to look at your pictures, and I'm anxious for you to see the progress I've made on the house." She grimaced at her own words. While it was true that her unpacking was progressing well, the house had a ways to go before the repair work could be considered done.

Winnie's gaze followed the path of drywall dust footprints, which coated the cardboard runner Dan had laid down to protect the carpet. She breathed a prayer that nothing would interfere with their schedule to complete all those repairs by next week.

"I suppose you're right, Mom. I'll see you when we get home then. Give Skipper an extra doggie biscuit and blow him a kiss for me."

Winnie glanced at the dog, which lay curled up at her feet. She had to admit she'd grown rather fond of the hound.

And Skipper proved to be surprisingly useful. Over the past two weeks, she came to depend on him to alert her on those occasions when her hearing failed to register a ringing door-bell or telephone.

"Okay, Sweetheart. Will do."

After exchanging good-byes with Carla, Winnie returned to her task of arranging a display on the plant shelf over the kitchen sink. She stood back a few feet to get a better view, taking care not to trip over the ladder she'd been using to reach the ledge. Her arms folded, she took a critic's stance, skewed her face, and studied the composition. The artsy mosaic of antique kitchen utensils, colored glass jars and bottles, artificial greenery, and little twinkle lights made her feel like she could finally call the place *home*.

"That looks nice—like a picture page right out of the latest interior design how-to book."

She startled to discover Dan standing behind her, since she hadn't heard him approach, but she quickly recovered her composure and offered him a smile. "Why, thank you. I'm quite pleased myself, actually. I only have to nestle this old toaster in that empty spot right there." She pointed to a place in the center of the display. "Then I'll be done."

"I looked this over the other day." Dan picked up the toaster off the kitchen counter and buffed a fingerprint from the stainless casing. "You may not be interested, since you're using it to decorate, but I enjoy tinkering with little projects like this." He raised the frayed electrical cord for her to see. "If you'll let me take this relic home to my workshop, I believe I can have it back to you in working order within a day or two." He chuckled. "No charge."

There he goes again. . .being too sweet and kind for my own good.

For a split second, she hesitated to let the vessel that represented so many of her cherished memories out of her possession, even for a brief time. Yet she knew she would find no one more reliable than Dan to whom she could entrust her treasure. When she accepted his offer with a profusion of thanks, he acted as if she were doing him a favor rather than the other way around.

"I'll dash out to the truck and put this in the cab so I don't forget it, then." The grin that split his face made him look like a kid with a new toy on Christmas morn. "But don't worry. I'll lock 'er up real good."

A giggle refused to be swallowed, and Winnie faked a cough to mask her juvenile response to Dan's enthusiasm. Such disconcerting reactions seemed to be growing in frequency on her part.

Over the course of Dan's day-in, day-out work routine, Winnie had found it increasingly difficult to keep her guard up around him. Even though she kept busy at the task of unpacking, while he labored on the roof and in the attic from sunrise until sunset, they shared little snippets of conversation over coffee and lengthy discussions during lunch. And, much to her shame, she'd begun to look forward to these moments with him.

Looking back now, her insisting on preparing the noon meal every day for the two of them to share might not have been such a good idea. Yet, to do otherwise railed against every rule of hospitality she'd been brought up to keep. She couldn't be downright rude and insist that this man, who was working so hard to help her, eat alone. He had offered to go to the Dairy Freeze or drive-through Sonic and grab a burger to eat, but that seemed like such a waste of both his money and limited time. Besides, she hated to think of a man Dan's age tanking up on all that cholesterol and fatty food. No, she had done the Christian thing by offering to cook for him. And not once since that first day, when she thought he had winked at her, had he behaved in any way other than that of a perfect gentleman. He had given no reason for her to regret her decision to share lunch every day with him.

She was the problem, not Dan.

She found him to be pleasant company. Very pleasant indeed. *Too* pleasant, in fact.

She had enjoyed sharing food and good conversation with a married man much more than she should.

Never in a million years would she allow their association to go beyond the sphere of Christian hospitality. Winnie knew better than to let her gaze lock with his and linger too long. She understood the wisdom of avoiding even the most innocent of physical touch between them.

Strong-willed and determined, she refused to give in to the temptation to seek out his companionship, his wide, warm smile—all the while reminding herself that even Jesus faced temptation and that temptation in and of itself was not sin. She tried her best not to dwell on her fleeting thoughts of what it would be like to someday, perhaps, let her heart fall for another man. Someone like Dan, with a tender heart, a Christian kindness, and a smile that made her feel like a teenager again.

This tug-of-war between desire and decency did one thing for her, though. It forced her to her knees. For the first time in a long while, she found herself praying more than a cursory bedtime prayer.

Winnie watched Dan as he passed by the kitchen window on his way to his truck. She longed for the kind of faith he had, a faith like she once knew. To see his fiery dedication to Christ left her longing for the spiritual vibrancy she had in her younger days.

Although she never turned her back on the Lord or walked away from her faith, after Bill died, she struggled with believing God truly cared for her. If He did, why would He take her beloved away before they could even begin to enjoy their retirement years? She and Bill had talked for years of travel and leisure and growing old together. Instead, she faced day after day of, first, agonizing grief and, now, consuming loneliness.

A deflating sadness washed over her, and Winnie sank into a kitchen chair. She gathered Skipper into her lap and stroked the length of his back as she stared, unseeing, out the window into the front yard.

She could quote all the right Scripture. In her head, she knew God loved her with an everlasting love, so much so that He purchased eternal life for her by sacrificing His own Son. She knew He had numbered the hours of her life, as well as Bill's. It wasn't for her to question Him. But her feelings took awhile to catch up to what she knew in her head. In those days, her heart developed a thick callous that both protected and denied.

She had not intended for her relationship with God to grow cold, yet she found a vibrant faith increasingly difficult to maintain. Since she lived so far out in the country, the effort of driving into town for church every Sunday became harder and harder to put forth.

In those tough days of fresh grief, rather than sharing her sorrow with the Lord in prayer, she pushed Him into the dark shadows of her daily life. Instead, she slipped into the habit of talking to an invisible Bill, drawing comfort from saying his name, imagining him near.

However, in the two short weeks since she'd been in Dan's constant, warming presence, she felt the arctic frost around her grieving spirit—the cold that had long resisted the fiery touch of God—beginning to thaw.

"Will you be coming to First Church again this week?"

"Scallions and spinach, Dan! You keep sneaking up on me like that, and you're going to scare me clean out of my skin." Winnie pressed her hand against her pounding heart. "What's that you were saying?"

"I'm sorry to startle you." As he moved so he could look down into Winnie's face, Dan mentally kicked himself for treading up behind her and scaring her. He kept forgetting she had trouble hearing at times. "I was wondering if you'd be attending worship at First Church again this Sunday."

Dan stepped across the kitchen and started to reach for

the coffeepot, but paused. "Mind if I help myself to a cup?" When Winnie granted her permission, he resumed his previous train of thought.

"I still feel bad about you slipping in and out of early service last week without me seeing you." With a full mug of coffee in his hands, he leaned back against the kitchen counter. "One of the few drawbacks of a church our size is that visitors sometimes get overlooked. I hate to think of you sitting all alone last Sunday, and I want to make certain that doesn't happen again."

Before Winnie could raise a protest, which she appeared as though she was going to do, Dan rushed on. "We'd love to have you join our Keenagers' Sunday school. We meet during second service time, then a group of us usually head to El Campesinos for their Sunday all-you-can-eat Mexican food buffet." Noisily sipping at his hot coffee, he studied Winnie over the rim of his cup. She seemed to be giving his offer serious consideration.

"If you'd like, I can even give you a lift so you don't have to drive."

The instant the words left his mouth, he knew he'd said the wrong thing. Winnie's eyebrows hitched in surprise, then she dropped her gaze and began to play with the spoon in the sugar bowl.

"Now, don't get me wrong," she said with deliberate slowness, "I liked everything about the service last week." She glanced up and back down to the spoon in her hand. Raising a spoonful of sugar, she let it trickle like snow back into the bowl. "The music provided the right blend of hymns and choruses for my personal taste and the pastor's sermon really spoke to my heart. I could feel the spirit of the Lord permeating the sanctuary so that I hated for the worship service to come to an end. . . ." Winnie sank the spoon into the sugar, then shoved the bowl aside. Squaring her shoulders, she looked him in the eye.

Dan braced for the "but. . ." he knew would follow and cringed when she spoke the offending word.

"But I'm concerned that I'd be attending the same church as my daughter and son-in-law. I just wonder if we wouldn't all be better off if I found a church of my own, apart from my kids. I don't want them to feel like I'm trying to horn in on their lives."

Judging by the guarded way she studied him, he could tell Winnie left unsaid what really bothered her about attending First Church. He wouldn't debate the issue, but her argument didn't hold much water with him. The church averaged several thousand in attendance each Sunday and had two worship services. It would be quite possible for Winnie to become active in her own circle of friends and never run into Carla and Jack at church.

He saw her defenses rise the moment he offered to give her a ride. Her mood had changed faster than the score of an OU Sooners' football game. She was pushing him away. Erecting a wall. Holding him at bay. For whatever reason he had yet to learn, she obviously thought he had come on too strong, and she was determined not to let him get too close to her.

The signal she sent him rang through loud and clear—*back off.*

"Forgive me if I came across as being pushy. I get a little carried away in my enthusiasm sometimes. I guess you can tell I love my church. But I also want to see you make new friends here in Milltown right away so you'll start to feel at home, and I know you'd get along well with the ladies in our Sunday school class."

The stress eased from Winnie's face and her shoulders slacked from their prior soldier-stiff carriage.

"Well, I suppose I could at least go again this coming Sunday since Carla and Jack are still out of town. . . ." Her lone dimple flashed for a moment across her right cheek before she raised her guard again.

Just that quick hint of a smile set off an explosion of pleasure through Dan. He raised his mug and took another sip of coffee in a hopeless attempt to wash down his rising emotion. What he couldn't do on his own, Winnie tamped down when she added a qualifier to her yielding to go to First Church again. "I'll drive myself, though, and probably won't be going to Sunday school or lunch."

A week later, Dan smoothed the last section of caulking bead around the windowpane and sat back on his haunches to appraise his work. As he did, he pulled a faded blue bandanna out of his back pocket, which he used to mop the sweat from his brow. Even in May, the attic temperature soared to nearly unbearable heights. Still, he regretted being done with this chore. The installation of the new glass signified one of his final tasks in Winnie's home repairs. All he had left to do was fix the fence, then his work here would be done. Right now, Winnie was applying a second coat of sage green paint to the bedroom walls. The carpet installers should arrive first thing tomorrow morning to replace the damaged carpet with new. Her daughter and son-in-law would be home in another day and a half.

And he'd be back to jigsawing lawn ornaments in his workshop at home.

His shoulders sagged at the thought of going through an entire day without sharing a laugh with Winnie. The idea of eating alone after sitting across the table from such delightfully feminine company these past three weeks left a bitter taste in his mouth. He hated the prospect of returning to life the way it was a month ago.

Dan crammed his bandanna back into his pocket and began to gather up his tools. He took painstaking care to return them, one by one, to their allotted spaces on his tool belt.

He would miss Winnie's silly little vegetable exclamations. And the way she inclined her good ear toward him to catch his words. He admired her loving heart and gentle ways and fierce determination to make it on her own. Even so, he wished he understood why she kept him at arm's length.

Within days of meeting Winnie, Dan decided the time had come for him to leave his loneliness in the past and pursue a future of happiness. He still had his strength. In fact, he could still outwork and lift more than most men half his age. He had his health and, Lord willing, a whole lot of living left to do. He needed companionship, regardless of what his daughter wanted or thought best for him. In the book of Genesis, God Himself had said it was not good for a man to be alone.

Patty would simply have to accept his decision to love again, he thought as he moseyed through the tasks of cleaning up after himself. He prayed he could somehow convince his daughter of the fact that taking another woman as his wife in no way brought disgrace to the memory of Esther. He was already praying for wisdom in how best to explain his thoughts and wishes to Patty; and he felt confident that, given time, she would come around to the idea. Yet, regardless of whether his daughter came around to seeing things his way or not, he simply had to follow his heart. When it came to knowing what was right for his own life, this was one area where Father still knew best.

However, the biggest hurdle to his hopes and dreams lay in persuading Winnie to consider the possibilities of a future with him. Winnie continued to spurn even the slightest romantic overtures on his part and, though he still couldn't figure out why, he knew better than to push. He also knew any progress toward romance would undoubtedly skid to a snail's pace in two days' time, since the only occasions he'd be likely to see her after that would be church events.

She mystified him. In the short time since he'd come to know her, he felt certain their relationship could go beyond friendship if she would only open her heart to the possibilities. His feelings for her had certainly gone to a deeper level in these past three weeks, and he felt fairly sure she held strong feelings for him as well. He feared she might be so tied to the memory of her deceased husband that she would never want to marry again.

An unending string of gruff, deep-throated barks pulled Dan's attention to the neighbor's yard directly below his attic perch. From his second-story viewpoint, he watched as the golden retriever that belonged to the couple next door buried his nose in the corner where the two yards met.

At first, Dan figured the hound had trapped a squirrel. But, upon closer examination, he recognized the furry form of Skipper clawing, nosing, and burrowing his way under the damaged section of fence that separated Winnie's front yard from the back. The agitation of the neighbor's hound served to spur the little rascal on to further mischief rather than send him back toward the house where he belonged.

The first day he started repairs on Winnie's house, he nailed several two-by-fours in place of the damaged fencerow in order to secure the yard for the dog. This allowed Winnie to let Skipper out to do his doggy business without having to escort him every time. Dan felt confident his makeshift measures had been adequate to confine such a little animal. He could see now he had misjudged the critter; his assumptions were wrong.

He raised the window, stuck his head out, and yelled down at the dog.

"Skipper! Stop that!"

The imp froze in his digging long enough to look up at Dan and give one short bark.

Maybe his eyes were playing tricks on him, but it looked

for all the world to Dan like the dog stuck out his tongue and grinned. Skipper returned to his escape attempt at an even more frenzied pace, ignoring all orders to stop. The thunderous barks of the golden retriever provided accompaniment.

When it became apparent that Skipper would pay him no heed, Dan tried a different tack. He stomped the heel of his work boot on the attic floor and yelled.

"Winnie!" He listened for her to respond.

The theme song from the musical *Oklahoma!* wafted from the CD player in the bedroom below him. He could hear Winnie singing along. "Ohhh-klahoma where the wind comes sweeping down the plains. . ."

Dan looked out the window again in time to see Skipper wiggle into his tunnel, under the two-by-four barrier, and out the other side to freedom. With a quick glance in Dan's direction, the dog barked once and trotted across the yard to the sidewalk, then broke into a dead run.

"Help! Winnie! Help!" He kicked at the floorboards again. But even as he pounded and yelled, he knew his chances of Winnie hearing him over her loud music were slim to nil.

Hampered by his inability to stand up straight in the attic space, Dan duck-walked as fast as he could to the pull-down stairs and scuttled to the main floor. He didn't bother to stop and explain to the oblivious lady of the house, but dashed out the door after the dog.

Chapter 5

Dan sprinted down the road after Skipper. He looked left and right. Under every car. Behind each bush, tree, and trash can. Around all the fire hydrants and lampposts in the block between Winnie's house and the end of the street.

Skipper had vanished into thin air.

When Dan exhausted all the likely places a fifteen-pound dog might hide within the Brook's Country housing development, he returned to Winnie's driveway, breathless and dripping with sweat. He climbed into his pickup and drove slowly through the neighborhood—starting the dog hunt all over again.

After an hour of fruitless searching, he turned back. He pulled in the drive to see Winnie standing on the porch, wringing a paint-smeared rag. Worry shrouded her features. She hurried down the steps to meet Dan before he could get out of the truck cab.

"Is Skipper with you?" she asked. "I went to let him in, and he didn't come, and he didn't come when I called." As she chattered, she craned her neck to look past him into the pickup. "Then I saw you'd gone somewhere in your truck, even though I didn't hear you leave. I thought you might have taken him out for a ride when you went on an errand of some kind."

"Winnie, calm down. Let's go back inside." He took her elbow and escorted her up the walk. The smell of turpentine that rose from her paint rag did nothing to clear the encroaching wooziness he felt after his mad chase through town.

"What is it? Dan, you're scaring me. Has something happened to Carla's dog?"

He closed the front door behind them and turned to face Winnie. The panic in her eyes made him gulp.

"I'm sure Skipper is just fine, but he got loose from the yard and ran off. I watched him from the window as he made his escape, but before I could climb down out of the attic and catch him, he was gone."

Dan watched the color drain from Winnie's face. Her complexion took on a hue that matched the sage green paint spatters on her baggy work shirt. She let the turpentine-soaked rag drop to the floor.

"We've simply got to find him. Carla and Jack will be home day after tomorrow. She would never forgive me if anything happened. . . ." Her sable eyes glazed with welling tears. "Oh, Dan, what am I going to do?"

"Winnie, please don't cry. Please." Helplessness crushed his chest. "Listen to me. I'll find Skipper if I have to turn this town upside down." He would promise her anything to keep her tears at bay.

"What with the move, then the storm, and now this. . ." She bowed her head. "I don't know how much more I can take."

A single teardrop trickled down the contour of Winnie's cheek, and Dan brushed it away. That lone tear dissolved his defenses. He fought an overwhelming urge to hold her close. Comfort her.

With a gentle tug of his finger, he raised her chin. "Sh-sh-sh, it's okay. I'll find him."

The sight of this beautiful woman in misery tore at his very soul. Before he could regain control, a swell of emotion washed away all common sense. He thought only of how right it would feel to kiss this woman who had invaded his heart. He leaned in, closed his eyes, and grazed her lips with his.

A whack of stinging pain exploded across the left side of his face. His eyes shot open to see Winnie glaring at him, her arms crooked at her waist.

"How dare you!" she sputtered. "How could you?"

She pointed to the door. "Get out!" Again, she jabbed her finger toward the exit behind him. He attempted to speak, but Winnie's fury refused to be contained.

"Your services are no longer needed here, Mr. Parker. Get out. Now!"

Dan held his hands up in a sign of surrender. Reeling with shock and confusion, he backed out the door and escaped.

He hurried to his truck, shoved the key into the ignition, and cranked the engine until it began to chug. Clutching the steering wheel with a white-knuckle grip, he bumped his head up and down several times on the back of his hands, then he rested his forehead against the wheel and closed his eyes.

A burning stripe traced the side of Dan's face where Winnie slapped him. Yet, the slap to his spirit stung more than the one that blazed on his cheek.

"Dear Lord, what just happened in there?" He prayed aloud the question that ricocheted through his mind.

Winnie's reaction to his kiss befuddled him. He'd intended to comfort her and convey that she wasn't alone, to let her know he'd be there to help her through yet another worrisome trial. Instead, he added to her misery. Judging by her response, one would think him a lecherous ol' coot intent on taking untoward advantage of a woman in the throes of emotional duress.

At least now he knew where he stood with Winnie. She left no doubt. All along, he'd misread Winnie's feelings for him; he'd been deceiving himself. She most definitely did not return his growing affections for her. He knew now his perception to the contrary represented wishful thinking on his part.

Only answerless questions sprang to his mind.

What do I do now? How can I ever fix this mess? Will I just make matters worse if I try?

Still, he couldn't sit around and wait for a lightning bolt of inspired wisdom to strike—not when Skipper remained AWOL. Visions of the runaway pooch lying, injured, somewhere along the side of the road sprang to Dan's mind. He refused to let this situation with Winnie stop him from fulfilling his promise to search for the dog.

Winnie awoke with a start but needed several more moments to get her bearings and gather her wits. She didn't remember falling asleep. She still sat curled in Bill's old brown vinyl recliner, which had been transplanted to the den of her new home. And she still wore Friday's clothes. But the whistles, pops, and beep-beeps of Saturday morning cartoons blared from the TV in place of the late-night news program she last remembered seeing on the screen.

Here, the very first night since the storm blew through when she could have slept in her own bed, and she never left her chair. She groped in the space between the arms and seat cushion of her chair until she found the remote control. Then, holding it like a saber, she punched the power button to turn off the television.

She dug the heels of her hands into her eyes and rubbed, which created an effect akin to using sandpaper to remove eye shadow. A much sharper pain pierced her heart. Not since Bill died had she shed so many tears.

If she could trust the TV programming and the sunshine that flooded through the patio doors as accurate indicators, thirty-six hours had passed since Dan broke the news. Thirty-six hours with no signs of Skipper. She was running out of options—and time. Less than twelve hours remained until her daughter and son-in-law returned, but the dog still remained at large.

Carla would be heartbroken to come home to find her cherished pet gone.

The house stayed much too quiet without that dog

around. To further compound Winnie's problems, the fact that she found herself forced to endure these thirty-six hours alone, without her friend, Dan, made her pain almost too great to bear.

Yesterday, in the midst of waiting for the carpet installers to arrive, she'd phoned the local newspaper. She placed a "Lost Dog" ad, which included the offer of a generous reward for his return.

When the workmen left, she drove the streets of Milltown for hours in a fruitless search. She happened by the pound and went inside to see if, by chance, the warden might have picked up a dog fitting Skipper's description. The woman who sat behind the receptionist's desk informed her they were already on the lookout for a sheltie by that same name. She remembered an older gentleman had come by before closing time the day before and filled out a report.

Winnie's heart pounded to think of Dan continuing his search for Skipper, despite their parting of the ways. She still felt bad for her violent reaction to his advances, no matter how inappropriate his behavior might have been. Never, in all her born days, had she slapped another human being—but she certainly gave him what he deserved. The thought made her lips tingle with the memory of his kiss. She doubted she would ever get over the shock. If she hadn't held Dan in such high regard and esteem, she might not have reacted with such emotion at that moment when he took her in his arms.

All she could figure was he had rationalized his guilt

away since his wife would likely never recover from her infirmities. No doubt he felt, in many ways, as though his wife had already died. From the days they spent in conversation, Winnie gathered how much he longed for female companionship. She realized Dan felt every bit as lonely with his nonresponsive wife in a nursing home as she did with her Bill gone on to his heavenly reward.

Given time to think it through, she decided she deserved at least a portion of the blame she so quickly laid at Dan's feet. How could she expect him to behave after spending so much time together with her, even if the reasons were perfectly legitimate? If the right opportunity ever presented itself, she would apologize for the part she played in allowing their relationship to escalate to the brink of his infidelity. Still, she never would permit herself to be alone with him again.

Winnie padded, barefoot, into the kitchen to put a pot of coffee on to brew. Then she remembered she would have to drink the whole pot by herself. Dan wouldn't be joining her for a morning coffee break today. She settled for a cup of instant instead. While she waited for the microwave oven to ding and signal her coffee was done, she heard a familiar barking on the porch.

"Asparagus and artichokes, Skipper, is that you?" She traveled the few feet from the kitchen to the entryway and yanked open the front door. Skipper dashed past her, headed for the laundry room, trailing a leash and the pungent smell of muddy, wet fur. Winnie let her gaze travel back to the porch.

Dan stood there with her old toaster in his hands. She fought to keep her expression grim.

Combing her fingers through her hair, she imagined the frightful image she must present to him after spending all night squirming in the recliner in her den. Thankfully, the navy knit warm-up suit she'd worn since yesterday didn't show wrinkles. She couldn't say as much for him.

The lines around his eyes and lips no longer laughed, but cut deep grooves into his face. His ball cap's bill cast a shadow on his face that served to intensify the effect. He looked as though he had aged ten years over the course of the past two days.

"Don't worry, Winnie." Hesitation tinged his words. He glimpsed at her, then down at his work boots. "I won't stay or ask to come in. I just thought you might want me to return these two vululiles to you."

Winnie surmised she'd misheard Dan's muttered use of the unfamiliar word, and in her mind, she translated it as *valuables*.

Stiff-armed, Dan offered her the toaster. She noted that a new cord dangled from the appliance when she accepted it from him.

More than anything she ever wanted in her life, she longed to invite him inside and pick up their friendship where they left off. But "where they had left off" included an embrace and a kiss from a married man.

I was standing in this very spot then. To remember that moment while, once again, in the presence of Dan brought flames to Winnie's cheeks. Even so, she would not give in and go against what she knew to be the moral and right thing to do.

"Jack and Carla's neighbor, Mrs. Pike, had Skipper all this time. . . ." He cleared his throat, but kept his head down. Winnie stared at the '89er logo on his ball cap. The red background had long ago faded to pink.

Dan glanced up and back down. "Evidently, when he ran away, he headed straight for home. The lady who lives next door to them heard Skipper barking. Since she was keeping their mail, she knew Jack and Carla were still gone, so she took the dog in to her place."

"I see," she said. "Well, thank you for bringing him back." Winnie intended for her words to sound curt.

He cleared his throat again and looked toward the side of the house. "If you want, I can fix the fence while I'm here. I wouldn't bother you or need to come inside for anything."

"That won't be necessary." Winnie kept her eyes trained on the doorknob and away from Dan. "I'll ask Jack to repair it when he gets a chance. After they take Skipper home tonight, it won't matter whether the yard is secure or not." She knew that every second he stayed on her porch, looking so forlorn, brought her closer to forgetting her resolve and welcoming Dan back inside. If she didn't cut this conversation short, she would soon do something she would regret.

"I'd best be going then. . . ." His words tapered off.

She stood in silence on the other side of the threshold.

Dan backed away two steps and turned, then slowly navigated the steps. He looked over his shoulder at her one more time before he got in his truck and drove off. Sadness laced his eyes.

It took all her inner fortitude to fight the urge to call after him. She forced herself to remember how much Dan had let her down. This man who purportedly claimed to be a devoted Christian could not remain faithful to his wife. She could never depend on his trustworthiness as a friend if he would dishonor his wife in such a way.

"Yoo-hoo? Mom? Skipper? You two here? We're home."

Winnie stood at the kitchen sink with her arms buried in soapy water up to her elbows. She looked over her shoulder toward the front door to see Carla standing in the entryway. The dog left his place at Winnie's feet and ran to his mistress, then let loose with a flurry of earsplitting barks while he spun in circles, chasing his tail.

"Come to Momma, Skipper. Come on, Boy. Come on." Carla addressed the dog in a falsetto voice like she might a human baby. "Are you happy to see me? How's my little boy, huh? Did you miss me? Were you a good puppy for Grandma?"

I am not that dog's grandmother, Winnie wanted to say, especially after the stunt he had pulled by running away, but she kept her comment to herself.

Skipper calmed enough for Carla to pick him up. However, when she held him close, he started to wiggle and squirm again. Instantly he coated her face with slobbery doggy kisses. "Yes, I missed you too, but I need you to be a good boy and be still now so I can talk to Grandma. Go get your blankie so we can go bye-bye, okay?" She released the dog and it scampered off toward the laundry room.

Drying her hands on the hem of her apron, Winnie greeted her daughter and they exchanged an embrace. Then Winnie held Carla at arm's length and they studied each other from head to toe.

"You look tired, Mom. Are you feeling okay?" Concern showed in Carla's brown eyes. "Just as I feared, you've worked yourself sick, haven't you?"

"Persimmons and parsnips! I'm fine." She waved off Carla's concern like she would a pesky fly. "I just didn't sleep well last night is all." Winnie rested her hand on her daughter's abdomen. "You, on the other hand, look great. Hawaii seems to have agreed with both you and this *real* grandbaby of mine. You're really starting to pooch out there now."

"Yeah, every time I went to the beach, someone mistook me for a beached whale." Carla gave her belly a light thump as if she were testing a watermelon for ripeness.

"Oh, no, Dear," Winnie shot back. "You're much too tanned for that." Mother and daughter shared a laugh.

"Listen, Mom, I know it isn't even dark yet, but we're jet-lagged. Bushed. Jack promised he'd try to wait up for me 'til I got back home with Skipper, but he made no guarantees, so I can't stay and gab. I'll come by in the morning after I've had a chance to unpack and start a load of laundry. I just had to pick up my little sweetie the minute I got to town." Skipper had returned with the blanket from his dog carrier. After stooping to lift him into her arms, Carla scanned the room. "Wow, you've really got this place looking great, Mom. Then again, I knew you would." She stroked the dog's fur as she spoke. "I do have a bone to pick with you, though." She pushed out her bottom lip into a pout. "I noticed when I drove up that my favorite pecan tree was gone. When you told me about the storm damage, you said a limb had come down. You never said anything about losing the entire tree."

"Well. . .you see. . .it's like this. . ." Winnie sputtered and raked her teeth across one corner of her bottom lip.

Carla heaved a sigh. "Oh, never mind. I understand. I suppose you know me well enough to know I would have let it spoil my trip, so I won't be mad at you for keeping secrets from me this time. Still, I just loved that big old pecan. Must have been quite a storm that blew through here."

Winnie offered only a nod in response.

"But, another thing. . ." Carla's forehead crinkled as she spoke. "Didn't you say you'd hired Handy Dan to fix the fence?" When Carla mentioned Dan's name, Winnie noticed how Skipper's ears perked up. "It looked to me like a section was still on the ground. I'm surprised Mr. Parker hasn't been able to get to a little job like that in three weeks' time. That's not like him. Is he ill?"

Averting her eyes from her daughter's inquiring gaze, Winnie studied the lace trim on her apron. "No, Mr. Parker is fine. He and I just had a little misunderstanding. It's a long story, Dear, and I know you're tired. I don't feel like getting into it tonight either. I'll explain everything tomorrow when we have time to really talk."

Carla looked crestfallen at Winnie's words. "What a shame. I thought sure you and Dan would be good company for one another. In fact—and don't be mad—but I had been planning on inviting the two of you over for dinner at our place once you were settled in here. I was a little disappointed when you told me on the phone that you'd foiled my great matchmaking scheme by calling him to do your repairs."

Winnie stared at her daughter in disbelief. "Carla, you can't be serious. Are you in cahoots with him? I know his wife is bedfast and all, but Dan Parker is still a married man."

"What on earth are you talking about, Mother? I don't know what you heard, but you heard wrong. Dan Parker's wife suffered a series of strokes that left her bedridden, then comatose for several months, but she's been dead for close to three years now."

"Dead? Are you sure? I'm certain Dan said. . ." Winnie replayed in her mind the first face-to-face conversation she'd had with him. She rewound the mental tape again and again. She was almost certain he'd said, with a hint of a Southern twang, that his wife had "been a-bed for close three years now." Had her bum hearing played a cruel trick on her? The prospect left her weak in the knees.

"I am one-hundred-percent positive." Carla bobbed her head up and down. "Without a shadow of a doubt. I was in charge of the sign-ups for the week's worth of dinners that our singles' Sunday school class provided for the family after the funeral. I distinctly remember, since Dad had only been gone about a year then. Seeing how the Parkers were struggling to come to terms with their loss brought back all of those horrible feelings of grief."

Slack-jawed, Winnie felt the blood drain from her face. She took two steps backward and crumpled into a kitchen chair. "Here I thought all along. . . So, when he tried to. . . His wife isn't. . . You mean to tell me Dan's a widower?" she finally managed to sputter.

"Most definitely. He's considered the most eligible bachelor among Milltown's fifty-and-older crowd."

Winnie floundered for a vegetable to punctuate her shock, but her frantic harvest for just the right word yielded none.

Chapter 6

D an dug through the dryer for clean socks and underwear, then carried the armload of clothes down the hall. He tossed his things into the nearly full suitcase that lay open at the foot of his bed.

"I give up," he muttered to himself. "As long as I live, I'll never understand women. I don't know why I bother to try." Moving to the bathroom, he emptied the countertop of his toiletries and stuffed them into a small duffel bag. As an afterthought, he reached into the shower and grabbed his dandruff shampoo.

From the time he returned from dropping Skipper off at Winnie's door, he'd fought the impulse to pick up the phone and call her. . .to explain. . .to apologize. He was still just as baffled as ever when it came to understanding why Winnie would be so determined to push him away. Maybe if he called, she would shed some light on her behavior toward him.

Looking back on it now, he admitted his kissing her might have been too forward, despite the emotion-wrought circumstance. No matter that he always was a sap when it came to a woman's tears. He should have reined in his emotions and exercised more self-control.

Even so, he didn't feel he merited the reaction he received at Winnie's mean right hook.

For the greater part of two days, as he conducted his search for the dog, he had prayed about his feelings for Winnie and her strange reaction to him. He had yet to figure out why she'd sent him packing without so much as a fare-thee-well. And, while he still had no further insight into why she responded with such harshness and severity, he felt a firm assurance that the Lord had heard his prayer. In his heart of hearts, he thought for sure when he went by her place this morning with Skipper in tow, she would welcome him inside and set him down so she could explain.

If Winnie had only given him half a chance and a second opportunity to prove himself, he would have vowed to move at her pace as far as the romance department was concerned. He'd given her ample opportunity to extend an invitation to talk, but she made it perfectly clear she had no intention of speaking to him ever again.

When it got to be suppertime, the urge to call Winnie was nearly killing him, despite his promise not to bother her. He had made a decision as he pulled the peanut butter and crackers from the pantry shelf. He knew if he stayed in this house—this town—one more day, he would drive himself plumb loco. After all the activity and excitement Winnie had brought into his life these past three weeks, he shuddered at the thought of going back to the old, lonely routine. And he wasn't about to spend another day moping around like a lovesick teenybopper, dreaming of asking the homecoming queen to the prom.

He decided he would drive to Dallas and surprise Patty and Brian and the boys. If he left now, he knew Patty wouldn't appreciate him dropping in on them tonight, unannounced, at the late hour when he would arrive. But if he loaded up the truck and was ready to leave before dawn, he could be at their house in time to have breakfast with the boys and see them off for school. The change of scenery would do him good. Maybe a bit of fresh Texas air would clear his head.

Dan zipped his suitcase shut and carried it to his truck. An Oklahoma sunset washed the horizon in multihued shades of orange and pink. After depositing the luggage in the cab, he opened the hood to check the oil and fluids in preparation for his trip. He had just wiped the dipstick clean when he heard the crunch of tires on his drive. Peeking around the open hood, he saw Winnie's red pickup pulling in behind his.

By the time he replaced the dipstick and swabbed the oil from his hands with his bandanna, Winnie had reached his side. The low-lying sun cast a fiery glow across her face and sparkled through her hair. He tried to assume an air of indifference when she greeted him, but his racing heart and sweaty palms belied his cool demeanor.

"Dan, I need to mend some fences," she said instead of exchanging the usual hellos. "And I'm not talking about the one in my backyard."

"How's that?" He lifted his foot, resting it on the front bumper, and crossed his arms. After all he'd been through in the past three days, he didn't dare raise his hopes just yet, but the way she started out sounded promising.

"Yes, you see, when Carla got home, she set me straight on something." She paused, but Dan encouraged her to go on with a nod. "So I've come over to clear up a huge misunderstanding on my part—and to offer you an apology."

She sighed and appeared to be studying his engine, then looked back at Dan and held his gaze. "I don't know if you've noticed or not, but my hearing isn't always so good. And, well. . ." She sighed again as though steeling herself in preparation for what she was about to say.

"I never really heard you say that your wife had died. Instead, I had the mistaken notion that she was in a coma in a Dallas rest home."

Suddenly, like the sun moving from behind a cloud, everything made sense to Dan. No wonder she'd hauled off and walloped him.

"So, when you tried to kiss me. . .I mean, I didn't think a married man had any business kissing a woman who wasn't his wife. Oh, what I'm trying to say is, if you'll forgive me for treating you so poorly and consider coming back around to my place to visit whenever you please, I promise to schedule an appointment with a specialist about my hearing loss and, if need be, get fitted for hearing aids."

Dan lowered his foot from the bumper and eased his defensive stance. Then he took a step toward Winnie to close the gap between them. "Of course I'll forgive you. There's really nothing to forgive." He could no longer keep his smile contained. In response, she broke into a grin. "It was all just a horrible misunderstanding."

"Oh, no—" She stammered in protest, but before she could go any further, Dan tapped his finger to his lips to silence her.

"Look at me, Winnie." He forced himself to assume an air of seriousness. "I want to make sure there's no miscommunication between us now." Her eyes grew round, and he could almost see the wheels churning in her head as she tried to guess his next words.

"Until you're able to see a doctor and get your hearing up to par, I'll just have to find another way to communicate with you—a way that will leave no doubt or question in your mind as to what it is I'm trying to say."

With no further talk or shilly-shallying, he pulled her into his embrace. Since she didn't protest or back away, he leaned down, closed his eyes, and grazed her lips with his.

When no slap answered his display of affection, he kissed her again, this time lingering to savor her sweetness, cherishing the warmth of her touch. He longed to spend the rest of his days with this woman he now held in his arms. He opened his eyes to see her staring up at him, her sable eyes sparkling, and her smile unreserved.

"Winnie, have I made myself understood? Did you pick the words *I love you* out of what I just said?"

"Zucchini squash and succotash!" She moistened her lips and smiled again. "I hear you loud and clear."

Susan Downs
Born and reared in Oklahoma and a descendant of Land Run pioneers, Susan Downs grew up in a place much like Milltown, the town in which her story is set. Her life as a minister's wife has taken her far from her roots, but she will always consider herself an Okie at heart. Susan currently lives in Canton, Ohio, where her husband serves as a district superintendent for the Church of the Nazarene. They have five children and are expecting their first grandson.

A Letter to Our Readers

Dear Readers:

In order that we might better contribute to your reading enjoyment, we would appreciate you taking a few minutes to respond to the following questions. When completed, please return to the following: Fiction Editor, Barbour Publishing, Inc., P.O. Box 719, Uhrichsville, OH 44683.

1. Did you enjoy reading *The House Love Built?*
   ❏ Very much—I would like to see more books like this.
   ❏ Moderately—I would have enjoyed it more if _____

   _____

   _____

2. What influenced your decision to purchase this book?
   (Check those that apply.)
   ❏ Cover   ❏ Back cover copy   ❏ Title   ❏ Price
   ❏ Friends   ❏ Publicity   ❏ Other

3. Which story was your favorite?
   ❏ *Foundation of Love*   ❏ *Once Upon an Attic*
   ❏ *Love's Open Door*   ❏ *Mending Fences*

4. Please check your age range:
   ❏ Under 18   ❏ 18–24   ❏ 25–34
   ❏ 35–45   ❏ 46–55   ❏ Over 55

5. How many hours per week do you read? _____

Name _____

Occupation _____

Address _____

City _____ State _____ Zip _____

If you enjoyed
The House Love Built
then read:

Aloha

Four Romances at a Hawaiian Hideaway

Love, Suite Love by Colleen Coble
Fixed by Love by Carol Cox
Game of Love by Denise Hunter
It All Adds Up to Love by Gail Sattler

If you enjoyed

The House Love Built

then read:

South Carolina

*Four Distinct Novels Set in the Palmetto State
by Yvonne Lehman*

After the Storm
Catch of a Lifetime
Somewhere a Rainbow
Southern Gentleman

If you enjoyed

The House Love Built

then read:

American DREAM

Four Historical Love Stories
Celebrating the Faith of American Immigrants

I Take Thee, a Stranger by Kristy Dykes
Blessed Land by Nancy J. Farrier
Promises Kept by Sally Laity
Freedom's Ring by Judith McCoy Miller

HEARTSONG ❤ PRESENTS

Love Stories
Are Rated G!

That's for godly, gratifying, and of course, great! If you love a thrilling love story but don't appreciate the sordidness of some popular paperback romances, **Heartsong Presents** is for you. In fact, **Heartsong Presents** is the only inspirational romance book club featuring love stories where Christian faith is the primary ingredient in a marriage relationship.

Sign up today to receive your first set of four, never-before-published Christian romances. Send no money now; you will receive a bill with the first shipment. You may cancel at any time without obligation, and if you aren't completely satisfied with any selection, you may return the books for an immediate refund!

Imagine. . .four new romances every four weeks—two historical, two contemporary—with men and women like you who long to meet the one God has chosen as the love of their lives. . .all for the low price of $10.99 postpaid.

To join, simply complete the coupon below and mail to the address provided. **Heartsong Presents** romances are rated G for another reason: They'll arrive Godspeed!

YES! Sign me up for Hearts❤ng!